The Christmas Princess

The Wedding Series
Prelude to a Wedding
Wedding Party
Grady's Wedding
The Runaway Bride
The Christmas Princess
Hoops (prequel to The Surprise Princess)
The Surprise Princess
Not a Family Man (prequel to The Forgotten Prince)
The Forgotten Prince

More romance by Patricia McLinn

Marry Me Series
Wedding of the Century
The Unexpected Wedding Guest
A Most Unlikely Wedding
Baby Blues and Wedding Bells

Seasons in a Small Town
What Are Friends For? (Spring)
The Right Brother (Summer)
Falling for Her (Autumn)
Warm Front (Winter)

Wyoming Wildflowers Series
Wyoming Wildflowers: The Beginning (prequel)
Almost a Bride
Match Made in Wyoming
My Heart Remembers
A New World (prequel to Jack's Heart)
Jack's Heart
Rodeo Nights (prequel to Where Love Lives)
Where Love Lives
A Cowboy Wedding

A Place Called Home series
Lost and Found Groom
At the Heart's Command
Hidden in a Heartbeat

THE CHRISTMAS PRINCESS

The Wedding Series
Book 5

Patricia McLinn

PROLOGUE

Washington, D.C.

"He won't fall for it." Hunter Pierce zeroed in on the gaping flaw in his boss's plan. "King Jozef might still be searching for the granddaughter everybody—including him—knows died decades ago, but he's not a complete fool."

From behind her utilitarian government-issue desk, Sharon Johnson sighed. "For someone working for the Department of State, you haven't learned much tact."

He grunted. "The point is, the Bureau of Diplomatic Security isn't in the business of making up fairytales."

"We're not making up a fairytale. We're simply saying we've found someone we think might be his granddaughter."

"We know she's not."

"Do we?" she asked in that There-Are-Mysteries-Greater-Than-Us voice. He hated when she did that. Almost made him wish she hadn't taken an interest in his career.

"You know as well as I do, she was spotted years ago and—"

"Spotted because of her uncanny resemblance to King Jozef's family, not to mention having the family characteristic."

"—researched again when she surfaced in connection with that science fiction author."

"Gerard Littrell. Yes, that was interesting."

He ignored her musing tone. "She's the only child of Melanie and Jeffrey Gareaux, both deceased. *Not* of Princess Sofia and Prince Leopold of Bariavak." The hand thing was a fluke.

"There are gaps in the record," Sharon said serenely. "That's why

I'm adding you to surveillance now that you're back from New York."

"Most of the gaps don't matter. The ones from around the uprising are because her parents moved a lot, not because she's a long-lost princess."

"Maybe, and maybe not. The gaps are enough to open the door. That's all we need. Possibility." The dark skin at the corners of her eyes creased with her smile. "It's for Christmas, just until he has the surgery."

"It's a cheap effort to curry favor with a strategic ally."

That was a low blow. Maybe higher-ups approved this hare-brained scheme with an eye only to extending the overflight treaty before the elderly King of Bariavak's surgery in January, but Sharon also liked the man. You'd think she had enough to do with her job, husband, three kids, two dogs, and a rabbit without taking an aged and ailing monarch under her wing.

"It's humanitarian, it doesn't hurt anyone, it'll give him happier holidays, and, yes, it might get overflight renewed, which would help our military," Sharon retorted. "So work your magic when you talk to her today, Special Agent Pierce, and get this rolling."

"What happens when he spots her as a phony."

"We'd let it drop. No harm, no foul. But he won't. Not with you in charge." Sharon sat back, a slow smile spreading. "Even you can't begrudge an elderly man a happier Christmas."

"The king of Bariavak."

"Still a man."

"A king."

CHAPTER ONE

April Gareaux emerged from the Washington, D.C., Metro station into a gloomy Thursday morning rush, and experienced a sinking feeling.

That was strange. She had no cause for a sinking feeling.

Unless it stemmed from the notion she was being watched.

No, no, she'd decided that was simply her imagination working overtime. There was nothing in it. Nothing at all.

She was engaged to a wonderful man. A wonderful, wonderful man. She lived with him in his gorgeous house.

Well, his mother's house, actually. And more of a complex than a house. A gorgeous, gorgeous complex.

This Christmas wouldn't be like the ones she'd come to love over the past fifteen years. Of course that made her sad, and she was sorry to disappoint Leslie, Grady, and the rest. But she'd be with Reese. And his mother.

True, the holidays were something special with her family. Well, not actually family, as Reese pointed out when he'd said her idea to divide time between her family and his wouldn't work. But she *was* related to Leslie, and since Leslie was married to Grady he was family. The others, too. Just not the way Reese was used to.

Reese had always had a home. The one he still lived in. He was secure, grounded. Yes, that came with age, though, really, the twenty years between them didn't matter.

And they were going to have a fabulous Christmas. Their first together.

So she had absolutely no cause for a sinking feeling.

Except that she was early for work.

That would give Jason more time to barrage her with unfunny jokes and Zoe more time to deliver sure-fire rules for success. At least Zoe's intentions were good, unlike Jason's. Like his pointing out— loudly—when she skipped the Brussels sprouts at Tuesday night's Vegetable Consortium reception at the Willard Hotel.

April passed a shoe store, then crossed the side street to a drug store with battered yellow and orange fake autumn leaves plastered on its window.

The reception at the Willard Hotel had been the start of this feeling that she was being watched.

Could Reese…? No. But possibly his Evil Ex.

Zoe, who was rarely wrong about such things, had told her Tuesday morning that Roberta Warrington was back in D.C. But even so, why would Roberta, who'd walked out on Reese a year ago, be tracking her?

April stopped in front of a jewelry store. Though there *had* been that odd sensation, as if her skin attracted rays of attention that condensed into a thread of awareness like … Like the shiver gathering at the base of her skull now. Next it would—

April whipped around.

Nobody was behind her.

Nobody was staring at her.

Nobody was paying the least attention to her.

She turned back to the shop window.

Then, forgetting the sense of being watched, forgetting the Willard reception, forgetting Reese's Evil Ex and mother, even forgetting Reese, April Gareaux smiled.

The jewelry store's window held a gleaming Santa sleigh filled with tiny beribboned boxes behind reindeer positioned for liftoff. A hand-lettered sign read: "Dear Kris Kringle, if Cupid and Blitzen are in the wrong spot, let us know—we aim to please!"

Spotting a white-haired man inside, she pointed at the sign referencing the opening of the original—the *real*—*Miracle on 34th Street*, and waved. He waved back and smiled.

She snapped a photo to send to Grady Roberts, Leslie's husband. He'd introduced her to that movie and so many others, just as he and Leslie had taught her to love Christmas.

The red of cinnamon and green of firs. The sweetness of cookies and tartness of cranberries. The prickle of mistletoe and the crackle of wrapping paper.

It would be different this year, but Christmas was still Christmas. They would have a terrific time, she and Reese. And his mother.

At that moment, gray skies opened, gushing cold rain on her head.

"April, you've got to do something with that mop." Zoe Holland opened April's top desk drawer, fished out her brush with one immaculately manicured hand, and thunked the handle into her palm. "Here, brush."

"Why?" It was nearly quitting time, and her hair had looked like this since this morning.

Still, discussing hair was a relief. When Zoe marched toward her desk, April had feared the topic would be Brussels sprouts.

Despite the thinnest resume on the planet for a twenty-eight-year-old woman, April *knew* she was good at some things. And maybe nobody would be *great* at lobbying for Brussels sprouts, but not one of April's cold contacts had produced a nibble—no pun intended. And then there'd been Jason's announcement at the reception for all to hear that she'd skipped the Brussels sprouts.

Tuesday. What a rotten day. It started with Zoe telling April about Reese's Evil Ex being back in town. Then Reese called her at work and said *they needed to talk.*

She'd reminded him about the important reception. Reese, who once called her plucky for working when he could take care of her every whim, had curtly ordered, "Skip it."

She'd refused.

"Why brush your hair?" Zoe repeated her question. "Because there is an absolutely delicious man waiting for you in the conference room."

April stopped brushing. "For me?"

Zoe flapped her hand as an order to keep brushing and rooted in the drawer where April kept her minimal makeup.

"He's from State." Using D.C. shorthand, like "State" for the Department of State—and knowing that was its official name, rather than the State Department—was a Zoe Rule. "They're looking for an expert on Brussels sprouts. God knows why. Here, put on some lipstick. Don't you have any blush?"

"I wouldn't say I'm an expert, Zoe."

"You listen to me, April. For this man, you're going to be an expert. Don't tell him what you don't know—dazzle him with what you *do* know. You're a talented woman. Look what you did for Gerard Littrell, but—"

"That had nothing to do with talent."

"—when it comes to men—Reese Warrington for God's sake! But never mind that now. How about mascara?"

"I'm wearing mascara."

"The stuff isn't rationed. Put it on like you mean it. C'mon, I've got emergency supplies in the ladies' room."

April took a quick breath then opened the conference room door. On the far side of the table stood a man in a dark suit, straight and still, allowing her a three-quarters view of his face. He appeared to study a photo of an avalanche of green peas as if he didn't quite trust them.

She saw men like him in D.C. Most often in the background at special events, infrequently during everyday errands, never at bars. Especially not the bars Mandy had dragged her to when April had still lived across the hall. The men at those bars talked loud and long about how important they were. And they smiled. Oh, how they smiled.

Like Reese.

No. Where on earth did that come from? Reese was nothing like that.

Nor, to be accurate, was he like these other men, either. These other men—the ones like this dark-suited man—seldom spoke and rarely smiled. But their eyes took in all that was around them. They saw things, yes, they definitely saw things.

Oh, and they had *the jaw*.

She'd tried to explain it, but Mandy had wanted to distill *the jaw* to size and angles and that wasn't the point. Leslie, on the other hand, had gotten it immediately. *The jaw* would never cave in. *The jaw* was something to rely on, something to believe in.

Reese had nothing like *the jaw*. But that was okay. He was very attractive. And surely living with the jaw would be uncomfortable.

This man, she saw as he turned, had one of the finest examples of *the jaw* she had ever—

"Ms. Gareaux."

"Yes."

With two strides he closed much of the gap, though far from cozy.

Automatically, she catalogued a description as she'd learned to do for Gerard. High, sharp cheekbones balanced *the jaw*. Neatly trimmed medium brown hair. Penetrating eyes, narrowed so much she couldn't tell their color.

Whoa!

What had she been thinking about men with *the jaw* seeing things? He sure did. He was cataloging right back. It felt like a beam of light, like—

A vibration started at the base of her skull and zinged down her spine. "You've been watching me."

His eyelids lowered and rose once. That was it. One blink. Otherwise, he could have been a lump of granite—albeit a nicely shaped lump.

Oh, God, *had* it been her imagination? All the times she'd looked around these past days, she'd never spotted anything or anyone out of place. And why on earth would this man with *the jaw* be following her?

"Ms. Gareaux, please sit down."

He pulled out a chair. She sat.

"My name is Hunter Pierce." He flipped open a passport-sized leather folder for a flash of a two-part ID with the top part including the Department of State logo and the words "Special Agent" and the bottom part showing a signature and photo ID. It was definitely the same man. He returned it to his inside suit jacket pocket. "I'm here on a confidential matter on behalf of the Department of State. This matter—"

"About Brussels sprouts?"

"No. About you."

"*Me?* Oh." Her stomach flipped. "*Oh, my God.* Leslie, Grady—."

"No."

"Nobody's hurt? Reese or—"

"No." He waited a breath as if to be sure his certainty had stopped her. It had. "For the sake of our country, you must never discuss with anyone what I'm about to tell you, whether you agree to cooperate or not. I need your pledge to that."

Her mind raced, trying to make sense of this. "Cooperate with what?"

"First, your pledge."

That was dirty pool. Dangle the sake of her country, make it all mysterious and 007ish—what was the chance of saying no after that?

"I pledge not to discuss whatever this is—unless it's going to get somebody hurt or something," she added.

He'd pulled out a paper with closely printed type beneath the United States seal, and placed it on the corner of the nearby table. He held out a pen. "Sign here, please."

She took the pen, but tugged the paper from under his fingers and brought it in front of her to read the legalese. "Hey! This says I can go to jail."

"Only if you divulge what you just promised not to divulge without permission. The appeals process—" He tapped a figure to the last paragraph. "—is spelled out if you feel permission would be or has been withheld without sufficient cause."

She read the words again. This was not a Monopoly "Do Not Pass Go, Go Directly to Jail" card, this was the real thing. On the other hand, if she didn't find out what this was about she'd be lined up right behind the cat under "Cause of Death: Curiosity." In which case going to jail would be moot.

She signed.

"What is this about, Mr. Pierce?"

He refolded the paper and tucked it away before saying, "Your country needs your assistance. This is not dangerous or hazardous duty. Quality accommodations and meals would be provided. All expenses would be covered. However, it would require a commitment until January second. That means—"

"January? That's *weeks* from now. I haven't worked here long enough for that kind of vacation—"

"An official request for your assistance would be made. A lobbying organization such as this would not refuse such a request."

"But you said this doesn't have anything to do with Brussels sprouts."

"It doesn't."

"What *does* it have to do with?"

"It has to do with you being a princess for the month of December, Ms. Gareaux."

It had made more sense when it was about Brussels sprouts.

"A princess?" she repeated.

"Yes. Until the first of the year. After that—"

"I'm not a princess."

"We know that. However, you bear a strong resemblance—"

April shook her head, trying to get things back in order. "Wait, back up. I'm not a princess and you know it? So people who know this princess would also know I'm not her. Uh, she." Wouldn't a princess get the pronoun right the first time? "Plus, people who know me will know I'm, uh, *me.*"

So not a princess.

"No need to worry about people who know the princess. And you wouldn't be around people you know. As I started to say, you will step away from your usual life. We would provide housing, any necessary wardrobe, transportation—"

"Transportation? So you're like the dog and horse who became the footman and coachman." She chuckled. "Although, actually the *mice* provided the transportation when they were turned into horses."

He didn't react.

"*Cinderella?*" she prompted. " 'Bibbidi-Bobbidi-Boo'?"

Come to think of it, if he provided the wardrobe that also made him the Fairy Godmother. Before she could swallow that image, he gave a single shake of his head. "I am not at liberty to further discuss arrangements until you have agreed to this, Ms. Gareaux."

He spread another form before her, but she didn't look at it. "Did Zoe hire you?"

"No."

She wouldn't put this past her boss, who'd hired a male stripper dressed—briefly—as a doctor for nine-months pregnant Lorene's baby shower and was forever saying April needed to get a little wild.

April eyed Mr. Jaw. He would look even better with his attire reduced to a single stretch of spandex than Mr. Stethoscope had. Though she'd never heard of a stripper impersonating a member of State's security. Not even in Washington.

But it had to be something like that, because otherwise it was real.

"Are you a friend of Jason's?" she demanded.

"No."

"If this is one of his so-called jokes, it's even less funny than the others."

"I assure you Ms. Gareaux, this is not a joke."

She stood. "If it's not a joke, I'm the absolutely last person you want."

He stood, too, picking up the form. Two of his fingers brushed across the back of her left hand.

It was a tiny fraction of the contact experienced each morning and evening with any number of strangers in standing-room only Metro cars. Yet the warmth of this contact against her nerve-chilled hands was like a close encounter with a defibrillator paddle. It certainly changed the rhythm of her heartbeat.

Ah. His hand jerked the tiniest bit too … didn't it?

Hunter Pierce's voice snapped her back with a thud. "You're the only possibility, Ms. Gareaux."

In that instant she knew it wasn't a joke.

"No," she said, retreating. "I'm sorry … No. I have, uh, a fiancé." Why hadn't she said that from the start? She couldn't possibly disappear for the month of December to pretend to be a princess.

She hadn't quite reached the door when he said, "April."

Reluctantly, she halted and faced him.

"Remember, you have sworn to tell no one about this." He tapped his jacket where he'd put the first form, over his heart.

"I remember."

Green.

His eyes were green.

CHAPTER TWO

"Miss April, Mrs. Warrington asks that you be taken to her upon your arrival," Barton said when he opened the entry door to her. She'd reminded Reese a week ago that she still didn't have a set of keys.

"I'll just go upstairs and…" Try emergency repairs to her hair.

"She asked to see you immediately, Miss April."

For an instant, she thought she saw sympathy in Barton's impassive face.

"Of course." No sense in getting him in trouble.

"Thank you, Miss April."

She hated being called Miss April by the staff. She'd asked them to call her April. Mrs. Warrington had countermanded her. Reese had suggested Ms. Gareaux. Mrs. Warrington had said, "We don't need to go that far."

He led the way to Mrs. Warrington's office. Tapped on the door, opened it, then closed it behind her once she was inside.

"Come in, April. Sit down. Your hair style is particularly unfortunate today."

She couldn't argue. She sat on the "guest" chair that would have been considered cruel and unusual punishment in several states. "How are you today, Mrs. Warrington?"

"I am in splendid health, as always."

April tried not to notice that the older woman didn't thank her for asking, nor ask in response. April also tried not to compare Reese's mother to her own great-grandmother. To many they would appear to come from the same mold, though Beatrice Craig was somewhat older. Her great-grandmother was a tartar, for sure. But she had a graciousness, a kindness, Mrs. Warrington lacked.

"I will not prolong this," the woman began.

Prolong what? April knew better than to ask.

"Roberta has returned." Mrs. Warrington said no more, apparently waiting for her to respond.

"Reese told me." After she'd asked him about the rumor Zoe had heard.

Mrs. Warrington grimaced. "If he had, we would not be having this conversation."

"I don't understand."

"No, you don't." The older woman's sigh held exasperation that she was required to explain. "She has returned to Reese. Roberta was always his proper match, and they have reconciled. Your things have been packed. Barton has called a taxi."

April understood the words. She even got the picture. Maybe at some level, with the way Reese had acted this week, she'd suspected. Those years after her dad died, with Melly swapping men as often as addresses, she'd come to sense when it was brewing, like feeling a change in air pressure.

Yes, at some level, she'd suspected. Still, she was shocked. And sad, of course. But she wouldn't cry in front of Mrs. Warrington. That's why her eyes were totally dry. Pride. "Reese is having his *mother* break up with me?"

"The ring, of course, will be returned to us, since it is a family piece."

"A grown man—nearly fifty years old—has his *mother* break up with his fiancée?"

"Reese regrets any pain you might have incurred."

"You incur debt. You *feel* pain." Or inflict it, in the case of this woman. April wanted to rail at her. Wanted to pound on the desk. Wanted to hunt down Reese and pound on him.

The spirit of Beatrice Craig—though still, thank heavens, safely ensconced in her great-grandmother's elegant and surprisingly sturdy form—entered April and infused her backbone with steel.

She stood.

She removed the ring.

She looked down at the woman, a bubble of something rising in her. "I hope you'll all be very happy together."

She closed the door behind her. Maybe now she'd cry.

Nope. Barton appeared in the hallway.

"Your taxi is at the door, Miss April."

Along with her luggage, no doubt. All very efficient. She slid her icy hands into her jacket pockets. The right one encountered the business card she'd placed there. Hunter Pierce. She'd thought about that strange encounter non-stop until the moment Barton had opened the front door. "Thank you, Barton. First, I'm going to the kitchen."

"Mrs. Warrington said—"

"I'm sure she did. But what she says no longer affects me."

She headed for the kitchen. Corrinda, the cook, was at the sink and Harlan, who kept the grounds and house running, sat at a table in the far corner.

"Oh, Miss April," Corrinda said, as soon as she saw her. "I'm so sorry."

Of course, they'd all known before she did. "Thank you. I wanted to say goodbye to you—to you both, and to thank you for your kindnesses to me."

"Common decency, that's what you got from us. It only looks like kindness in comparison to what you've received from the head—and tail—of this house's family," Corrinda said.

Automatically, April started to deflect criticism of the Warringtons, then reconsidered. "You're partly right. You both *have* been kind, but they have been awful. I was an idiot. Just like Leslie tried to make me see."

"Oh, now, never tell me that sweet lady said you were an idiot. She loves you. And so does that husband of hers. You go right to them and tell them exactly what happened. They'll take care of you."

Despite the phrase *they'll take care of you* echoing in her head like a discordant gong, April again said, "Thank you." She hugged the woman, then laid a hand on Harlan's shoulder. "And you, Harlan. Good-bye."

"You're better off," he said with a grunt, patting her hand.

On her way back to the front entry, she passed the open double doors to what Mrs. Warrington insisted be called the drawing room. It sure wasn't a *living* room.

And there sat the three of them, looking like a bad knockoff of those ancient Noel Coward movies Grady loved.

The Evil Ex was the first to spot April at the threshold.

"*This* is the piece of fluff you've entertained yourself with? Really, Reese."

Fluff? Her? A piece of fluff? The other woman must have seen things in her no one else ever had.

He half rose. "April?"

"Reese." Roberta and her mother-in-law spoke in unison.

He sank back down.

Had he even tried to break free? He'd said he would. But looking at him now, she knew he never would have succeeded. Mrs. Warrington was right. He and Roberta belonged together.

"Goodbye, Reese. Good luck."

At the front door, Barton watched closely as a taxi driver stowed two totes atop the two large suitcases she'd brought when she came here four months ago. The rest of her few belongings were in storage.

"The driver has been paid sufficiently to drive you wherever you would like to go in the metropolitan area. May I tell him your destination?"

"No, thank you. I'll tell him." When she came up with something.

"Will you be okay, Miss April?

"You can stop calling me that now. It's just April. And I'll be fine. Thank you for asking, Barton. Thank you for everything."

He inclined his head. "Goodbye, April."

When the door closed with her inside, the taxi driver slued around in the seat. "Where to?"

Somewhere she could think, without admitting how wrong she'd been. Somewhere she could feel, without being exposed. Somewhere she could be loved, without having to explain.

"Where's she going with all that stuff?" Derek Kenton asked.

Hunter Pierce didn't answer. Kenton was a rookie asking a rookie question. If they knew where subjects were going there'd be no need for surveillance.

Derek had been on day-time surveillance of April—the subject— for more than a week. Sharon had instructed Hunter to take the lead starting Tuesday evening. He'd picked up the subject at the Willard Hotel and had followed her here to the Warrington estate.

Wednesday and today, she left at eight a.m., dropped by a driver at the nearest Metro station, then commuted to her office in D.C. Returned by the same route.

Wednesday night she hadn't left. Tonight was different.

He contacted Sharon and reported April Gareaux's departure by taxi with luggage.

"Interesting," she said. She didn't ask if they were following. She knew they were. "I might start hoping she's changed her mind about our proposal, except she hasn't contacted you. Let me know where she goes."

CHAPTER THREE

For years April had volunteered twice a week at the Fairlington, Virginia animal shelter, visiting with the not-yet-adopted dogs and—more difficult—the unadoptable. That ended when she'd moved in with Reese, or rather, with Mrs. Warrington.

So that's where she went to be loved without having to explain.

But she'd certainly had no intention of adopting a dog that day of all days.

Sitting on the floor, petting two dogs at once and with a third curled up inside the curve of her bent knee, she'd reached into her pocket for a bag of treats and felt the business card.

"Well, at least somebody thinks I'm a princess," she muttered dryly, causing Dragon to cock his head at her.

Thank God she hadn't signed a government form saying she wouldn't think about Hunter Pierce's bizarre proposal. They would have hauled her off to jail a hundred times.

What she needed to think about was what to say when she called Leslie.

What she needed to *not* think about was what Leslie *wouldn't* say.

What Leslie *hadn't* said had been loud between them ever since she and Grady teamed up with Great-Grandmother Beatrice to give April a home.

April had been thirteen. Her mother had still been alive, though not much of a mother. Really, Melly had never been much of a mother. It became more noticeable when April's father died when she was six.

Sitting there on the floor, getting far more solace than she was giving and thinking this might be when the tears came, April tried to decide which was worse—Leslie not saying, or Great-Grandma Beatrice saying. God knew Beatrice Craig had not and would not hesitate to express her opinion, even—

That's when April looked up and saw the card.

"What is she doing at an animal shelter?" Sharon demanded.

Silence was the only possible response to that unanswerable question.

"Right," she said. "Let me know when something changes."

A date card on Rufus' cage. How had she missed that when she'd let him out?

The date was tomorrow's. And since the shelter was officially closing soon for the night, he had run out of time. In the morning—

She didn't hesitate, she put in the adoption papers.

She used the Warringtons' address. No one in the shelter's back office had seen her suitcases, so they had no reason to wonder. And her years of volunteering persuaded them to bend the rules, letting her take Rufus immediately. His near-death experience also contributed, she was sure.

Walking out with him suffused her with joy. She'd saved him. She had a dog. She got to take him right home.

She got to take him right home.

There was the snag. She didn't have a home.

Standing in front of the now-closed shelter with suitcases and a dog on a leash from the first-night-home goody bag, she considered her options.

If she called Great-Grandma Beatrice, a car service would pick her up before she could turn around.

April would have a lot to listen to once the car reached Charlottesville. That wouldn't be fun, but she could handle it. The sticking point was Rufus. He would not be welcomed. She certainly couldn't send Rufus back to a shelter. Even if she could find another place for him in the nanosecond her great-grandmother's tolerance of dogs lasted, could she let him go at all?

So that left Leslie and Grady.

No problem with Rufus there. They'd take him in. Never raise a fuss if he damaged anything in their beautiful home. The problem was they weren't in that beautiful home.

Oh, she knew the code. And they'd be fine with her staying there, even if she never called and told them she was doing it.

But that was too cowardly.

She'd *have* to call.

Then they'd want her to come to Illinois, where they were. Where they *all* were.

Every year they gathered for the holidays. An extended family that kept expanding like a balloon with marriages, births, and oddballs like her.

Grady had been best friends in college with Paul Monroe and Michael Dickinson, then Paul's younger cousin Tris joined them their senior year. Later, Paul married Bette, then Michael and Tris got married, and of course Grady married Leslie. But it didn't end there. There were all their kids, Paul's younger sister Judi and the family she'd married into, Paul and Judi's parents, assorted in-laws and connections.

All the people who'd taken her in nearly as much as Leslie and Grady had. They were Leslie and Grady's friends. They were her ... What? The people who'd hugged away her tears when she let them, cheered her successes when she had them, defined security and friendship and decency.

They would wrap her up in love and the holidays. They would distract her with their kids, who'd long viewed her as something between an aunt and a camp counselor. They would keep her too busy with festivities and traditions to mope. They would fix things.

They'll take care of you.

She looked down at the dog.

He looked up with melted milk-chocolate eyes, content and trusting.

She needed to figure this out.

Maybe Hunter took a little perverse pleasure in making his next report to Sharon, "She has a dog."

"What?"

"A dog. Four legs. Tail. Fur."

"I know what a dog—What is she doing with it?"

"Standing. In front of the animal shelter, with her luggage, making phone calls." And looking more disheartened with each call.

"She must be going to the Roberts'. She must be."

"They're out of town, aren't they?"

"Yes."

He looked over at Kenton. "You said she let herself into the Roberts' house at lunchtime Monday, right?"

"Yes. Watered the plants."

He spoke back into the phone. "So she'd go right there. No need for phone calls. One call maybe to see if it was okay, but she's made more than a dozen that were short, now three that have lasted—Wait a minute. She's flagging down a taxi. On the move."

"Crap!" Derek Kenton retreated three steps.

"Don't move," Hunter barked. He and Sharon had immediately gone still. Derek froze now.

April Gareaux rolled her shoulders as if she'd shivered, then pivoted away from the window she'd been staring out and carried a laundry basket across her friend's living room.

No one moved until the hallway door closed behind her, shutting off their view.

Derek cursed. "She looked right at us. How the hell did she know—."

"She didn't. She couldn't see you. We're a dark void to her." *You've been watching me.* No, she *couldn't* have known. Yet she'd been so certain … "But you know better than to move. Motion—"

"—draws attention," Derek finished with a grimace. "Sorry."

Hunter nodded. "Sharon, as long as you're heading out—" She'd said she came to see the set-up, but he suspected there was more. None of which he want to hear. Better to get her headed home to her family. "—check the laundry room as soon as she leaves."

"See if she's interacting with people? Or if someone else is following her? Good idea, but why not you?" All she had to do was pull rank, say "you do it." Typical that she'd rather poke at him.

"Hotel set-up, then—"

"Why? She turned you down."

Actually, the hotel was already set up. And double-checked. "Her initial reaction was negative. That could change."

"C'mon, that isn't why you want me to check the laundry room instead of doing it yourself." She squinted at him, then laughed. "God! Impervious Pierce isn't afraid of a little lingerie is he?"

He ignored her. "Don't make contact. Call me if anything needs to be added to the report. Please," he added belatedly.

Still grinning, she left.

Sitting on a folding chair with his screen masked so its light wouldn't show through the window, he opened the report, picking up where he'd left off.

The subject had loaded the luggage in the taxi, had a dispute with the driver about the dog, which she'd won, then headed out. With them right behind.

They hadn't gone far, pulling up to what he recognized as the address of the apartment she'd sublet when she'd moved to the Warrington estate.

Ah. Most likely her former neighbor across the hall. The background report had said they were friendly.

Supposition wasn't fact, so he'd dispatched Kenton to arrive as she finished getting everything into the elevator to watch which floor she went to. "Don't help her or she'll remember you," he'd ordered.

He confirmed with operations as soon as Kenton reported, and they were in this vacant unit across the street before she'd finished dragging her last suitcase into Mandy Roteen's apartment.

Mandy Roteen left shortly afterward, and April Gareaux divided her time between laundry and the dog.

You've been watching me.

He gazed past his laptop to the window across the street.

She couldn't have seen them a few minutes ago.

Just as she couldn't have known she was being watched.

He was good at his job. When he didn't want his presence known, it wasn't.

Yet she had been so sure ... until his lack of response made her doubt.

He shifted. Damned uncomfortable, these folding chairs.

He focused on the screen and completed the report.

He did not include the subject's comments about believing she'd been watched. Nor the gleeful descriptions of lace cups and high-cut legs Sharon called in. If she wanted that in the report she could put it in herself.

April wearily stacked cushions from Mandy's pull-out sofa on the floor.

There hadn't been a single hotel room within walking distance of the Metro system she needed for getting to work that would accept dogs and wouldn't bankrupt her.

Her next call had been to her best friend from college.

Amy said, "I'm so sorry I can't help, but Greg and I are in Colorado already for the holiday week, and the floors are being redone while we're gone."

That had delivered a double jolt.

Jolt A was realizing Thanksgiving was exactly a week away.

Jolt B was having no idea who Greg was, which showed how long it had been since they'd been in touch. God, nearly two years. She'd been so busy at the end with Gerard, then trying to find a job, meeting Reese … She'd let time—and the friendship—slide by.

She searched her mind for someone else she'd feel okay about calling for help.

It might be a bad career move, but she tried Zoe.

In response to the news of the engagement ending, she'd said, "Good riddance to the jerk. Now we can party."

In response to the news that April had a dog, she'd said, "No way. I'm allergic as all get-out. Hives, hospital, the whole thing. Not possible."

Zoe had promised to make calls on her behalf. But the evening had been slipping away. April would have to go to Leslie and Grady's place. Which meant she'd have to call them. Which meant she'd be in Illinois before she knew it. Which meant she—once again—would be rescued by the people she most wanted to show she was self-sufficient.

In desperation, she'd tried her former neighbor, Mandy. With reluctance clear in her voice, Mandy agreed to have April and Rufus stay for the one night's overlap, before she, too, left for the holiday.

Ahhh. That gave her more than a week to figure out the next move. April had felt like dancing. It was a good thing she refrained, because she needed all her energy to get her belongings in the cab, out of the cab, in the elevator, out of the elevator, and down the hall.

Mandy immediately announced she had plans this evening, which clearly didn't include staying home consoling uninvited guests. She said not to wait up, she wouldn't disturb April when she came in, and she left.

April washed clothes. That was a lesson from years with Melly. When you had access to a washing machine, you did laundry.

Next, she called Zoe to update her and check for any progress on a more permanent place.

"If you had a bigger budget…" The other woman didn't complete the thought, apparently recalling that it was what she paid April that limited her housing budget.

April plugged the awkward gap. "If I had more success lobbying for Brussels sprouts, I'd earn more and then I'd have a bigger budget."

Did princesses have an association? Maybe she'd be better lobbying for princesses. Especially if she learned about being a princess from the inside.

April touched the business card she'd transferred to the pocket of her robe.

"Don't be so hard on yourself. Nobody's done better at getting Brussels sprouts recipes in the papers than you—"

"Two! I've gotten two recipes in papers."

"As I said," Zoe voice twisted, "you've gotten more Brussels sprouts recipes in papers than anyone else. But maybe I've left you on this account too long. You could try broccoli for a while."

"Really?" April brightened. Surely, she could do a lot with a triple threat like broccoli—a salad ingredient, appetizer/dipper, or cooked vegetable. "That would be fantastic, Zoe. Who would take Brussels sprouts?"

"Jason could add—"

April's mood collapsed. "Jason? No. Honestly, Zoe, anyone else, but he's mean."

"To you?"

"About Brussels sprouts," she clarified.

"Honey, will you listen to yourself? You're feeling sorry for Brussels sprouts. This afternoon you could have used the little cabbage wanna-bes to get more face time with that hunk from State, but you let that slip right through your fingers. How about looking out for yourself for once? You've got to get a life, April. A little excitement."

April half smiled to herself as she crawled into the sofa-bed, one arm trailing down so she could touch Rufus, who was curled up on the floor. After today, she'd take less excitement, thank you.

A place to stay for her and Rufus, the routine of a steady job, and she'd be happy.

Only much later did she realize she'd fallen asleep without shedding a single tear for the end of her engagement.

CHAPTER FOUR

"Pierce. All hell's breaking loose over there," Kenton said.

He woke instantly. Had the close-up view in focus almost as fast. But it was dark. And there was a lot of movement. He thought the thinner form was April. But the other, that had to be a guy. A big guy.

He and Kenton couldn't get there, not fast enough. Damn. The hell with the operation if it prevented her from being hurt—

He grabbed his phone as he switched to night vision.

He put the phone down without connecting.

Five hours later, April sat on the cushions once more in place on Mandy's sofa, waiting for the clock to reach eight-thirty a.m. so she could call Leslie or Great-Grandma Beatrice without their thinking it was an emergency.

Taken from one angle, last night's scene was really rather funny.

Clearly, Mandy had forgotten about her guest. She and the guy drunkenly fumbled their amorous way through the dark—shedding clothes along the way, judging by evidence later visible—and fell onto the couch, April, and Rufus.

Rufus barked, Mandy screamed, the guy cursed, April desperately tried to corral Rufus to stifle the noise.

Too late.

The guy—April never had gotten his name—was still pulling on clothes when Roger, the building manager, rapped on the door.

"I know you're in there, April Gareaux. I heard your voice in all that ruckus. And I know what you have in there with you. One of those mangy, mutts you were forever sneaking in here. You know they're not allowed. You can pretend you're not there all you want—I'm calling the board. You know what they said last time—you know!"

Yes, she knew. Though, even if she'd known the man was terrified of dogs, there wasn't much she could have done differently.

She'd only brought that Chihuahua-mix she'd had out for a walk up to her apartment for a moment because she'd forgotten her sunscreen. But of course it was the precise moment Roger came out of a door, and started squeaking and squealing like a squeaky toy.

No wonder the dog thought he was playing, and happily jumped at him.

"And now he'll be on *my* case," Mandy had grumbled before she went into her bedroom and slammed the door.

Roger's threat became reality with an authoritative knock at quarter past seven this morning.

The board president wasn't cruel—he didn't allow Roger to come in—but he was firm. The dog had to go. Immediately.

Mandy, clearly hung over, said that was fine with her.

So she'd have to call Leslie or Great-Grandma Beatrice after all.

Her fingers slid into her pocket.

Unless she tried the one remaining possibility of dealing with this.

A princess for the month of December...

"Pierce." Sharon's voice came through his cell. "She's called the main number at State asking if you work here." Sharon didn't have to say who *she* was.

Smart move, April Gareaux. Any scam artist could have official-looking cards printed and get a crony to answer a phone. Going through the main number avoided that.

"Get the call sent to you, Sharon, and confirm. Set up a meet. Her office. One hour."

April watched Hunter Pierce cross the grassy area, approaching a gate that would let him inside this fenced-in area for dogs. His face showed nothing except a slight flush from the cold.

At least he wasn't impervious to nature.

When she'd called State this morning, she'd been put through to Sharon Johnson, who confirmed that, yes, she was Special Agent Hunter Pierce's supervisor. And, yes, she knew he had spoken with April yesterday about a certain assignment during the holidays.

Sharon had excused herself a moment, then relayed a message from Hunter about meeting at April's office, but she's said it had to be here. She hadn't mentioned that while her belongings could be left at the apartment building temporarily, Rufus couldn't be.

Sharon had chuckled and said, "Oh, this is going to be fun, watching him deal with you."

"He's going to? Deal with me, I mean. I thought he was…"

What? A princess recruiter? And now it turned out he was … a princess wrangler?

"He'll be in charge of the operation throughout."

"Oh." The operation? That sounded a lot more official than princess wrangling.

"Is that a problem, Ms. Gareaux?"

"I don't know. I don't know him." Yet, she already felt like she could ask this woman on the other end of the phone, "Can I trust him?"

"With your life," Sharon said immediately. "Not that it will come to that. The first phase might be a bit taxing. Then, if the king—"

A king. She supposed it made sense there could be king in the picture since she was supposed to be a princess. But what king?

"—doesn't agree to see you, that's that. We'll thank you for your time and effort, and you return to your routine. If the king does agree to see you, well, best case would be a matter of having pleasant holidays in his company."

And not with her family.

That thought produced a sharp pang, as she watched Hunter approach. She wouldn't have seen them if she'd still been with Reese, she reminded herself.

Rufus came flying toward them barking at Hunter, backing up so he was right in front of her.

Hunter looked at the dog, but didn't change his pace or his path.

"Rufus. Enough." The dog barked twice more, but with less conviction. She stood. "Sit." The dog sat. "It's okay, Rufus. Go play. Go on, go play."

The dog gave Hunter a sharp look before trotting off to rejoin two dogs he'd been happily tussling with.

April remained standing. If she offered to shake and he took her up on it, his hand might stick to her icy fingers like a tongue to a flagpole in January. She kept her hands clasped in front of her.

Hunter stopped at arm's length. And waited.

She cleared her throat. "I've changed my mind. I'll do it. What you asked me to do yesterday. I'll do it."

"What about your fiancé?"

"I don't have one anymore." His non-reaction seemed a little too perfect. She eyed him. "Why do I think you already knew that?"

He replied with a question of his own. "You don't want to spend Christmas with your family?"

"I … It's complicated." She rallied. "Besides, weren't you the one who wanted me to do this?" When he didn't respond, she went on, "I have two requirements. First, I have to be free on Thursday—Thanksgiving. As myself. The rest of the time I'll be your—" Her voice dropped. "—princess, but that day, I'm me."

He showed no curiosity about her demand. "Everywhere you go, you'll have a department escort."

"As long as they don't try to stop me from … my activities."

"Done."

"Second. Rufus lives with me wherever I am."

"That's not—"

"It's a deal-breaker, Mr. Pierce. And he might not be perfectly house-trained. Yet. I'll have to take him out several times a day."

He studied her face for one breath, a second, a third, then he turned toward the dog. "There may be places you go that don't accept dogs."

"Then I don't go there. I'm not talking about refusing to leave him alone for an afternoon or even a day, but he lives where I live."

"If at all feasible, and if it's not feasible, he'll be cared for."

"If it's not feasible, he and I will leave. I want that to be clear."

"It is clear."

"Okay then," she said. She suspected that wasn't how a princess would agree to something momentous, but it was all she could think of.

He sat, pulled a folded sheet from his inside suit coat pocket, spread it on the bench and extended a blue pen to her.

She didn't take her gaze from his as she also sat, then took the pen. She broke the look only to focus on the paper.

She spread her hand to keep it in place while she wrote her name. The paper felt warm. From being inside his coat, next to him. Her heart slammed—*one, two, three*—before she signed quickly, and returned the pen.

"Sharon—Ms. Johnson," she amended when something streaked across his eyes, "said you'd be handling this, uh, situation. So what is this all about? How am I going to convince anyone I'm a princess?"

"For operational security, you will only be told what you need to know. What I am authorized to tell you now is that we will begin instructing you in what you need to know immediately, while we attempt to arrange a meeting with King Jozef of Bariavak."

She pushed aside stomach-clenching thoughts at the second half of that sentence and focused on the first.

She'd just signed up for princess school.

CHAPTER FIVE

Over the following days, April came to feel exactly like a fairy tale princess.

Not the Disney kind, the Brothers Grimm kind.

The kind locked up in a castle—or in this case, a one-bedroom suite in an exclusive hotel across Lafayette Park from the White House—who has to go through many trials in hopes of being set free.

That first day, Hunter drove her to pick up her belongings at the apartment building, then to an alleyway entrance to the hotel. One of the most famous hotels in Washington, both for its history and location.

"I can carry—"

"Just your handbag. The dog and luggage will come up later."

"But—"

Before she got more out, he'd bundled her out of his anonymous dark car as if the sky were pelting rain instead of sparkling dry. He pushed open the back door into the hotel. She started forward—and walked directly into his back.

Instead of holding the door open for her to go in first, he'd stepped in front of her. She backpedaled. But the instant she broke contact with him he reached back and gripped her arm, sliding his large hand up the inside of her upper arm and drawing her whole body close to his back.

Warmth and a scent combining wood smoke and soap rushed around her. His body was as solid as the granite her thoughts had likened him to in the conference room yesterday. But granite couldn't have moved the way he did to keep her plastered against him, going through the doorway and into a small hallway.

When he released her she felt like a puppet who'd had its strings cut.

He gave her no time to recover, hustling her along with his hand wrapped around her arm, into a service elevator, up several floors, out the elevator, down a hallway, and into a room.

They'd moved so fast, she stopped inside the door catching her breath while he looked through the suite with efficient thoroughness. He clearly was checking for more than if there were enough towels in the bathroom.

"Are you going to tell me more about—?"

"I'll be right back."

And he was gone, locking the door as he left.

Without moving position, she looked around the suite. Her eyes took in the classic sofa and two easy chairs. A small dining table in the corner by windows that showed only bare tree branches from where she stood. An open door revealed a pristine bedroom and the elegant bathroom beyond.

Her brain pounded with two thoughts: She should have asked more questions. What had she gotten herself in to?

Before she could unstick herself from the spot or the thoughts, he was back with Rufus on a leash and a couple of the bags. He gave her a sharp look, apparently recognizing she hadn't moved.

"What were you looking—?"

"I'll be back shortly. Stay in the suite. Do not call or communicate in any other way with any of your friends or relatives. Do you understand?"

"Yes, but—"

He was gone again.

Rufus rushed around her, wagging his plumy tail, until he had wrapped her ankles in leash. That finally broke her out of her trance.

When Hunter returned with an African American woman probably in her late thirties, a Jaw-in-Training man in his mid-twenties, and the rest of her belongings, she was still in the suite, and she had not called or communicated in any way with friends or family.

So Hunter Pierce had no reason to glare at her. Just because she was putting soaps and toiletries in the bathroom while Yolanda from housekeeping sat in the easy chair, petting Rufus.

As soon as the hall door closed behind Yolanda, he added words to the glare. "You were alone thirty-one minutes, and all you had to do was stay in the suite and not talk to anyone. One slip and this can be over before it's started. If you told her any of your history—"

"I didn't."

"I suspect April was asking questions, rather than telling secrets," the woman said. "I'm Sharon Johnson. Nice to meet you in person. And this is Derek Kenton."

Hunter interrupted their hellos and handshakes, demanding of her, "Is that true?"

She shrugged. "Yolanda needed to sit down. She works two full-time jobs, takes care of her family, and now her mother-in-law's moved in. Plus, she has a bad back. There wasn't time to talk about my history."

His frown darkened. There was no pleasing the man.

Over the following days, she learned how true that was.

She'd thought Zoe Rules were tough? They were anarchy compared to Hunter Rules.

Starting with a handshake.

Closing the space and remembering to smile were just a start, as she learned when he instructed her to demonstrate a handshake with Derek Kenton. Over and over and over.

Don't grip that hard. Now it's too limp.

Don't let your arm flop like a fish. Not that stiff, either.

Don't tuck your elbow in at your side. That looks like you're holding him at arm's length because he smells.

"Do it again. No." He stepped in, and Derek dropped into a chair with apparent gratitude. "Half a step closer. Now, thumb up. Make sure your fingers go under the other person's palm. Palm to palm until base of thumbs meet. Curve your thumb over the back of the other person's hand, otherwise—" He straightened his thumb. His hand was so much larger that his thumb slid under the cuff of her shirt, brushing her wrist.

He was right. It was too—No, not *intimate*. *Personal.* She rotated her hand, but that rubbed his thumb across the pulse-point at the inside of her wrist.

"No crushing, no limp fish, no stiff arm," Derek said from the sidelines. "Two or three shakes. Smile and make eye contact."

Automatically, she looked up, making eye contact.

"Sorry. Did I grip too hard?" Hunter's voice was harsher than usual.

She'd pulled her hand from his grasp. "Bit of a cramp."

"Been using the same muscles all morning," Derek said sympathetically.

Right. Her princess muscles.

Hunter turned away. "We'll switch topics."

A switch, but no break. Because what followed was the first in seemingly unending sessions on diplomatic and royal no-nos.

She'd awakened two mornings in a row to her own voice mumbling, "Mr. Ambassador, Sir or Excellency, but never Ambassador Jones. Your Majesty, but His Highness."

In between, she studied stacks of photos of the Bariavak royal family, including Princess Sofia and her dashing husband, Prince Leopold—the long-dead parents of the lost princess—as well as dignified King Jozef.

The upside was that she had no time or energy to think about her family or her job or where she and Rufus would live after New Year's or even the end of her engagement. Princessing was hard work, mentally and physically. She'd be so tired by the end of each day that brushing her teeth seemed like a major achievement.

At this rate her hair would grow long enough to let out the window and climb down from the fifth floor suite before she'd satisfy Hunter Pierce.

"Was Rapunzel a Grimm's fairy tale?" she asked Derek abruptly.

He blinked at her, then looked at Hunter, who was on his computer at the table by the windows. Hunter shrugged, apparently granting permission for Derek to say, "What?"

"Never mind. I'll ask Sharon when she comes next time."

The only time April had any freedom was when she was alone with Sharon.

They'd made clandestine expeditions down the service elevator to the hotel kitchen, becoming friendly with the staff, especially Ferdinand, the chef, and Manny, their regular room service waiter. Sunday evening, in a moment of daring, they had slipped outside with Rufus and walked around Lafayette Park. Who would have thought visiting statues of General Von Steuben and President Andrew Jackson could be such a treat?

But Sharon only came once or twice a day. Mostly, apparently, to order Hunter to take a break. She'd made him walk Rufus one time, though more often that task fell to Derek, who was not amused but diligently took the poop bags with him.

Officially, Hunter and Derek rotated on 12-hour shifts. In practice, it was Derek for 12 hours and Hunter for 24. Oh, he had to leave sometimes, because he'd be clean-shaven and in fresh clothes when she came out of the bedroom in the morning. But since he apparently waited for her to fall asleep before he indulged in those forays, what good did it do her?

"Shall we get started?"

She was sorely tempted to answer "no," but by now she knew that wouldn't stop Hunter.

"What are we doing today?" she asked.

"Dancing."

She groaned.

CHAPTER SIX

Manny wheeled in the room service lunch cart on Wednesday for her, Derek, and Hunter with professional aplomb. But when he spotted Rufus, he broke into a smile. The dog started to wag his tail.

"Got something for you, too, my man," Manny said to the dog. "Straight from Ferdinand."

April's stomach dropped.

Manny removed the cover from a small bowl and placed it on the floor, then looked up at her. "We didn't think you'd mind. Boiled rice and beef. Nice and mild. Shouldn't interrupt Rufus' training at all."

Hunter's narrow-eyed gaze shifted from waiter to dog—now immersed in the bowl's contents—to her.

She moved so her back was to him, giving Manny a warning look.

"Please thank, uh, whoever that was you said was thinking about my dog. I suppose the housekeeping staff must have mentioned Rufus' presence," she said with emphasis.

"Yeah. Housekeeping. Housekeeping did mention it," Manny said, watching her.

She nodded. "And I suppose someone in the kitchen empathized because he—or she—loves dogs, too."

"Yes. That's exactly what happened. Hope that's okay."

"Of course it is," she said before Hunter could respond. "And please tell whoever provided the treat for Rufus how much it is appreciated. By me as well as him."

Manny departed, pausing only to shoot her a quick eyebrows-raised look when the door masked him from the rest of the room. She smiled back blandly, aware of Hunter watching her.

"Let's eat," Derek said. "I'm starved."

Hunter said nothing throughout the meal.

As soon as she finished, she jumped up and said, "We better get back to work."

She and Derek took their positions on the cleared area being used for a dance floor and Hunter had his finger on the button to start the music when he said, "He knew Rufus' name. The waiter."

"I called him by name."

"Not until after the waiter did."

"Yolanda knows his name. She must have mentioned it. Are we going to continue? Or are you satisfied with my dancing?"

He made a noise that didn't say much for her dancing, but, still, he didn't start the music. "You will not break your pledge, April Gareaux."

It was a command.

"I won't tell anyone anything ever—*ow*."

He'd started the music, she was slow moving her foot at the first note, and Derek stepped on it. Hard.

An hour later, and it still throbbed.

Boy, had she been wrong thinking of the Disney version of Cinderella. Hunter was no Fairy Godmother. She was no graceful Cinderella waiting to show her true self, and there was no magic wand. If there had been, she'd have used it on her foot. Or her dancing skills.

Yes, she was definitely a Brothers Grimm kind of princess.

"We'll go back to the waltz," Hunter announced, switching off "They Can't Take That Away From Me" that they'd used for the fox trot.

April flopped on the couch. Derek eased into a chair as if his leg hurt. She hadn't kicked his ankle *that* hard.

Hunter fiddled with the speakers, and ordered Derek, "Again."

Before Derek could respond, April said. "Let us rest. If my passing for this princess depends on my ballroom dancing, we're cooked anyway. We'll have to rely on the resemblance you say I have to the royal family."

She didn't see it herself. What she *had* seen in those photos was sadness in King Jozef's eyes, even before his granddaughter went missing.

"You resemble them," he said.

She huffed. "Why you won't tell me details of how this princess came to be lost—No, don't bother. I know. Operational security."

But he hadn't started to say that. Not this time. He'd gone still.

She zeroed in on him. "There's something more, isn't there?"

A nanosecond of awareness connected them. Possibly surprise on his part that she'd picked up on his reaction. But he damped it down, and April put it at fifty-fifty whether he would ignore her question.

He extended his hand to her. "Derek, put the music on."

Derek scrambled to obey. She didn't budge, chin sunk on her chest, looking at that strong hand in front of her.

"I request the honor of this dance," he said formally.

She stuck her hand out, because there wasn't any reason—any rational reason—not to. He slid his palm under hers, wrapped thumb and fingers around her palm and drew her inexorably to her feet. Not a handshake, yet the contact had some of the same muscles trembling.

Because they'd been overworked.

The same old music started—she used to sort of like Strauss—he put one hand at her shoulder blade, used the other to clasp her hand, and hit the beat perfectly. *Show off.*

But as they moved around the open space, her ill humor faded. His hand on her back was larger than Derek's, firm and in control. His hold on her hand guided rather than pushed or pulled. His confidence and ease flowed into her. They were not two independent operators in constant danger of collision, but a single unit negotiating space and time and music. Flawlessly. Breathlessly.

The music stopped, and they stopped with it—something she had not achieved with Derek.

Hunter released her and took a half step back, dropping his head momentarily, almost in a bow. Regarding the thick glossy brown at the crown of his head she quelled an urge to curtsey.

He took her left hand in his. Their hands had been clasped throughout the dance, but now she was aware of this single contact as she had not been within the intricacies of their dual movement. She felt the warmth and faint scratchiness of his skin, sensed the power he could wield.

For one insane moment she thought he would kiss her hand. Instead, his grip shifted so only her ring finger and little finger rested atop his hand.

"This is the something more."

The dance must have deprived her brain of oxygen, because she had no idea what he was talking about.

"Along with your resemblance to the king's family, you have this mark—the Bariavak Hand. The little finger on the left hand being as long as the fourth finger."

She looked down, her own hand feeling oddly unfamiliar.

"It's hereditary," Hunter continued. "A very strong gene in the Bariavak royal family. Others have it as well, but it is not a common trait. That combined with your overall resemblance…"

April felt something rush through her. She was worn out, emotionally, physically, mentally. Yet this rush was like a mega-jolt of caffeine applied directly to her nerve-endings.

He thought this might happen. He thought all they'd done might actually lead somewhere. And oh, my God, he also thought she could pass herself off as this princess.

Hunter stood in front of Sharon's desk.

He'd timed it so she'd just cleaned the last folder from her desk, ready to start the long holiday weekend with her family.

That would keep this short.

So would being direct. "You've got to stop undercutting my operation by taking her outside the suite."

"You're working her hard. All that handshaking, moving across a room, titles, diplomatic intricacies, dancing." She raised her brows at the last one. "Even dancing with her yourself, I hear."

He didn't react to the teasing. "It is necessary to show her how to stand, how to walk."

"Why? She's not supposed to have been brought up as a princess, right? She's supposed to be an everyday person."

"Those are facts. If he agrees to see her, you don't want the focus to be on facts. You want the focus to be on emotion. Therefore our focus now is on emotion."

She snorted, and muttered, "Hunter Pierce, focusing on emotion."

He ignored that and continued. "We smooth over the facts by giving April confidence in small skills he would expect of a princess, helping him accept that she *is* a princess."

Both of Sharon's eyebrows went up and her eyes opened wide at the same time her mouth curled. She stood, picked up her briefcase and came around the desk. "I do believe you're starting to feel something for our make-believe princess."

She reached up and patted his cheek as she passed him. "Happy Thanksgiving, Hunter."

CHAPTER SEVEN

The fourth Thursday in November arrived amid a reprieve of warm, sunny days that recalled earlier autumn.

Hunter drove through holiday-quiet streets, following April's directions, clearly heading toward the neighborhood of her old apartment. A return to the animal shelter?

No. She instructed him to park in a municipal lot, then led him away from the shelter, saying how good it felt to stretch her legs after never getting out of the suite.

As if he didn't know she and Sharon took jaunts around the park, not to mention to the hotel kitchen. So far April had been discreet, telling no one anything of what she was doing here or of who she really was. Instead, she got these people talking about themselves.

When he'd agreed to her requirement to spend Thanksgiving as herself, he'd known he'd cover the shift, relieving Derek early so he'd get to Delaware for Thanksgiving dinner with his family. Giving other people holidays off was good for morale. Hunter could protect the operation no matter what she had in mind.

But he hadn't expected this.

The sign on a bland cement-block wall beside the door April was about to open read: "Dinwiddie Shelter. Thanksgiving Dinner, 1 p.m."

"What's the matter?" she asked.

"Nothing."

She tipped her head, unconvinced. Damn. He was falling apart if he let April Gareaux see that something—No. No, nothing was wrong. He was here to do his job. Like always.

He checked their surroundings again before stepping in front of her to open the door and enter first.

Scents and noise crested over him, but it was the undertow of memory that could take a man down.

On the far side of the kitchen a flow of people carried stacks of plates, napkins, and tins of utensils out a set of swinging doors. For an instant, tent flaps replaced the doors in his mind.

April's voice came to him. "Hang your jacket here."

She hooked her coat and purse over a peg before he reacted.

"That's not a safe place for your purse." He said it more to give himself time—to hang up his jacket and regain his mental footing—than from hope of changing her mind.

"It'll be fine."

Focus on now. On the job.

The maelstrom of activity centered on a small black-haired woman holding a clipboard. People rushed up to her, asked a question, she consulted her clipboard, and gave an answer that sent the person scurrying back into the flow. At a trio of huge ovens, people filled metal containers with steaming food. More headed out the swinging doors.

April waded into the fray without a backward glance. One step behind, Hunter stuck out an arm to keep a man with a huge tray of uncooked rolls from knocking into her. The man harmlessly bounced off his arm and continued his journey, never bothering to see what redirected him.

Hunter came up behind April in time to hear her say, "I'll do potatoes again, Maria."

"I don't know, April. Last year I thought you were going to drop from piling those mashed potatoes on the plates. That's heavy work for—Who are you?"

A pair of dark eyes pinned him.

April glanced over her shoulder. "This is Hunter. He's with me."

"Is he now?" A large black man swathed in a white apron turned from the nearest stove and smiled. "Tell us all about it, April."

She faced away from Hunter, but he knew she was blushing because the tip of her right ear showed pink.

"Not now, Jameel," countermanded the woman as she consulted the clipboard. "No time. We sure can use the extra pair of hands. You look strong enough, so you do the potatoes, and let April do green beans."

"He's not here to work. I mean he already is … uh…"

"I can handle the potatoes," he told Maria. "As long as they're next to the green beans."

"Oh, ho!" crowed Jameel.

Maria kept to the point. "If that's the condition to your helping, I won't argue. If that's not the way they're arranged—"

"I'll take care of it."

She looked up. "I believe you will." Then her attention shifted to someone by the refrigerators. "No, Henry—cranberries go in the other unit."

Hunter followed April through the swinging doors, into a wide aisle behind a metal counter with rectangular holes to receive the containers he'd seen in the kitchen. Tables with paper turkey and pumpkin decorations cluttered the rest of the room.

April handed him a large chef's white apron made of paper. He'd managed to get it on without shredding it when the kitchen doors popped open and a parade of potholder-wearing workers started carrying in metal containers.

At the far end of the room, someone opened the main door. A line shuffled toward them, gathering trays, plates and utensils on the way to the food. The leading edge of the line reached him, and he kept his head down and dug a metal scoop into a snow bank of mashed potatoes.

Beside him, April wished each person "Happy Thanksgiving," some by name. Those simple words expanded into conversations about half the time.

He took a plate, overflowed the scoop and added it to the turkey and cranberries.

"You're not leaving any room for the green beans," April protested.

"I don't mind, lady."

Hunter looked up and saw the owner of the plate was a boy of about seven. His dark hair was slicked down except for a curling tuft at the crown of his head.

He winked at the boy, shocking the hell out of himself.

The boy gave a quick grin, then moved on down the line, as if nothing extraordinary had happened.

As if it wasn't odd for Hunter Pierce to be serving instead of receiving. To have the power to decide how much went on each plate instead of hoping for enough.

Plate after plate they came. Age, race, gender varied. Some came in families, others in pairs, most alone. What never changed was the plate they held out to him. The same dim white, the same portions of turkey and cranberries in the same positions.

Plate after plate, he piled on potatoes.

"Whoa, man! That's a heap of potatoes," the man named Jameel boomed from over his shoulder. "If you keep on like that I'll have to get back to making more."

Hunter stopped in mid-scoop. His brain knew he had no reason for the guilt making his heart jump.

"If you didn't make the mashed potatoes taste so good, Jameel, people wouldn't want so much." April's voice seemed to come from a distance.

Jameel laughed. "All right, all right. But I'm telling everyone I hogtie to do the peeling that it's all your friend's fault."

The leathery-faced man in front of Hunter extended his plate.

"Don't you mind that old Scrooge Jameel, young man. You listen to our April and heap those potatoes on here like you been doin'. You're the most popular soul up and down this line today."

"Why, Robert, you said I was your favorite last year," April teased.

"You was, last year. But look what you're serving up this year—beans. We still love you, April. But this man, he knows how to dish up potatoes to make a soul happy!"

Everyone around them laughed.

Hunter put his head down and focused on the next plate shoved in front of him.

The sound April made in her throat jerked him out of a non-thinking stupor like the snap of a hypnotist's fingers.

"What?" No one was in sight on the empty street.

She brushed the front of her top, visible between the open flaps of her coat.

"Green bean juice," she muttered, disgusted. "Not very princess-like."

"Princesses do charity work. Just not usually heavy labor."

She looked at him. Not until he saw the surprise in her face did he realize he was smiling. Relief at leaving the shelter.

They had reached the corner by her old apartment building. Down the side street he saw a man's form slumped at the base of a wall.

"Wait here," she said.

"I'm coming."

"No you're not, or Leroy will disappear. I want to bring him and Ham their Thanksgiving dinners." She hoisted a plastic bag with leftovers from the shelter. "Leroy and Ham don't like going to the shelter."

"So you deliver."

She shrugged. "Why not?"

"And you skip Thanksgiving dinner yourself."

"No. That's the bag you're carrying."

She headed down the sloped sidewalk toward Leroy, who now stood at the far end of the building. Hunter surprised himself by not following her. But if Leroy hiccupped wrong…

He didn't. He barely let April come close enough to hand over the bag, then he scurried off, while April called out wishes for the day.

"Two more stops before our dinner," she said when she returned.

She signed in at the back entry of the animal shelter, which was officially closed, but apparently not to her. She tucked mini-baggies of treats in her pockets, and held one out to him. "They'll love you forever if you give them treats."

"No, thank you."

She looked at him an extra beat, then added that baggy to her pocket.

She started with the cats, giving them treats, letting them wind around her ankles, talking to them, petting them. Even the ones that had "Caution" marked on their cages got a treat or two and some conversation.

She washed her hands at a utility sink. His momentary hope that they were done ended when she opened a door that revealed an aisle between dog runs. She greeted each animal by name and with enthusiasm. As with the cats, she let most have a few minutes out of the run.

But the last dog was clearly a favorite. Hunter knew it from her voice and her face when she opened the cage.

"This is Dragon," she announced. "Dragon, say hi to Hunter."

The shaggy animal gave an excited yip. But it was clearly for her, not him. She dropped to a cross-legged seat on an old towel on the floor. Wriggling with energetic joy that belied his white muzzle, the dog circled in front of her, so she could pet all of him while she stayed still, talking to him, praising him, and using his name every other word. The dog backed up so she could better scratch his flanks. He raised his head and a shiver of ecstasy wriggled along his backbone.

April sneezed. Three times in quick, hard succession. Hunter stepped around the dog for a look at her face. Her eyes were red.

"You're allergic."

He wrapped one hand around her arm to pull her up.

"No, it's fine. I'm—"

As soon as she resisted, the dog advanced so his body partially blocked April's, and growled. Hunter didn't know dogs well, but he knew a warning when he heard it. He had to admire the animal's positioning—protective, and equally poised for offense or defense.

"Dragon! Shame on you. Don't you growl at Hunter."

The dog stopped making the sound, but he stayed right where he was and his eyes didn't waver from Hunter.

"Really, I'm fine." She sneezed again.

"Right."

"It's not Dragon—or any of the dogs. I'm allergic to cats. I guess I didn't wash my hands well enough. It'll stop." She gave her arm a slight tug. He released it and Dragon relaxed. "If I weren't so allergic, I'd have had a cat years ago."

Her voice dropped. "Don't tell the cats, but I'd rather have a dog, anyway. My apartment building didn't allow dogs. The building manager caught me keeping one for a weekend, so I could show him to a family who couldn't get to the shelter during regular hours. And it worked! The Flannerys adopted Homer. They sent a picture of Homer bounding through the grass and you could see how happy he was. Uh, what was I saying?"

"The building manager caught you breaking the rules."

"Oh. Right. After that he watched me like a hawk. One time he insisted on looking in my laundry basket—"

Dirty-minded super probably hoped to see what Sharon had described with such glee. Lacy cups, High cut—

"—As if I'd hide a dog under all those towels."

He eased his hands open. Towels.

"The machine here was broken, so I said I'd do them. Roger tried to say I wasn't allowed to do commercial laundry under terms of the lease. I told him it wasn't commercial since I wasn't receiving money. He had no argument for that." Her smile faded. "More recently, I've only been able to visit sometimes on my lunch hour."

"While you lived with Warrington?"

He hadn't meant to say anything—certainly not to ask a question. And most certainly not one with a rough edge to it. But there it was—a rough-edged question spoken aloud.

Her hands stilled as she tipped her head to look up. "Yes."

He looked at his watch. "It's getting late."

She resumed petting the dog. "A few more minutes. Poor old Dragon here needs a good home. People who love him as much as he loves them. People as loyal to him as he is to them. Is that so much to ask?"

He had no answer. He went to the cage's wire door and swung it open. Behind him, April sighed, and he heard her getting up.

Beneath the name "Dragon," a card attached to the door listed feeding requirements and check marks for when he'd been fed, watered, walked. At the bottom was a date.

"What's December 27 on here for?"

Her hesitation gave him a moment to wonder why on earth he'd asked.

"He's got until then to be adopted."

What she didn't say was that if he weren't adopted, that would be the end of the animal that so clearly had caught her heart. Did the woman specialize in lost causes?

"Why didn't you adopt Dragon last week?"

"Rufus' date was the next day. Dragon has more time to be adopted. And he will be," she added fiercely. "Someone will see how wonderful he is. Someone will adopt him."

On the way back to the car, April checked her cell phone. "Oh."

"What?"

"Family. I haven't—I need to call them."

"You can't tell them anything about—"

"I know. But I haven't told them … I haven't talked to them in a while. It's Thanksgiving. I have to call them back."

"I'm going to listen."

"I won't—"

"I'm going to listen."

She jerked one shoulder. "Fine." She stabbed a number on her phone.

Apparently it answered faster than she expected. "Leslie. Hi, it's me. Happy Thanksgiving to everybody. We went to the shelter to serve meals. … Uh-huh. Everyone said hello, and Maria says thank you for the contributions. And after that, we went to the animal shelter. … Reese? No." Her eyes flicked to him, then away. "Yeah. A sort of, uh, colleague. One of a group of colleagues," she added quickly. "Oh, and Leslie, I haven't told you the best part. I have a dog. I adopted Rufus from the shelter last week. He's doing great. He's only had one accident with his house training, and he's terrific on the leash. He already knew sit and lie down, and he's got stay at least 80 percent of the time, and he hardly ever barks, and never without a reason. … Yeah…. Uh-huh … Of course, I want you all to meet him as soon—"

She broke it off and her gaze came to him again. "Though it might be a while. You know with work and, uh, everything. But as soon as we can we'll get together, for sure. … I don't know. When you get back from Illinois we'll talk and—Oh, I hear them saying the turkey's ready, I'll let you go now. Love to everybody. Hope Mr. M's leg is better. Bye!"

She ended the call and let out a breath. "Okay. Last stop. My storage unit at the apartment."

"You shouldn't tell them they'll meet me," he said. "You shouldn't tell them anything about this."

She looked at him blankly for a beat then chuckled. "Not you. Rufus. I want them to meet Rufus."

At a Lake Forest, Illinois home nearly bursting with good smells and happy voices despite its size, Leslie Craig Roberts stared out a set of French doors toward the frothing gray of Lake Michigan that could be seen beyond bare tree branches.

"Ready, Leslie?" Tris asked from the doorway, then immediately stepped into the room, "What is it? Was that April? Is something wrong? Is that why she hadn't called back earlier?"

Leslie caught her bottom lip between her teeth. "Yes, it was April. She says everything's fine."

"She says," Tris repeated, clearly understanding the significance of those words. They'd been friends before their marriages. With their husbands part of a trio of college friends, they'd become even closer over the years.

"She said she served dinner at the shelter and went to the animal shelter today with a *colleague.*"

"Not Reese?"

"Not Reese," Leslie confirmed.

"Well, that shouldn't break your heart. Though it does seem odd that Lois Warrington would allow it. Wasn't her complaining about dog hair the reason April cut back her volunteering at the animal shelter?"

"Yes. And that's something else. April's adopted a dog. Rufus."

Tris' eyebrows rose. "A dog? Especially a dog named Rufus? In Lois Warrington's house?"

Leslie smiled briefly. It was gone when she said, "Something's going on, Tris."

"Yes. But she's an adult, Les. You can love and support and be available when she wants your help, but you can't interfere."

Leslie made a face. "You might be able to convince me of that, but if Grady gets an inkling…. Let's keep this between us, for now, okay?"

CHAPTER EIGHT

There was a small fake Christmas tree lighting up a table near the hotel's back elevator that had April "ohhhing" as soon as they came in.

He felt something like relief at the sound.

The trip to the storage unit hadn't gone well.

At first he'd thought she was putting things in the hall in order to get at something else.

"Tell me which box you want, and I'll get it," he'd said.

"I want them all."

"Why?"

"So I can put up decorations."

"Where?"

She'd straightened, blinked. "The suite."

He tipped his head toward the labels on two of the bigger boxes. "Tree stand? Lights? Ornaments? You can't put up a tree in a hotel suite. They won't allow it."

She'd stepped into the hallway, her head down. She might have been checking the labels of the boxes. Or not. "I suppose they won't."

"You wouldn't have put up this stuff if you were still engaged to Warrington. So it's really not any different."

Her lips parted, then clamped shut.

He said, "I'll put the boxes back and——"

"No. I'm taking some."

He would have been better off letting her take all the boxes and doing the sorting at the suite. It took so long that both their stomachs were growling, and he was fully aware that his exercises in reason—pointing out she couldn't put up a tree in the suite and she wasn't missing out on anything because she wouldn't have had this stuff at the Warringtons'—had not been appreciated.

"Stay here," he ordered.

"They're my boxes. I'll carry them."

"Stay here," he repeated grimly, refraining from commenting that actually many were her trash bags, since she'd pulled items out of boxes and put them in bags.

She turned away as he went back outside.

And damned if she wasn't talking to that waiter who clearly knew her and Rufus better than he should when he returned, schlepping the remaining boxes and bags from the car.

The waiter handed over the leash attached to the dog and seemed to be giving a report on his behavior. Hunter frowned. He'd thought Vanessa from housekeeping had been in charge of Rufus' care while they were gone.

The waiter spotted him and melted away.

She looked over her shoulder, her gaze practically daring him to comment. Then her stomach growled.

"Let's get upstairs and heat up these leftovers," he said.

Rufus gave a happy yip.

At least one of them was happy.

They watched Chevy Chase in *Christmas Vacation* on TV while they ate leftovers from the shelter, followed by pumpkin and apple pie Manny brought from the kitchen for dessert. Hunter sat in an upholstered chair and she on the couch. Neither of them had said much.

Once when she laughed at Chevy Chase marooned in the attic, he looked at her as if she might have belonged at the business end of a scientist's microscope, but later she noticed him smile at the squirrel rampaging in the house. So that was progress. Not that she was trying to reform the man or anything.

It was simple human compassion to be concerned.

Especially after that reaction at the shelter's Thanksgiving Dinner.

He'd looked as if he expected to be shot any second. And as if that expectation made him all the more determined to stand his ground.

The news came on, led by a piece about another shelter giving out meals.

"I don't think I thanked you yet for helping at the shelter," she said.

"No problem."

But it had been a problem. She was sure of it. Something about it had bothered him and—

He didn't move, yet she felt the shift in his intensity. She realized the anchor was teasing a piece to come after a commercial break about the King of Bariavak's surgery.

"Why are you doing this?" she asked abruptly.

He looked at her, then back to the screen as if the merits of the breakfast food being extolled there required great concentration. "Media gives us an idea of what the general public knows."

"I don't mean watching the news. This." She gestured around the suite. "Me. Princess school."

"Princess sch—?" He'd almost grinned. At least she thought that's where his mouth had been headed until he clamped down on it. His voice was even. "It's my job."

"Why? I mean why do you do security for State," she added quickly, because she guessed he was about to answer the *why* with *because my boss told me to.*

"It's a good job. And I'm good at it."

"There are a lot of other government agencies involved in security or law enforcement or—"

"News is coming back on. Don't you want to see this?"

Damn him. Of course she did.

As she watched the clips of the King of Bariavak and listened to information about his being in D.C. in preparation for serious surgery after the first of the year, another part of her mind wondered if Hunter's ability to shut down her questions was part of being good at his job.

CHAPTER NINE

Hunter arrived in perfect time Friday morning. She'd showered and dressed and was beginning to open the boxes and bags they'd brought from her storage unit yesterday.

"Good, you're just in time to help me."

He gave the open box in front of her a dour look. "We have work to do."

"But it's Christmas—"

"It's the day after Thanksgiving. You asked for Thanksgiving, and you got it. Now it's time to get back to work."

"Don't you have any Christmas spirit?"

"No."

She sat back on her heels, challenging him. "What do you do for Christmas?"

"I work."

"All day?"

"Often."

"But not every year and even when you work all day you have to go home eventually. What do you do then?"

"I sit on the couch, drink a beer, and watch an NBA game."

"You don't have any traditions?"

"I told you. I sit on the couch—"

"Fine. What about a special meal?"

He shook his head.

"Turkey?"

Head shake.

"Beef roast? Ham?"

Head shake.

"Pie or cookies? Ah." The head shake had faltered. "Cookies."

"Sharon gives cookies to a lot of people." He sounded defensive.

"Homemade Christmas cookies. That's nice." She brought her gaze back to him. "Sharon knows you very well, doesn't she?"

She could have almost sworn he jumped. A small jump, like a nerve ticking under his skin. "No."

"Sure she does, because you're friends."

"We've worked together a long time. She's my boss."

"One doesn't preclude the other. I worked for Gerard Littrell and we were friends. I'm friends with Zoe and she's my boss."

"We're not." The dour look was back in full force. "It's time to get to work."

Feeling oddly cheerful she said, "No dancing or handshakes, since Derek's not here to do the grunt work."

"We'll go over terminology and etiquette."

She groaned. There went her cheerfulness. His, on the other hand, appeared to increase.

"Plus Bariavak's geography and history."

She narrowed her eyes. "Then I get at least an hour to ask questions about the king."

He looked back at her without expression. "Yes, all right."

"And you *answer* the questions," she specified.

He raised both hands, palms toward her. As if such a dodge had never occurred to him, but the twitch of his mouth gave him away. "What I can tell you within operational protocol."

April closed her eyes and leaned her head back against the top of the couch cushion.

Her mind felt like what was left over after winemakers squeeze every last bit of juice out of a grape. Smashed, deflated, empty.

Boy, she'd thought Great-Grandmother Beatrice's lessons in deportment were tough.

She considered that with her eyes closed. Well, they were tough. They'd seemed downright impossible, not to mention unreasonable when she'd first encountered them as an adolescent. Now … they were still tough, but they covered a lot of situations, and covered them well.

The ones Hunter kept hitting her with were just so detailed and arcane.

That pretty much described what he'd told her about Bariavak's history, too. Lots of dates, treaties, and dodging enemies thanks to the mountains that nearly surrounded the country.

He'd taken the same approach with her questions about King Jozef and his family.

"In 1962, his father—"

"No more dates. Tell me what his father was like. Better yet, what was his daughter like?"

"I never met her."

"You never met any of these fusty old treaties, either," she snapped, and saw the twitch of his mouth again. "Okay, you say you can't tell me any details of how the baby princess went missing because of operational security. But what do the reports of Princess Sofia's character and personality and relationship with her parents and husband say?"

Getting it out of him wasn't quite that simple. But she did begin to get a sense of a young woman whose mother had died when she was a girl, who had rebelled against her father strenuously in her teens, then had reconciled with him, especially after her marriage.

April empathized with Sofia—the death of a beloved parent as a child, the period of rebellion, the reconnecting and mellowing. One place where their stories diverged was that Sofia had married a man her father approved of in what appeared to have been a love match.

Her family hadn't voiced overt disapproval of Reese. Then again, it turned out he hadn't been a love match.

That was interesting … She said the phrase inside her head again. *He hadn't been a love match.*

Nope. Hardly a twinge.

And she never had gotten around to crying over the end of the engagement. Not even about him having his mother doing the breaking up.

It was like she—

"Have you thought through what you will tell King Jozef if he'll see you?" Hunter asked.

Her eyes popped open. "Tell him?"

"About yourself."

"The truth."

His brows dropped into a frown. "This might not be the time for the whole truth and nothing but the truth."

"I'm not going to…" *Lie to him.* But she was. That's exactly what she was going to do. By presenting herself as a *possibility* that she didn't believe in.

"You don't have to tell him a lot." Apparently he'd interpreted her phrase differently. "But you do need to be prepared for him to ask you questions. About your childhood. What you remember of your parents."

"But won't that—"

"No. If the princess survived the kidnapping she'd have been too young to remember anything about it or life before it. So your memories of your parents don't rule you out. Neither does the paper trail."

She nodded slowly. "Because my parents moved around a lot and didn't keep records. I remember Great-Grandma Beatrice and Leslie having trouble getting me enrolled in school when I started living with them."

"You had to have been in school before you were thirteen," he objected.

"Oh, yeah. But when they asked for records, Melly would keep stalling and stalling them. If we didn't move on anyway, she'd buy time by pulling me out of that school and putting me in another."

"That's not easy."

His voice was even, but she knew with absolute certainty that he understood. Because he'd experienced something similar?

"No, it's not."

"But you don't let it define you."

Now she really wondered if he was talking about her or himself.

Either way, she confirmed, "No, you don't."

Hunter stopped outside the hotel suite's bedroom door and listened. April was restless tonight.

As if she might be wondering what she'd gotten herself into.

She couldn't say he hadn't given her a chance to back out. Even after she'd said she'd do it.

You don't want to spend Christmas with your family?

He never should have asked that. And she'd homed right in on it.

Weren't you the one who wanted me to do this?

Answering with the *No* that had been in the back of his throat wouldn't have been a good idea on many levels.

He paced across the living room, standing at an angle to the window to look down. Every other street light had a large green representation of a red-ribboned wreath hanging from it. The alternate poles held flags with red and green and gold.

Decorations had popped up all over, like an army of Aprils had been at work.

He'd kept her too busy to do much, but she'd still managed to set out a dozen or so decorations.

He shouldn't have let her bring all this stuff from her storage unit. He shouldn't have let her go to the animal shelter. He sure as hell shouldn't have served up food beside her to those people.

Memories tried to encircle him like the hazed light around each pole below.

He pivoted, strode to the couch, snagged a red and green quilted pillow from the corner and tossed it to a nearby chair so it wasn't in his way, and sat.

He put his feet on the coffee table, pressed his shoulders against the cushion to stretch the muscles in his back. This was a heck of a lot more comfortable than a hundred other places he'd spent a night, or—if it came to that—the bed in the apartment he rented off Connecticut Avenue. He'd sleep fine when he was tired enough.

April's decorative pillow showed a Santa in a rustic red coat in profile with a bag of toys over his shoulder and a dog standing at his side. The dog looked like that dog at the shelter. Dragon, that's what she'd called him. Or maybe the pillow was getting old and frayed.

He grabbed the pillow from the chair and shoved it behind his back where it would do some good and he wouldn't have to look at it.

"How're you getting along with Hunter and Derek?"

Sharon spoke into a silence broken only by occasional tapping as they did online shopping side by side on the suite's couch. Online was the way to shop for anyone in princess school.

April looked over at her. "Fine, I guess. Derek's very pleasant. And a hard worker," she added, remembering she was talking to his supervisor.

"And Hunter? Is he a hard worker, too?"

"Relentless."

Sharon chuckled.

"He's very—" She leaned over to stroke Rufus, who was curled up between their feet, buying time to think before she spoke this time. "—dedicated to his job. He could, uh, relax a little. The way he acts going in a door … I'll probably have bruises from him yanking me behind him when we got back from the shelter last night."

She smiled, but Sharon's expression had gone serious. "You know why he does that?"

To be annoying? "No."

"If there are two operatives, one covers front, one rear. But if there's only one, he or she assesses the known—wherever you are now—for dangers. Once assured there are none, he or she enters the unknown first. So if there are any dangers there, the operative takes the risk, not the protectee."

"I didn't…" She swallowed. Sharon meant serious dangers and risk. "I didn't realize. He never said—"

Sharon emitted an abbreviated chuckle. "And he never will. Not Impenetrable Pierce."

"That's his nickname?"

"Not one you want to call him, April. He doesn't like it."

"But you use it?"

"I'm privileged. I've known him since Day One in DS—Diplomatic Security—and he doesn't scare me the way he does the rest of them. I tell you, if more Special Agents had three-year-olds, they'd be a lot less intimidated by Hunter. You should have seen my Ben when…"

Sharon told the tale well. And the next one. And the one after.

April was interested. Very interested. She asked to see photos of Sharon's family and home because she was interested. Truly interested. She only wished she could have found out more about Hunter Pierce first.

It was a sure thing she wouldn't get any information from him.

Hunter walked into the suite mid-afternoon to find April and Sharon side-by-side on the couch, apparently surfing the Internet. Rufus raised his head, saw who it was, gave a couple thumps of his tail and settled back down.

Hunter frowned. "Kenton's supposed to be here."

"Hello to you, too, Pierce. I stopped by while Ross has the kids at a football game this afternoon, and as long as I'm here, I gave Derek a couple hours off. You haven't given anyone—" She flicked her gaze toward April. "—time to breathe this week."

"We're Christmas shopping," April said, smiling. "One of my favorite things."

Sharon snorted. "Don't you keep up with the news? It's all a commercial plot. Christmas—the holidays—are terrible for us. We eat too much, drink too much, stress too much. We rush around trying to pack too much into too few days, travel great distances in bad weather and all to see people who can drive us crazy in the shortest amount of time known to man. People—intelligent people, mind you—who *know* you're a grown up, yet can't seem to get past the fact they changed your diapers in some distant, dim past, leaving you forever locked in that stage in their minds."

Hunter watched April's face as she stared at the other woman. Was she feeling bad because of the reminder that she wouldn't be spending these holidays with either her now-ex-fiancé or her family?

"Sharon—" he tried.

"Oh, and we spend money we can't afford," she continued, "because our mercenary offspring have been brainwashed by the megabucks machine of advertising conglomerates. We stay up until 3 a.m. wrapping heaps of packages—not to mention the impossible task of inserting Tab B2 into Slot 5AA—and the little heathens have all the paper shredded and the packages ripped apart by 5:02 a.m. Twenty minutes later they're looking around for something new.

"And dinner! Don't get me started on Christmas Day dinner. We've gotta have all of Ross' family dishes and then there's the real dinner—*my* family's dinner. I feel like I cook for a month, then they plow through it in four and a half minutes. Except for the cookies, of course. Those they eat until they could fuel the entire Eastern seaboard with their sugar high."

April's lips compressed.

He tried to change the subject. "It's time to—"

Neither woman paid any attention. April spoke over him. "And you love it all, don't you, Sharon?"

His boss opened her mouth, and he braced for a flow of hot words. Instead, she held her breath a second then released it in a puff. "Yeah, I do. It's a great time."

They smiled at each other.

He would never, in his life, understand women.

"So, what do your kids want for Christmas this year?" April asked her, leaning over to look at her screen.

"Oh, God, what don't they want?" Sharon said. "Deposit the inventory of a ToyRUs warehouse in our family room and we'd be all set."

He sat in the closer upholstered chair. "No more talk of shopping or Christmas. There's too much to do."

Sharon chuckled. "Hunter Pierce, the *real* Grinch."

But April's eyes were pinned on him, and they had gone huge.

"Hunter." She sounded a little breathless. Almost as if she'd read the news on his face or in his voice somehow. But that wasn't possible. People didn't read him.

"The king will see you tomorrow. Three o'clock."

CHAPTER TEN

Sharon whooped. "Hot damn!"

Rufus sat up, looking around, probably checking if he needed to bark at something.

April's eyes widened even more. "He wants to see me?"

"He's agreed to see you."

She didn't seem to notice his correction. "Tomorrow."

"You'll do fine."

She met his eyes.

Then she looked away, stood, and walked into the bedroom.

When his gaze shifted back from the still-open door, Sharon held up one stop-sign hand before following April.

Rufus stared at him a moment, then trotted after the women.

Hunter waited. Maybe five seconds.

"I can't do this. You have to postpone," April was saying to Sharon as he entered the room. "Better yet, call it off."

"What's the problem?" he demanded.

April snapped. "Problem? For starters, let's try that I have no idea why I'm doing this. All your talk of operational security. You've told me hardly anything about this king who's—"

"We spent hours on him yesterday."

"—supposed to be my grandfather. Dates. Facts. Not who he *is*. How can I—?"

"It would make him suspicious if you knew too much. The princess was taken when she was a baby in a crib. It's not as if he'd expect her to have memories of him, the family, or that life."

"That is not the point. I can't believe I've gone along with this.

Was I nuts?"

She opened her tote bag, pushing around the contents in an apparent search for something. All the while she muttered about being nuts, as well as something about a jaw and adventure. More accurately, *stupid adventure.*

"Hah!" She pulled out a Metro card from the bottom of the tote. "It's been interesting, but I'm out of here and—"

"You're scared," he said.

She whirled on him, bringing one end of Rufus' leash with her. "Scared? Damn right I am, along with about a dozen other things."

"April—" Sharon started.

"No, I'm sorry, Sharon. You've been great, but Mr. Silent Sam over there put me on the wrong side of his need-to-know-line, his operational security, and I went along with it. But now all I can think about is this king—this elderly man I'm going to meet and lie to. Pretend I'm the granddaughter he's been searching for all these years. I can't do it. Not without a better reason than I've been given so far."

He opened his mouth.

"Don't say it, Pierce. I won't tell anyone anything anytime anyway. Or I'll go to jail. I wouldn't tell anyhow—who'd believe it?—but the jail thing clinches it. Besides, how much do I really know? Why's a mystery to me and who or what aren't much better. So your precious operational security is safe. But I'm leaving."

"You can't take the Metro," he said.

"I sure can. I can—"

"You're right. *You* can. *Rufus* can't."

She snapped her mouth closed.

"Sit down, April." He pointed to the bed. "Please," he added.

Her glare went on another beat before she put the Metro card and leash down with a show of keeping them within easy reach.

"There was no reason for you to know more unless King Jozef would see you. Now there is. Like I told you yesterday, Bariavak is nearly encircled by impenetrable mountains with one pass through them. That pass is what this is all about. The pass makes permission to fly through Bariavak's airspace important. Without it, planes have to detour hundreds of miles or risk the peaks."

"A lot of planes have been lost in those mountains," Sharon filled in.

He continued, "Like I said yesterday, Bariavak has withstood the conquests that have swept the region over centuries because of its location in this mountain stronghold. However, there was a little-known conflict there almost thirty years ago. The U.S. and other allies sent select troops to help the king retain power when threatened by insurgents fostered by a neighboring country. Parliamentary reforms have—"

"The complete geopolitical ramifications can wait, Hunter," Sharon interrupted. "The woman wants the real skinny."

"For starters," April said, "what does my pretending to be a princess have to do with flying through the pass?"

"King Jozef is considered friendly to the United States and our allies. However, as you know, he's scheduled for major surgery in early January, complicated by his age. His heir is unreliable. Our government wants the king to sign an extension of the overflight agreement before his surgery."

"He's said no?"

"No. But he hasn't said yes." Hunter sounded absolutely detached. "He has said that at this stage in his life he would like more than anything else to find his granddaughter."

"But ... you're setting all this up to trick him? To—"

"To give an old man a happy holiday season? Perhaps his last?"

At Sharon's question, April snapped her head around.

"It's all in how you look at it," Sharon continued. "He hasn't had the easiest of lives. The king and his wife lost a number of children as babies. Then his wife died. His daughter, his only child to reach adulthood, had given birth to her first baby, a girl, when the uprising started. The baby was kidnapped from the palace—right out of her nursery—the very night victory over the insurgents was declared."

"I don't remember anything about this princess being kidnapped."

"You were a baby when it happened," Hunter pointed out.

"But you'd think a famous kidnapping … I mean everybody's heard about the Lindbergh baby and that was decades before I was born."

"It was kept quiet," Sharon said. "There was never a ransom demand. It's believed that agents of the defeated rebels took—possibly killed—"

"Probably," Hunter inserted.

"—the baby as a final act of revenge. The king's son-in-law had been assassinated three months before by rebels. When her husband was killed, the king's daughter went into labor early, so the baby was a month premature. But the baby was healthy, and it seemed at least the princess would have her daughter. A year after the baby was taken, the princess died, too. They say she gave up. And the king was alone."

Empathy flickered across April's face. "But why did he keep it quiet? If he'd told the world, maybe they could have found her."

"More likely, the rebels would have killed the baby, if they hadn't already. Better to get rid of the evidence," Hunter said. "Plus, he would have been flooded with false reports. Keeping details secret has made it easier to debunk false claimants."

"There have been leads over the years," Sharon said. "Enough so he could never stop hoping. And now he faces this surgery. Doctors didn't want him traveling for several weeks before the operation, so he's here alone for the holidays and—"

"Sharon wanted to give him a fairy-tale for Christmas."

Two pair of reproachful eyes turned on him. The irritation-tinged reproach in his boss's brown eyes should have concerned him more. Instead, it was sympathy-washed reproach in April's blue eyes that twitched his muscles into motion.

He walked toward the door, turning back before crossing the threshold.

"You have to make up your mind, April. Right now. We can contact the embassy and explain we were mistaken about the woman we thought might be his granddaughter. Or…"

She stood. Her gaze steady.

"I'll meet the king."

Hunter stifled any reaction. "We have a lot of work to do—"

"No," Sharon interrupted him. She squinted at April. "She should go to a salon—someplace great—be pampered, be treated like a—"

"No salon. Too visible," he interrupted in turn. "Besides, she's not supposed to have been raised as a princess, remember?"

"Just born as one," April muttered.

"Princess or no princess, the right hairstyle can make a woman feel more at ease than six months of protocol lessons."

"No. Too high profile."

"I do have split ends," April said. "I should have had a trim last month. It doesn't have to be fancy…"

"Sure," Sharon said, with entirely too much good humor. "Take her to that little place where you get your hair cut, Hunter. Nobody would ever crack him. And that place would certainly be low profile enough."

Hunter's hair was cut at a barbershop, owned and operated by Mack Dubronski, a retired Marine. Sharon was right that Mack would never breathe a word.

A vision of the brawny barber leaning over April, his hands in her sudsy hair, her eyes closed in response to the touch, popped up like an evil hologram.

"Maybe Sharon could trim the ends," April said.

"You can't send a woman to meet a king without having her hair done," Sharon said in the I'm-the-boss voice she used so seldom in the office, unless she was on the phone with her kids.

He pulled out his cell phone as he walked out to the living room. "I'll make arrangements."

"What are we doing here?" April asked.

Even after Sharon left and Derek returned, they'd kept her so busy she hadn't had time to think about tomorrow. At least not much.

She hadn't questioned where they were going when Hunter escorted her out the hotel's back door and into the waiting car Derek was driving.

Now they'd pulled into a narrow alley almost before she'd registered they were in the toniest part of Georgetown.

Hunter looked at her like she was dim. "Getting your hair cut, like you asked."

"But I thought … When you said about making arrangements, I thought it was with the man who cuts your hair."

He retreated into his I-show-nothing mode. Why?

"This is better," was all he said, before scanning the area, opening the door, and preceding her. She was starting to get used to that.

He glared into the alley beyond her as he reached back, wrapped one hand around her arm to draw her close behind him. Remembering what Sharon had told her—only a few hours ago?—she clutched both hands around his arm, suddenly afraid for him.

He glanced at her with a flicker of surprise. Then faced forward again, pushing open the door.

She gaped at the name stenciled on the door as she passed it. "Hunter. Etienne's? *Etienne's?* Do you know how expensive—?"

He shut the door behind them, still staying between her and the hallway beyond. "He owes me a favor."

She goggled at him. Which was why Etienne, the favorite of Washington glitteratidom, first saw her with her mouth hanging open.

"Pierce," he said.

"Summit."

Etienne had a last name?

They nodded at each other. There wasn't an ounce of emotion in either man's voice. They didn't shake hands. Yet April had the strangest impression of a bond between them.

"Saw Maurice last week. Said to say hello if I saw you," Etienne said.

Hunter grunted acknowledgment. They looked at each other a

moment longer, then Etienne turned and started away.

"This way." As soon as they'd entered a room at the back of the otherwise empty salon that apparently was his private domain, he focused on April and said, "Walk."

"Where?"

"Anywhere. I must see how you interact with space. How could I possibly cut your hair without that?"

She walked. "Shake your head. Again." She obeyed, even when he added "Turn" and "Faster."

"Color," he pronounced.

"No."

She stopped to look at Hunter, surprised the word had come from him.

Etienne glared. "This is my world, Pierce—"

"No, please," she said. "I don't want to have to keep up coloring."

"Walk. Turn," Etienne said to her, frowning. "More."

Before she complied she caught his assessing look at Hunter.

"Highlights, then," he said as if conceding a great deal. "Subtle. By the time they grow out, you will have natural ones from the spring sun."

"Okay."

"Walk! Turn!"

She was dizzy when Etienne abruptly clapped his hands, and breathed out, "Ready."

Dizzy, yes, but not so dizzy that she didn't catch a peculiar expression skidding across Hunter's face. She had no time to consider it as Etienne whisked her off for a smock, shampoo and the works, as he said.

To her astonishment, Etienne did everything himself.

To her great relief, Hunter did not accompany them into the station behind the privacy screen.

As much as he knew about her already, she wasn't prepared for him to see her hair sticking out in packets of foil.

Sharon Johnson was not only a credit to the Department of State's Bureau of Diplomatic Security, she was one wise woman.

April felt like a new and vastly improved person.

Hunter opened the salon's back door in his usual fashion, looking around before reaching back for her.

She now recognized how he positioned himself so she was protected on one side by the open car door and on the other by his body for the heartbeats before she was inside the car.

As she slid in, a gust of wind caught her hair, and swung it wide, before it rippled against her cheek on the way to falling back in place. She sighed. She would never again get it to look the way Etienne had, but boy, for tonight, it felt great.

Impulsively, she turned to Hunter, who sat next to her while Derek drove.

"Let's go somewhere, Hunter. Look, right over there—we could go in and have a glass of wine. We can sit in a corner. No one will see us. We can watch the bright lights and have a glass of wine. That's all."

"No."

"One time, Hunter. To pretend…" Pretend what, exactly? She didn't know. It didn't matter. His refusal encompassed all possibilities.

"No."

"Fine." She turned away. But she couldn't have been too angry, because she also felt a little zing of pleasure at the way her hair swung in response to her motion.

"You agreed—"

"I know. You're right. I signed the dotted line, so no glass of wine, no bright lights. Just haul me away."

She extended both wrists to him in melodramatic pantomime.

His gaze went to her wrists. Slowly he raised his gaze to her face. So slowly, so intently, that her wrists started to bob and knock against each other, and then she felt heat spreading up from her chest.

"I'm sorry, April."

She dropped her hands to her sides. "No, I'm sorry. I don't know what came over me."

"You've been working hard. People like you want to get out and have fun, meet people. The king might take you places."

She kept her eyes down. The moisture filling them was inexplicable.

"It doesn't matter," she said, truthfully.

"You're wound up. Don't worry about tomorrow. The idea is to let them see who you really are."

She blinked away the last of the moisture and looked up. "An interesting statement coming from someone who's been trying to teach me to be who I'm not."

"You're talking about title, rank, position. I'm talking about what's in here."

He touched his fingertips to her forehead. They were cold. She knew that for a fact. He wore no gloves and the temperature was dropping fast. She felt the cold at first contact. She was sure she did. Yet heat bloomed from that point across her face.

"And here." Hunter said, his fingers dropping to her collarbone above her heart. Coat, sweater, blouse, all separated his touch from her skin, yet she felt the heat there, too. At the same time that, in a paradox that no physics could explain, she and Hunter froze.

April moved first, looking past him to where Derek was turning into K Street. Hunter's hand dropped.

"Well," she said with would-be lightness, "if they see who I really am, it sure won't be a princess."

Hunter said nothing.

Not until they were in the alley behind the hotel, just before he opened the car door to get out and put his body between her and any risks. "Depends on your definition."

April came out of the bathroom to find the bedroom almost dark. She could have sworn she'd left the light on...

And then she saw that the curtains had been opened. And before the window sat the table from the corner. The flame of a single candle reflected in the window glass and off a metal bucket.

Another step closer and she could see a split of champagne in the bucket, a solitary champagne flute waiting.

She turned slowly, making sure she hadn't missed anyone in the shadows. He wasn't there. The door to the living room was firmly closed. No light showed under it. A clear message.

She sat at the table and poured herself a glass of champagne.

She thought of that sensation of an internal defibrillator jolting her heartbeat when their fingers brushed that first day. She thought of the conversations, of the handshaking lessons, the dancing. His face when they entered the homeless shelter.

Movement from beyond the window drew her attention. It was snowing.

Fat, dawdling flakes meandering past the lights of the city, blurring them at the same time they caught their sparkle and magnified it.

Her glass of wine and bright lights.

Something caught in her throat at the same time a smile broke free.

She poured another glass of champagne and toasted the snow flakes.

He heard her come into the room.

Maybe he'd been listening for it.

She walked past the sofa where he was and went to the drawn curtains. She pulled them open slowly.

Facing the window, she said softly enough that it wouldn't have awakened most people, "If it were rain, we'd all complain, even though it means it's not all that cold. Worse if it becomes sleet. Miserable, stinging, sloppy. But then it turns even colder, and freezes each drop into an individual crystal, and suddenly it's … magical."

She turned from the window, recrossed the room. At the door to the bedroom she paused.

"Thank you, Hunter." Then she was gone, without ever looking toward him.

CHAPTER ELEVEN

April had a vision of a rubber band, stretching tighter and tighter. And the one doing the pulling was Hunter, even as he remained silent and still on one side of her.

He thought she was going to fall flat on her face. He was steeling himself for the fiasco. That had to be where this tension was coming from.

Oh, God, why had she agreed? She had to get out of this. Would they believe her if she said she was sick? That wouldn't work. Even if they believed her, Hunter would get that duty-at-all-costs expression, and expect her to carry on.

A contagious disease. Malaria? Or—

"Ah!" April jumped from the contact of a hand on her knee.

Her gaze went to Hunter, but he was still sitting stiffly upright, looking out the window.

Sharon. She'd reached over and patted April, offering a physical reassurance she now backed with words. "You'll do great, April. Don't worry. You'll be fantastic. Won't she, Hunter?"

He turned slowly from the window, which showed the lineup of impressive structures dubbed Embassy Row as they turned off Massachusetts Avenue. "If you follow what we've taught you, you'll be fine."

Their eyes met, and she knew with abrupt clarity that he was not only the puller, he was also the rubber band. His taut discomfort practically hummed in the air.

But … Did that mean it didn't have to do with her?

Sharon grimaced. "Please, Hunter, stop gushing. You'll make a mess in the limo."

He scowled.

April chuckled, her tension easing.

The limo slid through a gate that opened before it and glided to a stop in a cobbled courtyard. Before her nerves could gather themselves, the door opened. Hunter stepped outside and reached back in to offer his hand.

The woman who opened one side of the imposing double door was what Lois Warrington wanted to be.

Dignified, cool, inscrutable.

"We have an appointment," Sharon said simply.

"Come in."

After closing the door, the woman led them down a broad hallway toward the back of the building. April could swear she heard the rustle of taffeta. The woman had that feel of timelessness.

Opening an impressive door into another hallway until, finally, she knocked at a closed door. They all heard the "Enter" in response.

The woman opened the door, then stepped back. Sharon went in first. April hesitated.

She felt a firm warmth at the small of her back and knew it was Hunter's hand. Not pushing. Simply there.

She stepped forward.

She'd been right to think of this in terms of showtime, because the stage was set.

At the far side of the room sat a massive wood desk before the partially drawn velvet curtains of a bay window. Behind the desk sat the King of Bariavak.

April's first impression was that he reminded her of the actor Patrick Stewart with hair and a short beard. He was flanked on one side by two middle-aged men in finely tailored suits and on the other side by a man not much older than her.

The woman who'd guided them here closed the door to the hall, skirted around them, and went to stand beside the young man.

"You may approach," said the king.

That left them what seemed like a football-field worth of oriental carpet to cross. Briefly, April felt Hunter's hand once more. Then they started the trek, three across, with her in the middle.

At least she didn't have to make the trip under the king's scrutiny. He turned to the people on either side of him and addressed them in a language she didn't recognize. Instructions from his tone, pleasant but firm. One of the middle-aged men started a response, and the king's tone grew more firm.

The three men moved away from the desk. The woman stood her ground.

"Madame Sabdoka," the king said. Then he sighed and added something else.

She gave one nod, then followed the three men. From the corner of her eye, April saw that the woman closed the door behind the men, then took a seat on a straight chair near it.

"Now," said the king in accented but excellent English, "we shall talk."

April glanced at Hunter.

He looked straight ahead, apparently at the curtains. His expression was impassive, but she could almost hear the hum of tension coming from him.

"It is a pleasure to see you again, Ms. Johnson."

"Your Majesty."

King Jozef's gaze came to him next. "Hunter."

He dropped his head in a curt nod, not a gesture anyone could mistake for a bow. "Your Majesty. This is April Gareaux."

The King of Bariavak continued to regard him, his still-bright eyes glinting out through narrowed lids under bushing eyebrows.

Odd. Hunter would have expected the king to have immediately zeroed in on April.

Possibly to take an extreme position by embracing her. Or the opposite extreme by repudiating her. More likely to steer the intermediate course by peppering both her and him with questions about her background.

Finally, the older man turned his head slowly toward April.

"How do you do, my dear. Won't you sit down?"

April smiled. "Thank you. I would like that very much, since my knees are shaking."

Hunter heard a faint sound behind them, like Madame Sabdoka had sucked in a breath, but the king not only smiled, he got up and came around the desk, taking April's left arm and leading her to a chair in the conversation group by the fireplace under the painting of the coronation of King Poterzo in 1523.

In a seemingly courtly gesture, King Jozef seated April. Hunter noted it gave the king an excellent view of the relative lengths of the last two fingers on her left hand.

"No, you stay, Hunter," the king ordered as he'd taken a step toward the door. He turned to Sharon, gesturing to the chair next to April. "I hope you will stay as well, Ms. Johnson. And you there, Hunter."

That put April and Sharon on one side of the coffee table, the king on the sofa opposite, and Hunter in a chair at the far end of the table. Part of the group, yet sidelined.

What was the old man up to? Calling him Hunter as if they knew each other. As if—

"What do you ask of me, my dear—? No, I cannot keep calling you my dear. Shall I call you Josephine-Augusta?"

"No!" April's gaze came to Hunter. He gave no response. She needed to find her own way. He would not be here to smooth moments like this. She looked back to the king. "I've been called April as long as I can remember."

"Very well." Neither the king's tone nor expression changed. "What would you ask of me, April?"

"I would like to get to know you if that's all right."

He studied her a moment before the grooves around his mouth eased. "Is that all?"

"I'd like to hear about ... your family, if you don't mind talking about them."

"So all you that care to ask is to hear an old man talk about himself and his past?"

"They could be my family, too."

Hunter should have felt like applauding. She didn't overplay the moment. She neither staked a claim nor demurred. The simplicity made it powerful.

Her sincerity also made it dangerous. If she let her feelings get too deeply entangled ... Yes, even though he'd be at a distance, he'd watch that carefully. Only because it could affect the operation.

"What of the celebrations and galas of the diplomatic holiday season here in Washington?"

She frowned. "I hope to celebrate Christmas with you. But as for the diplomatic season, you should rest with the operation coming up."

"You know about that, do you?" The king's sharper tone matched a chilled expression he aimed at Hunter. Hunter looked straight ahead.

April said, "Anyone who reads the *Post's* Style section knows it."

His Royal Majesty, King Jozef of Bariavak burst out laughing.

"Ah, sometimes with all our games of intrigue and negotiation and diplomacy, we forget the direct and open approach. Is that not true, Hunter?"

"Yes, Your Majesty."

"Yes. It is a lesson I will be happy to have you teach me, if you can, April. And I shall be honored to have you as my guest for this holiday season. I would give a great deal—." The rumble of his voice hinted at depths beneath those bland words. "—to be able to show my granddaughter a true Bariavak Christmas. However, as you note, my approaching surgery makes remaining in the United States advisable. So we must settle for the pleasures this city provides us."

"There are many Christmas things we can do. We'll get a tree, and decorate it. I can bake cookies and—"

Madame Sabdoka didn't make a sound or move as far as Hunter could tell. Yet waves of disapproval rolled off her so strongly that he thought for a moment they might knock over April.

She looked around at the older woman, then toward him, then to King Jozef.

"Aren't trees and cookies part of Bariavak's traditions?"

"They are. However, the staff here deals with such matters," the king said.

"Oh."

"At this time, the staff is quite depleted. As you saw, I have sent the last two of my advisors and my assistant secretary home to Bariavak, joining most of the embassy staff. The embassy retains here only a skeleton staff."

"Then it makes even more sense for me to do those things."

From behind him, Hunter felt the power of Madame's reaction— like a teakettle about to blow. But he kept his eyes on April and the king, looking across the coffee table at each other. Sizing each other up, he thought suddenly. Neither backing down. Anyone who didn't know better might think they were related.

The king gave a small, noncommittal smile. "Perhaps an arrangement can be made. In the meantime, I would like to have you come to stay here with me."

April's expression snapped to shock. "Stay here?"

"Yes. I am told I can be very demanding. I will want to spend what time I have free with you so that we may become well-acquainted. I do understand you have commitments, activities of your, shall we say, previous role."

"Thank you, Your Majesty, but I have arranged my few obligations so I could be free in hopes of getting to know you. But—"

From the corner of his eye he caught a flicker of surprise from Sharon, which meant she'd been caught off-guard by that final word, too.

"—I'm afraid it's not possible for me to stay here with you."

"Not possible?"

"No, Your Majesty. I have a dog."

"A dog?"

"The dog can stay with—"

She cut off Hunter. "No. Rufus can't stay anywhere except with me."

"The dog shall come, too," said the king.

From by the door, Madame made a sound like lips clamped hard over a sucked-in breath.

"Tomorrow." Although the king continued to look at April, that added word clearly had been directed at Madame.

Now he turned to Sharon. "I also request the services of Hunter Pierce until I depart Washington. You are his supervisor, are you not?"

Hunter stiffened.

"I am. He can be assigned to your security detail—"

Hunter interrupted. "Your security staff is more than capable, Your Majesty."

"If they were not, I would not have them. However, if an emergency should arise and they spoke Bariavakian under stress, April would not understand. I require that you be on hand, since you know English even better than your native Bariavakian."

He felt the startled look April shot him. He kept his attention on the old fox, who wasn't done yet.

Returning his attention to Sharon, King Jozef said smoothly, "As for an assignment to my security detail, that would not be satisfactory. I should prefer to have broader access to his abilities. His language skills would serve me as well. My English is not as certain as I should like." Then he wanted to be Shakespeare. Because he rarely hesitated, much less misspoke. "In addition, he has lived in this city for many years and spent a great deal of time among these diplomats who are sending me invitations. He can help steer us away from the most boring. So, I request Mr. Pierce be available at all times, and thus will need to reside here, in the embassy."

Hunter twitched. If King Jozef suspected April wasn't the real thing, wouldn't he want Hunter out of the picture so he could quiz her? And if he thought April *was* the real thing, he'd be even more likely to want her to himself. Yet Jozef was clearly intent on keeping

Hunter on call. Why?

"I can, of course, make this a formal request at the highest levels…" Although he never looked away from Sharon, it was as if a challenge had landed at Hunter's feet. A challenge he could not afford to pick up.

Neither could Sharon. "That will not be necessary, Your Majesty. This is an extraordinary circumstance, and we want to assist in any way we can. I am happy to assign Mr. Pierce to your household for your time in Washington."

CHAPTER TWELVE

From the window, King Jozef of Bariavak watched the trio get into the limo.

The young woman had been slightly flustered at his request that she stay here.

His cynicism had soared at that. It was more than she'd agreed to in whatever bargain they'd struck.

But then it had appeared her reluctance was because of a dog.

So then he didn't know what to think. That was a rare occurrence of late. He rather liked that he didn't know.

Madame Sabdoka stood behind him, having returned from showing them out.

"Speak," he said. She would accept the invitation only as an order.

"What do you hope to gain from having her—*them*—here?"

"Enlightenment, Madame." Thinking about the glints he'd seen between April and Hunter, he added, with another bit of surprise, "And, perhaps, enjoyment." Those glints could well be from sparks suppressed with determination. He knew about such sparks and such suppression.

Madame's mouth pursed even tighter.

He had rarely had a private word with her in more than fifty years, yet he knew this pursing was her method of keeping words inside.

It reminded him somehow of the rigid control of young Hunter Pierce.

He suddenly wished Madame Sabdoka would let her words out. Perhaps he wanted even for Hunter Pierce's words to come out.

Too much had been held inside for too long.

"I believe it's going to be a most memorable Christmas, Madame Sabdoka. Most memorable."

"Could it have gone any better than that?"

Hunter answered his boss's patently hypothetical question. "Yes."

"What more do you want?" Sharon demanded.

It wasn't more he wanted. It was less.

Less of April's heart in her eyes.

And *none* of his staying in the embassy at Jozef's beck and call.

What was he up to?

King Jozef had barely given Hunter Pierce a glance when he'd been assigned to his detail during a brief state visit to Washington.

Fresh out of training, Hunter had been given the assignment because of his knowledge of the language. He'd never needed to use it, because the king, after acknowledging the introduction with a regal nod, had not interacted with the American security man.

That had been fine with Hunter. He'd half expected a repeat today. Instead, the king had made it clear he knew who Hunter was and then made that bizarre demand for his presence.

"From an operational standpoint," he said to Sharon, "it's better if she doesn't become emotionally entwined with this role or with him. If she lets her feelings rule, it could complicate the end of the operation. That's the important thing. The only thing. She needs to moderate her feelings."

"If I weren't so astonished at you talking about feelings, I'd blast you for being a cold-hearted jerk. She—."

"Hey." April waved a hand. "You do know I'm here, don't you?"

Sharon grinned. "Sorry."

"I do appreciate how much you have done for me, both of you and you, Derek," she pitched her voice to reach the front seat. "Thank you all."

"I would be even more terrified than I am now—" Her smile went lopsided. "—if you hadn't given me such a good grounding. Now I have to do it."

Her gaze came to him.

"I have to do it," she repeated. "That means it has to be my way, not your way any longer, Hunter. Even if I could close down or separate my emotions the way you think I should, I wouldn't. I won't cheat King Jozef that way. I won't cheat myself that way. I'm going to do this—and I'm going to do it with feeling." She straightened in the seat, her head held high. Then she launched one last salvo at him. "And if you don't like it—tough."

"Hold up, Hunter," Sharon said, drawing him back out of the suite where they'd just returned April, to Rufus' delight.

She closed the door and walked a dozen steps down the hall. He followed.

"Look, I know it's gotten more complicated, with King Jozef wanting you to stay at the embassy. I want you to know I didn't plan that."

He said nothing.

"And it's not going to be easy for you with April, either," she said.

"There's no need for you to be concerned. We can get along."

"No kidding you can get along." Her smile faded as she studied his face. "Oh, God, Pierce tell me you're not trying to pretend you don't feel anything for that woman."

"I don't know what you mean."

She swore under her breath. "Then I'll have to take a picture of your face when you touch her."

"I don't tou—"

"Oh for heaven's sake, Pierce, don't waste my time. Let me tell you, what that picture of your face would say is that you like touching April Gareaux. You like it a lot."

Hunter stared at the ceiling.

It took a moment to realize why it seemed unfamiliar. It was the ceiling over the bed in his apartment, but for the past ten days he'd spent most of his ceiling-staring time at the hotel. A much higher quality of ceiling to stare at.

Sharon had ordered him to go home tonight, pack his bags, and make any other arrangements necessary to stay at the Bariavak embassy until after the first of the year.

Not much more than a mile from his apartment. A world away.

Damn Sharon.

Not for agreeing to Jozef's request. *Request. Right.* The man demanded, he didn't request.

No, that was part of the job. Hers and his. He didn't damn her for that.

It was what she'd said in the hotel hallway. Now she had him thinking about touching April.

Not that kind of touching. Not his hands on her body, stroking the heat of those legs, all the way up to——

No, dammit, he wouldn't. All he'd done was take her arm to guide her. Into the car, a building, a doorway. He wasn't going to stop doing that. It was security protocol. There was nothing in the touch. Simply making sure she got where she needed to be. That all.

And that's all it would have stayed if Sharon hadn't started playing with his head.

Packing took far more time than April expected.

First, there were all the Christmas things from the storage unit that had to go back in their boxes and bags.

Plus, she hadn't realized how much she'd spread out in the suite in a little over a week.

Derek helped, especially gathering the papers and photographs that had been her study materials. He also reached up to hand her decorations that had been placed high up.

And he answered the door.

Somehow, hotel employees had heard they'd be departing and one by one they came up to say good-bye, give her a hug, and give Rufus going-away treats. Judging from their relaxed smiles when the door opened, they also seemed to know Hunter wasn't here.

Which made it impossible to ask him how he had never mentioned that he was a native of Bariavak.

And that might be a good thing, because as the night went on, she thought that not asking might be better. At least for now.

When the last of the hotel staff visitors left it was late, and she still had all the bedroom to deal with. She closed the door behind her so the light wouldn't disturb Derek if he stretched out on the couch the way she'd suggested, and started in.

She was leaving with the same amount of clothing as she'd arrived, but somehow it wasn't fitting back into the suitcases. It was as if all her possessions had fluffed themselves up like Great-Grandma Beatrice's down comforters released from the bondage of summer storage.

Great-Grandma Beatrice. Leslie. Grady. All the rest. She missed them. She wanted to sit with Grady. To feel his acceptance, as always. She wanted to talk to Leslie. To hear her calm, southern-tinged voice dispensing soothing wisdom.

But she couldn't. She had to use her best judgment and move ahead. Reese had been a mistake, but Gerard Littrell hadn't worked out so badly.

This would work out, too.

If she could just get this suitcase closed. She pressed the top down with one hand, and advanced the zipper bit by bit with the other.

There. Closed.

Now, on to the next one.

Until she finally could fall into bed, by then so tired that she'd had hardly a second to think about where she would be sleeping tomorrow night. Or about how strange it was to not have Hunter on the couch outside her bedroom.

CHAPTER THIRTEEN

King Jozef came into the main back entryway at the height of the chaos. April hoped he was good at unsnarling knots.

Because there were too many people, too many suitcases, too many bags, and a substantial dog crate all jammed into a restricted area where four hallways and two staircases converged.

On top of that, Madame was giving what sounded like orders to the man who appeared to be a driver, which apparently involved him picking up things and heading through the obstacle course with them. But one of the bags held Rufus' treats, and the dog expressed his displeasure with piercing and repeated barks.

"No, please. Don't take that. Don't take anything yet," April said.

"The bags shall be taken to your rooms," Madame said. She waved at the driver and he started off again.

"But some things should stay down here, like Rufus' food."

"A moment, Rupert," King Jozef said. "April has a point."

Madame drew herself up. "That animal will not stay here. Or in the kitchen."

"He'll sleep in my room, so the crate can go up." April frowned. "But he can be a messy eater, so I wouldn't think you'd want him to eat in a bedroom."

Madame glared. Sharon's expression went impassive. King Jozef rubbed a hand across his mouth, which didn't hide his amusement.

Hunter stepped in. "Rupert and I'll take a load up of things you know are going up. That will leave more room, and you can decide about the rest."

"Rupert shall carry everything," Madame said.

"I need to see the set-up for security," Hunter said. "Might as well carry things with me as I go."

The king nodded.

"The periwinkle room," Madame said.

The two men picked up suitcases and headed up the back staircase, with Rupert leading the way.

The King of Bariavak extended a hand toward Rufus. "What breed of dog is this?"

"A mutt." April saw a flicker of confusion and added, "A mixed breed. No one knows which ones. His name is Rufus."

"Hello, Rufus."

The dog sniffed cautiously. He advanced nearer, and the king scratched behind his ears.

April felt as if she'd expelled about a dozen breaths all in one. "You like dogs."

"I do."

"He's a good dog and I'll do my very best to see that he doesn't disturb you, but—"

"No matter. We will be in the greatest informality for this time. I have already discussed with Madame Sabdoka that meals will be simple and of a family style. No ceremony or protocol."

That, clearly, did not please Madame.

Perhaps to divert attention from that disapproval, the king said, "I confess to curiosity for what these boxes and bags contain."

"Mostly Christmas decorations. A few things I've gathered over the years, a few things from my childhood."

"Indeed. I should particularly like to see those items from your childhood."

She looked up, knowing they treaded closer to the dangerous territory of her birth, but she smiled into his sad eyes. "I would like to show you and to share them with you."

"The embassy decorations are under contract," Madame said.

Her brisk tone broke the moment's connection.

King Jozef said as the two men came down the stairs, "I'm sure we can arrange something once April is settled. In the meantime, Madame you will find a place for these decorations, as well as Rufus' accoutrements."

"The crate should go where I'll sleep, also this tote."

Madame nodded at Rupert. He headed back upstairs with a second load.

"I must close myself up in the office shortly for a remote meeting with members of my government who are in Bariavak. But I hope you will join me for tea at four. How will you entertain yourself in the meantime?"

"I want to take Rufus for a walk to, uh, avoid accidents. Then I'll go up and unpack."

"I shall unpack your cases," Madame said.

"Oh, no. I can—"

"I unpack your cases," she repeated, her accent stronger and her tone implacable.

"That is the way it is done," King Jozef said.

April's eyes met Sharon's. She got the message: This was not a battle worth waging. "Thank you."

Madame inclined her head and started across the room. At the stairs she turned back and declared, "I shall not, however, tend to that animal."

"No, of course not. Rufus is my dog, and my responsibility." She had to pitch her voice louder, because Madame was ascending the stairs. "I'll feed him and take him for walks—"

"With escort," Hunter said.

"I don't need an escort."

"You're getting one. Any time you leave the grounds."

Suddenly aware of the king's scrutiny, she faced him. His expression was neutral, yet she had the notion he'd just finished smiling.

"I am to my office now." He nodded to both of them.

That left Hunter, Sharon and her in the entryway.

"I should put these somewhere, so they're out of the way," she said, gesturing toward the boxes and bags.

"Not unless you want Madame on your case," Sharon said.

She clicked her tongue. "That's embarrassing, isn't it?"

"What?"

"Having someone unpack your suitcases. Especially someone like Madame." She turned to Hunter. "I bet you won't like it one bit."

He said nothing.

"Wait a minute—you're saying she won't unpack for you?" Actually, he wasn't saying anything, but she went on. "Why not?"

"I'm not a princess." Hunter looked at her for a moment, as if waiting to see if she'd say that neither was she, then he pivoted and headed to another of the hallways, tossing over his shoulder, "Don't leave the building without me."

Caught.

April knew it the second she realized Sharon was watching her watch the direction Hunter had gone.

"Oh, April, honey." Sharon shook her head. "Don't."

"I'm not." Heat rose from her chest up her throat. "I'm trying not to."

"Try harder. It's a dead-end road. I'm telling you, an absolute dead end, with a cliff at the end of it. I strong-armed Hunter into going out with one of my friends to celebrate his getting out of training. That was the first of three women who ended up as sobbing puddles on our sofa. Each and every one of them fell for the guy, sure they could rescue the man behind the iron mask, and each ended up with a bruised heart, battered ego, and swollen eyes. That's when Ross—my husband—said no more. He *said* it was because of mascara stains on the couch, but it's really because he doesn't like to see people hurt.

"The last time I fixed Hunter up with one of my friends was a few years ago. I love Dee, but I've got to tell you, this woman is the Genghis Khan of dating. She sweeps in, takes no prisoners and moves on. She'd destroyed more hearts than a solid diet of butter would in a decade. Ross kept saying not to do it to Hunter. But I thought if something could shake him up, get through to him there'd be hope. And I thought if anything—anyone—could do it, it would be Dee."

She shook her head. "No dice. Genghis had met her Waterloo, if you get my drift. At first she was all the more determined, certain she could conquer Hunter. Before long, though, she was on the phone to me twice a day, asking what was wrong with her that Hunter wasn't interested. It was sad, really, to see this romance carnivore reduced to a twitching rabbit. Though, in the end, it did *her* a lot of good. She became much more empathetic and lost her zest for conquest. She met a nice corporate lawyer—if that's not an oxymoron—and they just had their first baby.

"Still, I wouldn't wish Hunter on my worst enemy as a romantic interest."

"Hunter wouldn't…" Or would he? What did she really know of him?

"Break hearts intentionally? No, he wouldn't. It's not that Hunter's mean, he's simply implacable. No, it's more than that…"

Sharon frowned, looking down as she fiddled with the bracelet on her wrist.

April waited.

Sharon looked up, decision made. "I've wondered, with his background … You've read about some orphans from Russia, Eastern European countries who are neglected as babies, never held or given any loving, and when they're adopted they don't know how to love or be loved—attachment disorder they call it. I wonder if Hunter, with his background…"

"His background," she repeated, nodding sagely. "In Bariavak."

Sharon shot her a look, and April feared she was about to have her bluff called. Instead the other woman echoed her nod and said, "Yeah, with being orphaned so young during that uprising. He never talks about it."

"Oh, my God." She wasn't sure her words were audible through suddenly numbed lips.

"It's a miracle he survived," Sharon continued. "They say he wouldn't have lasted much longer if he hadn't been picked up by a patrol of U.S. soldiers across the border. They were part of a multinational force patrolling the border to keep more outside fighters from coming in.

"The story is, one of the soldiers rescued him, fed him from his own rations, took him under his wing, and kept him under the official radar. Then Hunter's guardian-angel soldier was killed, and he was sent to a refugee camp. Somehow, eventually he got to the States. Charities supported him. He also got scholarships and jobs, getting himself through school, college and grad school. Then he signed up with Diplomatic Security. He could have gone with any of the big ones—ATF, FBI, CIA, but he chose State. Hunter Pierce is an honorable, reliable man. And one hell of an agent."

"You haven't given up on him. As a person, I mean. Forming attachments."

"No, but I'm a tough bird. Besides, I'm whacking away at his wall trying to reach *friendship*. Trying to dig all the way down to his heart?" She shook her head.

"I'm not—"

Sharon's look stopped her words. But then she smiled. "Come on, let's go see your room. It's got to be capitalized, don't you think? The way Madame says it: *The Periwinkle Room*."

CHAPTER FOURTEEN

The room was not only the color of periwinkles. The blooms also appeared on the bedspread, draperies and upholstery.

April woke with the uneasy feeling she'd dreamed about being smothered by periwinkles.

Sharon's departure yesterday afternoon had been followed by an uncomfortable hour while Madame gave her a tour of the building, detailing how it was divided into three zones—official reception rooms, embassy offices, and residential.

Only the king, the ambassador, and Madame Sabdoka had a say over all three zones.

April now knew it had been built in 1912 by a lumber baron, and bought by Bariavak in 1927 from his widow. Sixty-five rooms. One of a minority of embassies that also served as the ambassador's residence. It had been updated two years earlier, the third major renovation during its time as Bariavak's embassy. Each devoted to blending historic accuracy, modern function, and a dignified presentation on behalf of the people of Bariavak.

April had hoped Hunter would join them any minute on the tour, but when she'd interrupted Madame's monologue to ask about him, the older woman had looked down her nose and declared he was, no doubt, establishing himself in his quarters.

Hunter hadn't been any more forthcoming during their dinner with the king.

A king whose lined face seemed infinitely sad to her. When he'd laughed yesterday it had sounded almost rusty.

The atmosphere between the two men practically twanged.

Sharon had said Hunter was born in Bariavak and had been or-phaned there. But surely, this tension came from something more personal than monarch and former subject.

A week of preparing her to pretend to be King Jozef's granddaugh-ter and he'd never thought to mention he knew the man? That was too much to swallow as an accidental oversight. Even for Hunter.

So he'd kept the fact to himself for a reason.

Now, how was she going to find out?

The king dropped a series of bombshells Tuesday, yet didn't even seem to know he was doing it.

He and April had breakfast, the two of them at a small table in a bay of the kitchen—a much more relaxed meal than dinner had been.

Madame stood well back from them.

"Approach," King Jozef said.

"Is everything satisfactory, Your Majesty?"

"April?"

"Yes, wonderful. Thank you, Madame Sabdoka."

The older woman gave the smallest nod. "The digest, sir." She set a page to one side, within the king's easy reach.

"Ah, you add my secretary's duties to all your others, Madame. I am sorry to have burdened you further."

"Not at all, Your Majesty." She withdrew.

The king picked up the paper, taking out his glasses. "I receive the most important news of my country when I wake, but this is the complete digest of reports that have arrived overnight." He put on glasses, read it. "Nothing urgent but I must start my day. This has been most pleasant, April."

"Thank you, Your Majesty."

He stood.

She started to rise, trying to remember if any Hunter Rules specifi-cally covered breakfasts.

"No, no, my dear, we shall not stand on formality here. Ah, but one thing I had nearly forgotten: Your wardrobe will be supplemented as needed for the engagements you attend in my company."

"That's so kind of you, but I'm sure I won't need anything. I'll enjoy quiet times with you here at the embassy. Perhaps we could watch some movies."

"I shall enjoy watching movies with you that you enjoy. However, even with this not being an official visit, there are obligations I shall fulfill and I would like you to accompany me. As for your wardrobe being sufficient, Madame says otherwise. It will be taken care of. Have a pleasant morning, April. I will be occupied until lunch, but hope to then have some time to spend with you."

And with that he was gone.

April started the morning trying to write out exactly how she would explain to her relatives that she wasn't with Reese or working— without saying where she was or what she was doing. After she'd erased more than she'd written, she found herself examining her clothes hanging in the huge closet of the Periwinkle Room.

She realized she was staring into the open closet without seeing anything in front of her.

"This is ridiculous."

Rufus lifted his head at her voice.

"Yes," she said to him. "You're right."

She bundled up for the raw wind, grabbed Rufus' leash and headed outside with him.

Before they'd gone a block, the walk's mind-clearing benefits diminished as she realized Rufus kept looking behind them. She turned and saw Derek.

She stopped and he stopped.

"I don't need an escort," she said.

"Pierce's orders. Any time you leave the grounds."

She started to say more, but Derek wasn't the one to discuss it with. "At least walk with us so Rufus doesn't get a sprained neck trying to keep track of you."

He grinned, and joined them. They walked a couple miles, talking pleasantly, mostly of dogs and his Thanksgiving visit with family. She meant to tell him about her Thanksgiving, then a memory of Hunter's face at the homeless shelter stopped her.

In the hallway headed to lunch, she spotted Hunter ahead of her and caught up. "I need to talk to you."

"No walks alone," he said. So Derek had reported to him.

"That's ridiculous. I could understand you wanting me out of sight before meeting King Jozef, but now?"

"Somebody decides you're a princess and they're not going to wait for a DNA test."

"Wait." He wasn't going to budge on solo walks and they were almost to the dining room door. She wrapped her hands around his arm to slow him. He looked down at her grip, and her breath came faster, but she needed to tell him this. "We'll talk about that later. Before we go in, I want to tell you, the king is talking about supplementing my wardrobe. I can't let him do that."

"I'll handle it." His tone was precise and crisp.

Now she was *really* worried.

But there was no time to try to find out what he intended—or to dissuade him.

The king was already seated at the table, greeting them with a smile and a speculative look that had her saying, "I ran into Hunter in the hall."

Hunter glanced at her but said nothing.

Conversation during the meal centered on the news of the day. Stiff, but at least a conversation. With the dishes removed, the king said, "I should like to go over these invitations now, April. Unless you are otherwise engaged."

The last sentence didn't erase the command in the first.

On the cleared table, the king set three stacks of invitation cards.

"These I have no interest in," he said of the largest.

"There is a dinner planned this Saturday and the day after Christmas is the annual Receiving Hours here at the embassy when Bariavakians are welcomed. That I must attend. In addition, these—"

He tapped two cards that accounted for the smallest pile. "—I intend to accept." That left one stack. "We can assess these together."

"April doesn't have to go to anything she doesn't want to," Hunter said.

The king looked at him levelly for a long moment. "Of course not."

He handed the two invitations to her.

"I'm sure I'd be happy to accompany you to—Oh, yes, this concert at the National Cathedral should be wonderful. I'd love to go with you to that." She flipped to the second card, looking up quickly. "The White House? Really? The *White House?*"

He smiled at her. "Yes. As I said, there will be some events that require a different wardrobe."

"We're taking care of any extra wardrobe for April," Hunter said.

The arch of the king's eyebrows reached haughty in a heartbeat, but the eyes beneath them had a roguish glint. "You are, Hunter?"

"The United States government. It is our intention that neither the country of Bariavak nor you, personally, incur expense from this introductory visit." Hunter's voice was as formal as his words.

The king leaned back, the haughty arch remaining, the roguishness gone. "How considerate of the government of the United States. I assume that should I acknowledge April as my granddaughter that this government will concede that I have the right to clothe her and otherwise provide for her."

"If the acknowledgement occurs after a reasonable process of assessment, certainly."

"I don't want either one of you 'clothing' me," April said. "I have clothes."

"She needs to be presented in a manner appropriate to Bariavak's dignity," the king said, still looking at Hunter.

"She will be."

"You do not have the knowledge to see to that. Madame will make arrangements—"

"April's going to Maurice's tomorrow night."

"Maurice's?" she repeated, stunned.

For the first time King Jozef's gaze came to her. Then it returned to Hunter, whose gaze had never left the king's face. "You can arrange this?"

"Yes."

"Since it pleases April, it is acceptable. Now, these other events." He picked up the middle pile of cards.

Hunter left as soon as decisions were made on the invitations.

The king lingered, sipping coffee from a fine porcelain cup while they chatted about the holiday events they would attend.

When Madame left the room after assurances that the lunch had been excellent, his eyes followed her. Then he lapsed into silence.

Snippets of moments, gestures, and looks clicked together. The ramifications of the conclusion she formed had to wait, however, because the king abruptly asked, "What do you know of Bariavak, April?"

"Very little. I know where it's located, the mountains that ring it, and how they've prevented it from being conquered for all the centuries that your family has ruled."

"Hah. Ruled. The royal family is more ruled than rulers. Our lives are in service of our people. Whatever the sacrifice."

His gaze went to a portrait that Madame had told her during their tour was of King Jozef's grandfather.

"So Hunter told you that our country was never conquered be-cause of the blessings of geography. He does not do his ancestors justice. The people of Bariavak do not rile to anger easily, so few have true cause to find fault with us. Yet, once aroused, our people are ferocious fighters, especially in defense of their home. As a result, few have risked invading our mountains. Mountains forbidding to an outsider, but beloved by those of Bariavak and those who love us."

He shot a look at her before adding, "Our people can be much like our mountains. There are those whose hearts are strong enough to brave the rugged terrain of our mountains and find the sweet valleys and meadows hidden away from most of the world."

"I'd like to learn more about your country," she said as calmly as she could. If she wasn't mistaken, this monarch was pushing her toward exactly what Sharon had warned her against. She felt like a piece of taffy being stretched. "Madame mentioned a library during our tour yesterday. If I have your permission…?"

She must have taken a wrong turn on her way to the library after walking Rufus with Derek. She thought if she went past the king's office and turned left she wouldn't have to backtrack. Maybe. Madame's voice coming from an open doorway down the hall—the office—stopped her.

Instinct told her they were discussing her.

"…for you or even for our country is not mine to say. Here, though—here is mine to say. Such ignorance of the ways of such an establishment, or of our country—"

Something she and Madame agreed on. It was the reason she was searching for the library.

"—Such disruption—"

"Such life," the King's voice said. "It has been a long time since such life." He said another word that April did not recognize.

The pause that followed both made her wish she could see their faces and know that she had to withdraw. Now. This was private.

April hadn't left the embassy since walking the dog. Hunter was sure of that. For starters, her coat was still in the closet by the back entry.

But she wasn't with the king. She sure as heck wasn't with Madame. She wasn't in her room, the family dining room, or any of the official rooms.

Wherever she was, Rufus was with her.

He opened the closed door to the library. She was sitting on the floor, her back to a window seat on the south wall, the area around her cluttered with books, but with a space carved out for Rufus, who was stretched out along her leg, with his chin resting on her shin. The dog had heard his entry, judging by the flickering of his ears, but didn't stir. Either he'd identified the new arrival or he was a lousy watchdog.

"What are you doing?" he asked.

Her head snapped up. Now the dog raised his head, too.

"Hunter. You startled me."

"The time to be startled is before I'm five feet away."

She smiled. As if he'd been joking. "Did you need something?"

"As a matter of fact, I come with a message from Madame. It's okay, you can relax. It's actually a directive from the king, which he's relaying through Madame so she knows it's what he wants."

"I'm not sure that makes me feel any more relaxed."

He grinned. "We're supposed to call him *sir* when we address him in informal circumstances. Instead of Your Majesty."

"Are there any informal circumstances?"

"Figure any time you're talking to him in the embassy or one-on-one outside it. So, what are you doing?" he repeated.

"Reading. About Bariavak." Her brows dropped. "What's the matter?"

"Nothing's the matter."

"What's wrong with my reading about Bariavak."

He had no idea what she was talking about. "Nothing I know of. Don't know why you'd want to, though." He looked around. "Seems to be plenty of other reading choices."

"It's interesting. The country's history, I mean. Maybe I got an interest in history from Leslie. Oh, Leslie's my—"

"I know who she is."

"Ah. Well, she works in preservation."

He knew that, too. He sat at the end of the window seat, so she didn't have to crane her neck. The dog had settled back with a sigh. Hard to tell if it was contented or irked at the interruption. "This is only for a couple weeks. No need to learn the history of a country you'll never see."

She started to say something. Stopped. Then said mildly, "Have to do something to keep myself occupied. Can't do what I did for Gerard Littrell.

"What *did* you do?"

She slanted a look at him, clearly taken aback by the question. "Like you don't already know," she said. Smart. She'd bought herself time to gather her thoughts, rather than blurting out the first thing that came to mind.

"Tell me your version."

She turned to look at him directly. "Unless you're trying to hint at those ridiculous rumors that we were lovers."

"I rarely hint. Tell me your version," he repeated.

"He was a talented writer who had many more stories to tell, but his health, his personality, and his lack of organization had made writing nearly impossible for him. And that made him feel dead before he had to be. I smoothed his way wherever I could, then bossed and cajoled him into overcoming the obstacles I couldn't smooth away. Most of the time he tolerated me, sometimes he railed at me. But at the end of each day he loved that he had written when he wouldn't have otherwise."

"How'd you start working for him?"

She grinned. "I was working part-time for the alumni newsletter my senior year. There was a standing assignment to try to get an interview with Gerard Littrell. He always said no. But when I re-searched him, I realized that the foundation Leslie and Tris—" She raised her eyebrows. He nodded, yes, he knew who Tris was, along with the foundation that employed her and Leslie. "—worked for had helped save his family home in Old Town Alexandria. Which is where he still lived then.

"When I was here for a break between graduations and going full-time with the newsletter, I used that to get in the door and to start talking to him. His computer wasn't working—you would not believe how old that thing was. I took off the back, blew out the dust, put it together, and it started up again. Then I made him a peanut butter and jelly sandwich. He demanded I return the next day. I did. And I never went back to the newsletter."

"Did you get the interview?"

"No. But I did do an article eventually. With his knowledge. I let him read it before I submitted it, but told him I wouldn't change anything." The memory made her smile. Then something killed the smile. "I still miss him. At first, it was … so hard."

Hunter knew she'd met Reese Warrington barely two months after Littrell's death. She'd just moved into her apartment. From the reports, she hadn't known many people, because she'd devoted herself so much to Littrell.

"Then the Vegetable Consortium," he said.

He knew all this. Why was he getting her to talk about her past?

She nodded. "I'd been job-hunting for months. Nobody was looking for a nurse-nanny-nag. King Jozef said at breakfast that those skills would make me an excellent assistant to an ambassador."

Ah. That must explain it. At some level, he'd realized it would benefit the operation for him to know how she was answering the king's questions about her life. Even though he'd bet King Jozef had as complete a file on April Gareaux as he did.

The difference was, the king hadn't followed her for days, hadn't lived with her for more than a week, hadn't stayed outside her bedroom night after night.

Her wry smile faded. "I'm so grateful Zoe's giving me a chance."

"A chance to sell the world on Brussels sprouts? Dream job."

"They have Vitamin C and protein and fiber and antioxidants."

"And taste like bitter cardboard."

"You have to cook them right. If you overcook them, that's when they get bitter and—What?"

"You don't like them, either."

She sucked in a breath, clearly ready to defend them. Then the breath came out in a rush and she slumped. "No, I don't. And I'm terrible at trying to pretend I do, and being all enthusiastic about them.

I'm afraid lobbying for Brussels sprouts is not a good career path for me. Only job I've ever been really good at was helping Gerard. In a way, this—" Her gesture took in the embassy. "—came at a good time. To get my thoughts straight about what I want to do, what I can do. Oh, and about the end of my engagement to Reese, of course."

She was so transparent. She'd as good as forgotten her ex-fiancé. How on earth had she gotten engaged to the jerk?

He watched her hand idly stroking Rufus. The animal's coat already looked better. The food or the love?

Abruptly, he said, "You're right, you can't do here what you did for Littrell. Madame would see you as a rival and probably poison you."

Her mouth twisted. "Before or after poisoning me for being an interloper?"

His mouth twitched. "Same time. She's a very efficient woman."

CHAPTER FIFTEEN

"What do you mean she's gone?"

"She and Sharon—"

"Sharon." Some of Hunter's adrenaline retreated. "When did they leave."

Derek squared his shoulders. "She left with Sharon in the embassy car at 2:12. Rufus, too."

Their leaving right after he'd gone into a meeting with the Bariavakian security detail the king had depleted with his leave-giving was no accident.

Of course she took the dog. "Where?"

"Sharon didn't say—" Hunter would have asked, but Kenton wouldn't. Sharon knew that. "She told Madame that April would be back here for dinner."

Sure, leave him in the dark, but wouldn't want to upset Madame.

Tris knocked on the open door as she stepped into Leslie's office down the hall from her own at the historic preservation foundation.

"Here's the file from 1954 on that eighteenth-century church in Texas. We have *got* to get all the archives digitized."

Leslie kept typing as she said, "Every time it's in the budget, we end up using the money to save more buildings instead. And you're usually leading the charge."

"Those buildings were now-or-never. Digitizing can wait." Over Leslie's chuckle, she added, "Heard anything more from April?"

Leslie stopped chuckling, stopped typing, and turned to face Tris.

"No. This isn't like her. She was really good about checking in when she was working for Littrell and when she started seeing Reese Warrington."

"But she hasn't been good about it since the summer."

"It's natural that she didn't stay in touch as much once they got serious."

"Especially since Reese is doing his best to isolate her from us. I know, I know, that's not a battle you're prepared to have with her right now. But, really, Les—"

"But remember the dog. If Reese—and more important his mother—are okay with her adopting a dog, maybe it's better than we've feared."

Tris gave a slow nod. "Maybe. And I will say, it's not like she could go missing without her fiancé noticing—I'm kidding. Don't look so worried. Just because she wasn't with us for Thanksgiving and she's not calling as much doesn't mean there's anything wrong. This time I mean it seriously, because I know that's what's at the back of your mind, Les. But Reese Warrington would have raised the alarm. She's living with him for heaven's sake. Not to mention the people where she works—What?"

"I called her office. Left a message. Then I tried her boss, Zoe. I heard her tell her assistant to say she wasn't in."

"She wouldn't do that if April were missing," Tris said with certainty. "She'd want to find out from you where April is. See? It's okay. April's just busy."

The friends looked at each other. Logic didn't wipe out concern.

Leslie let out a breath. "I've made a plan. I'm going to try her again tonight. I haven't wanted to fill her phone with nagging *call me* messages, but this time, if I don't get her, I'll leave a message."

"And if she doesn't call back?"

"I'll give it forty-eight more hours, then I'm calling the Warringtons."

If April could have window-shopped at any establishment in Washington, it would have been at Maurice de Chartier, Clothier.

Except Maurice's, as it was known to customers and wish-they-could-be customers alike, was entirely too self-confident to have a window. That was for plebian establishments that needed to lure people in.

Instead, April knew from walking past it many times, it had an austere black door between frosted sidelights that gave the illusion that a passerby might be able to see in if she pressed her nose to the glass. Simply entering that door was often worthy of inclusion in the about-town columns and blogs.

April wondered if anyone had ever been mentioned for going in by way of the alley.

Not that she was complaining. Griping that Rupert drove right past the acclaimed black door, and turned into the alley would be petty.

Besides, who would she gripe to?

Hunter had been more distant than ever since she and Sharon returned just before dinner. King Jozef had invited Sharon to join them. He and Sharon had chatted amiably, April had done her best, and Hunter had been silent.

He'd walked Sharon to her car, parked inside the gates, and they stood there, despite a light rain beginning to fall. From a back hall window, April had watched them. Hunter stiff, Sharon at ease.

At one point Hunter spoke loudly enough that she was pretty sure he'd said, "Then take me off." Sharon said, "No."

When Hunter pivoted to start toward the building, Sharon gave a brief, grim smile, then got in her car.

April turned away from the window, meeting King Jozef's eyes as he did the same from a window farther down the hall. He nodded, with a hint of a smile, then turned and went the other direction.

Now, Hunter told Rupert he would call when they were ready to leave, got out of the car, gesturing for her to follow out the same door. As soon as she'd slid across the seat and started to straighten into the bracing cold, he clasped her arm. She was starting to get used to that.

Really she was.

With the cold rain heavier now, he guided her into the alcove by the back door before reaching back and shutting the car door with his free hand.

The metal security door opened. Hunter's hold on her arm, and the memory of previous collisions, kept her a step behind him as he entered the building first. He pulled her closer to his back.

"Ah, *bonjour*. It has been so long, Monsieur Pierce. I had thought, perhaps, that you no longer found Maurice's designs suitable," intoned a deep, accented voice from somewhere beyond Hunter.

But all she could see was the back of Hunter's overcoat, and the way his thick hair curved into a comma at the base of his skull, as if it would become a curl if he let it grow.

"Hope springs eternal, huh, Maurice?"

She gawked. She must have misheard. As hard as it had been to believe that he knew Etienne, it was impossible to imagine he knew Maurice, *too*.

Hunter closed the door and stepped aside, opening her view of the utilitarian hallway.

Maurice de Chartier was tall and slender, his hair close-cropped. He wore jeans and running shoes—like an ordinary person. The sleeves of his lemon shirt that appeared to be made of the finest wool she'd ever seen were folded back to reveal powerful wrists and hands the color of tea. His smile was rueful as he looked at Hunter.

She followed that gaze and couldn't look away.

Mischief—honest to God mischief, and with a sprinkle of amusement, no less—sparked Hunter's eyes golden.

"This is the young woman I called about, Maurice."

Reason told April that to understand this interaction she really should look at how Maurice de Chartier responded, but she couldn't take her eyes off Hunter. With his eyes glinting and his wide mouth twitching up, his jaw softened. Oh, it was still reliable and strong, but not quite so domineering.

"Your coat, ma'am?"

She blinked at the low voice and found at her shoulder a dark-skinned woman who was probably Zoe's age but looked younger.

"Oh, yes. Thank you."

"Would you care for something to drink? Our special carrot juice refresher? Sparkling water? Wine? Latte? Tea?"

"It all sounds good. Perhaps later?"

"While you decide, may I take your bag?" The woman's voice was so smooth it was hard to tell, but April thought there might have been a criticism of the canvas bag she carried in addition to her purse.

"Yes. It has muffins in it I baked this afternoon. They're wrapped in towels to keep them warm, and I need the towels back, because they belong to—" She stifled the urge to glance at Hunter as she stumbled to keep from mentioning details. "—uh, someone else."

"Muffins?" The woman's voice was as low and smooth as before, but the cool distance was gone. "You baked *us* muffins?"

"Where?"

She ignored Hunter's question and nodded to the woman. "Cranberry. I hope you like them. They're a small thank you for being so kind by working this evening to help me."

The woman looked toward Maurice de Chartier, apparently for a decision. April looked toward him, too, and almost jumped.

He was watching her with an intensity that rivaled some of Hunter's looks. She forced herself to look back steadily.

Maurice de Chartier burst out laughing. The sound was deep and warm—and unexpected. "An original! You are a complete original and I will dress you to show all the world that quality. Tonya!"

"Yes, Maurice." The woman smiled.

"You like cranberry muffins, do you not?"

"I love them."

"Then let us have cranberry muffins and tea before we begin."

"We will talk about this later," Hunter said to April as they entered a cluttered office.

She and Tonya talked about recipes and baking. After his first muffin, Maurice watched her steadily, his gaze sharp yet abstracted.

Hunter also said nothing. But he ate two muffins, his focus seeming to take in the entire office without zeroing in on any one thing, or person. Certainly not on her.

After twenty-two minutes—but who was counting?—of Maurice de Chartier staring at her and Hunter Pierce not, she could have cheered when Maurice abruptly stood.

"This is most unorthodox, but it has been helpful," he said. "I have seen the woman inside and have now a concept deeper than form, deeper than color, of how to dress her. Now," he pronounced, "we start."

April was considering his words and how similar they were to what Etienne had said, which reminded her that Etienne had said something about seeing Maurice. *This* Maurice? Could there be another one that both he and Hunter knew? But what possible connection could these three men have?

Ideas tumbled through her head as everyone else stood. April followed Maurice out, but not before noticing Hunter snag the last muffin.

"Those were for me and Tonya," Maurice said, aggrieved.

"I'll make mo—"

Hunter passed her, so close in the narrow hall that his breath stirred her hair. "You will *not* make more unless you make them at the embassy, and we both know that won't happen," he said in a low tone.

"Why do you frown so?" Maurice demanded. He put a large palm to the small of her back to hurry her through a doorway after Tonya.

"A little nervous, I guess," she said. And it wasn't a lie, now that she thought about it. "This is all rather intimidating."

"Intimidating? This?" Maurice's gesture encompassed the room.

It had a trio of angled mirrors in each corner, plus two mirrors spaced out on each wall, even the back of the now closed door held a mirror. Between the mirrors narrow closets alternated with shelving that held bolts of fabric. Hunter had taken a chair in front of shelves toward the left rear and Tonya stood at the ready with an empty padded clothes hanger.

"Now, let us see what we have," Maurice said, circling April. "Take off that jacket."

Oh, no, nothing intimidating about this. But, having weathered Etienne, she was better prepared for Maurice. She took off her jacket and handed it to Tonya.

"Shoes off. Let us see your true inches."

She toed off her shoes. They were flats, so not much difference there.

"Now the sweater."

She hesitated an instant then grabbed the hem of the v-neck pullover and doggedly dragged it over her head, while keeping the hem of the cotton turtleneck underneath from riding up.

She barely had her head free when Maurice complained, "What? Another layer?"

"It's cold out," she defended herself, trying to shake her hair into order.

"There are ways to stay warm other than wrapping yourself like a mummy. Take it off."

April concentrated all her willpower on not looking toward Hunter. "No."

"I must see what I dress! I cannot guess at the form under all this. This is impossible!"

"Maurice," murmured Tonya, taking his arm and continuing her comments in his ear. His eyes shifted from her to Hunter's corner.

"Yes, all right, all right," he said after a moment. "Go with Tonya."

April gladly followed the other woman to a mirrorless cubicle. Tonya had her strip to her underwear then pull on a pale t-shirt and matching leggings. In no time, Tonya ushered her back to the room.

April took two steps toward the center of the room where Maurice waited. The mirrors threw her reflection back at her and she halted.

Surrounded by herself, she tried not to look anywhere. It was impossible. Everywhere she saw reflections of herself, the thin layers of form-fitting cotton offering no more protection than her underwear would have. Worse, every other reflection provided a new angle of

Hunter sitting in his chair, his fingers steepled, his face so impassive it appeared rigid.

And damn, damn, damn, that internal defibrillator was going nuts again.

"What possesses you to wear those—those wraps to your chin? You have beautiful lines. Everywhere, beautiful lines, but the most beautiful, yes, definitely is here—." Maurice's hand sketched an arc without touching her. "Chin, throat, chest, to your bosom. Yes, you have a fine, high bosom, and we shall show that off."

"No."

Hunter's voice was low and sounded strangled. Everyone stared at him. April felt both shivers and heat from the depths of her *fine high bosom* to her hairline.

"Pah! The jealousy of men who want to hide a woman from everyone but themselves."

"That's not the situation, and you know it." Stern and unmoved, Hunter sounded like himself again.

April wondered if Maurice de Chartier had ever had a customer sink to the floor in a Wicked Witch of the West puddle—without Dorothy, Toto, the bucket of water or being a witch.

"Conservative, Maurice," Hunter warned.

Maurice spun on him. "Do I tell you how to guard a diplomat? Do I tell you where to look for dangers? No! Because I respect that you know your business. As I, Maurice, know the business of dressing women for this city. You think I would put this one in spangles and glitter? No!"

Hunter raised his hands in a gesture of half surrender. It didn't stop Maurice.

"I tell you, you are to sit silent in that corner. This one is to stand here in the center. And I shall work magic."

CHAPTER SIXTEEN

She sank against the car seat, more mentally tired than she would have believed she could be. But if she didn't take advantage of this opportunity with Hunter alone, there might not be another time. "I have to ask. How do you know Maurice? Etienne *and* Maurice? Do you only have friends with single names?"

The corners of his eyes crinkled, then returned to neutral. "They're not friends. Not the way you're thinking. Not watching a football game and having a beer friends."

"What kind of friends are they then?"

"Left over from when we were kids."

Kids. The way he said it brought a sudden, vivid memory of a sail Grady had taken her on one early morning on Lake Michigan. She could smell the sun-warmed breeze skimming across night-cooled water, feel the rocking of the small boat, and the smooth firmness of its side when she grabbed it after that rocking. She'd been so unhappy. So lonely. So armored against anyone—especially any adult—poking beneath her crust of sneering cool.

"Kids," she repeated slowly. "Being a kid's not always the easiest time."

He didn't respond.

"I hit a real rough spot at thirteen. Don't know if that's in your reports?"

"Your great-grandmother and your mother's cousin became your guardians when you were thirteen," he said, not answering her question.

She could have left it there. That would be easier.

Then she thought of Grady.

Not taking her on that sail would have been easier for him. But he had.

"That was the beginning of things getting better," she said. "Before that was … the worst. Maybe it was my not-yet-formed brain, but I seriously thought suicide might be a good option."

Grady had known.

He hadn't asked questions. Not to start. Instead, he'd talked about his own childhood. And how he'd taken a sailboat out alone one night.

She'd been the one to ask the first question: *Why'd you come back, when nobody'd missed you?*

I would have missed me. … You know, though, about the time I decided all this, the wind kicked up and I had to fight like hell to stay afloat. It was almost as if the lake was telling me deciding's not enough. You've got to work at it.

"We met at a kind of boarding school," Hunter said abruptly.

From the corner of her eye, she knew he was staring out the darkened window. She didn't look at him, didn't turn toward him. She waited, quiet and patient. The way Grady had that morning on Lake Michigan.

"Not the kind where rich families send their sons. More of a place to put kids who didn't fit anywhere else. Guess we were lucky it wasn't a reform school."

The tilt of his mouth carried little humor.

"None were criminals—yet—but definitely misfits. The three of us were misfits among the misfits. Maurice was already showing his talents. Sketching and sewing didn't go over big with the other boys. Neither did Etienne. Gay and a foreigner. Me, I was just a foreigner. Maybe they'd have overlooked that." One shoulder twitched in a brief shrug. "Preferred being alone, mostly. I encouraged the others to leave Maurice and Etienne alone."

He was silent so long that she ventured, "You've stayed in touch with them ever since?"

"Not really. Run across each other now and then."

"But if they're a couple—"

He turned toward her, suddenly grinning. "Maurice and Etienne? No way. Maurice likes women. A lot of women. He adopted Etienne's accent and some of his mannerisms for business. The mystique, he calls it. Etienne calls Maurice a heathen with an inexplicable talent. Told you, we're not really friends." The grin faded. "We just know each other from way back. We've done each other favors now and then."

She wondered if the favors Etienne and Maurice had performed on her behalf were partial repayment for Hunter "encouraging" others to leave them alone as kids.

The car slowed to enter the embassy gates, then slid to a stop with her side closer to the building. "Wait for me to come around to your door."

"Hunter." He looked over his shoulder at her. "I want you to know. I won't say anything about what you've told me."

Something that might have been surprise came into his eyes. Then the grin returned briefly. "In that case, I can also tell you that Maurice's real name is Marvin."

He held her arm.

Not the way he usually did, since they were inside the gates. Instead of her being behind him, he'd brought her to his side. Sure, he was still scanning the area, his head away from her now.

But it was almost the way a man would escort a woman with the paved surface they were crossing made slippery by rain now freezing as it hit the ground.

"Getting icy," she said, turning to him.

He'd turned to her, too.

Their eyes met. Both went still for this moment. Inches apart. A stream of his breath, then hers in the cold air. Forming a cloud between them, around them. Was it obscuring them from each other, or shutting out anything beyond the two of them?

Streams of breath, each separate and alone, coming together, mixing and melding until it was impossible to tell what came from him, what came from her.

"Inside," he said, his voice harsh.

Ahead of him, Hunter watched the king open the door into the library.

With workers putting up decorations inside and out, April had spent most of Thursday here, coming out only for lunch.

"Come, come, April," the king said. "We shall all go to see the embassy's Christmas tree now that it is completed."

April and Rufus were considerably more cheerful about heeding the order than he—or, he suspected, Madame—had been.

Together they all left the private quarters and emerged into the main reception room of the public area.

April's face went blank.

Hunter stepped to the side, letting the king's bulk block most of his view of April while giving him a clear view of the official tree. He knew nothing of Christmas trees, but he could swear he could feel the temperature drop near this creation. Weren't Christmas trees supposed to remind you of family, hearth, and home? He didn't know anything about those either, but he was pretty sure this wasn't how they felt.

Sure didn't look like the things April had put around the hotel suite.

The tree was tall and rather narrow, which allowed it to fit in a space encircled by the bottom of the curved staircase. The lights were white, but tinged with blue, giving them an icy glow. The ornaments were the same color and all the same; round saucer-sized medallions with the royal crest of Bariavak on one side and a bas relief of the embassy on the other. A narrow silver garland wound around the tree, and some sort of silvery-blue tinsel hung from the branches.

"What do you think, April?" King Jozef asked.

Madame's erect posture went so stiff she might have been a specimen scientists found in a glacier.

April shot a look toward the king that Hunter didn't quite catch. But he saw the king incline his head slightly, perhaps in an encouraging—or commanding—nod.

"It's … very dignified."

Madame's shoulders relaxed, but Hunter saw the king give April a close look.

"You don't like it."

Her voice was careful. "Your Majesty, that's not for—."

"You don't like it," King Jozef insisted.

Madame had returned to her personal ice age.

"It wasn't put up for my pleasure, was it, sir," she said with straight-forward logic. "This tree is meant to formally welcome visitors to the embassy and to mark the season with dignity and decorum, befitting official functions. Madame has produced a tree that does those things perfectly."

That would have been that … if she hadn't drawn a breath and kept going.

"I do prefer more relaxed, informal decorations, as I'm sure we'll have in the living quarters."

The silence that followed shouted as loudly as any words.

"That is, if you want decorations. Not everyone does, of course," she said quickly. Her gaze flicked toward him. The king's followed.

King Jozef then turned to Madame. "I shall want decorations in the living quarters after all, Madame."

"Please don't change your plans for me. I—"

"You are my plans, April." He took her hand in both of his. In these few days the king's manner to her had unbent to an ease she returned. "And I am delighted to have you change them from nothing to something."

"But to add more work for Madame. I can't—"

The king quashed April's protest. "You are right, my dear. So, I ask that you take charge of this project."

April shot a look toward the older woman, whose posture and straight-ahead stare would have suited a man about to be shot.

"Will you do that for me, April?" King Jozef asked.

Her mouth opened. Closed. Opened again. "Yes, sir."

Madame wasn't as easy for the royal bulldozer to flatten.

"There are no decorations to use in the living quarters."

King Jozef turned to her, still holding April's hand. "Come now, I can't believe the Ambassador and his wife have not decorated in the years they have remained in Washington for the holidays. I know Gregor and Lilette and they have always enjoyed such things."

"They do decorate," Madame conceded, then added with relish, "With personal items. Family heirlooms of great sentimental and personal meaning."

"Oh, no, we couldn't use their personal things," April said immediately.

Hunter doubted they'd heard her. The king and Madame were locked on each other.

"It does you credit to consider the feelings of Gregor and Lilette," the king said.

She returned his look without blinking. "Thank you, sir. I try to be conscious of their comfort as part of my duties."

"As you have been—and will continue to be, I'm sure—conscious of my comfort."

Score one for the king.

"Of course, sir," Madame said through lips that barely moved.

"And since it will add to my comfort to decorate for Christmas, I am certain you will see to it."

"Very well." There was a glint in her voice like light off of a polished sword. "I shall have the cartons with spare materials from this tree brought up once more from the basement, and erect a tree in—"

April made a quickly cut-off sound at the reference to *spare materials from this tree*. The king had heard it.

"A different sort of tree for the living quarters," he said. "Relaxed and informal, as April said."

"The embassy possesses no such decorations." Which was as it should be, judging from Madame's tone.

"Ah, but we have other resources. You will want to use the ones you brought," he said to April before returning to Madame. "Then whatever else is needed, you shall buy."

"I have no information on where one might purchase such *relaxed* and *informal* decorations as might please Ms. Gareaux. Nor do I have the time—"

"I'll get them. It's only right—" April said quickly. "Since it's my idea. And I can find whatever we need so much easier than Madame, who is already working so hard with Hunter and me being added to the household, and the staff reduced. Truly, I'd like to get the decorations. And a tree. A real tree." Her smile left no doubt that she meant it. "I'd like to do that."

His face softened as he looked at her. "So you shall. It is all settled then. Where shall we put it?"

"The library."

"Not the small recep—Ah, no. Not in such a formal room."

April smiled at him. King Jozef smiled back.

Madame's voice broke the moment of unity. "His Highness has allergies to trees."

"Not firs," he objected. "And only in the spring. From the pollen."

"The scent everywhere. Your breathing. The doctors." Hunter had to admire the woman. She did not give up. "So close to your surgery, it is not wise."

"Bosh," King Jozef said, or a noise close to that word.

"Oh, no," April said. "If there's any chance that you could have a reaction or your breathing—"

"There is nothing wrong with my breathing." He was focused on Madame again. "And if there were, the scent of fir trees would have killed me many decades ago. You might well have forgotten, but at one time, you had every reason to know that."

And damned if Madame Sabdoka didn't blush.

"A real tree. In the library." Then, His Royal Majesty, Jozef, King of Bariavak, added as if it had just occurred to him, "And Hunter shall help you."

"I talked to Grady about April this morning," Leslie told Tris as they took an afternoon coffee break. Tris had been out of the office until now.

"I want to hear about that. But first I have to ask, you manage to have a conversation in the morning that's not interrupted by emergency signatures being needed, forgotten homework being completed, and missing books being found? You two are bona fide miracle workers."

"Oh, no, all that happens over, under, and through the conversation. Though this one was pretty brief." Leslie scrunched up her face in a way Grandma Beatrice decried, but Grady loved. "As for what we talked about … Wouldn't you know it? Here I've been avoiding the topic with him for fear he'll go all protective and march right up to the Warringtons' front door demanding to talk to April, and, instead, he says to give it until the weekend. That she's all grown up, probably busy with life and love, and she'll call back soon. She *is* grown up. I know she is. She has a good head on her shoulders, and she's smart."

A small frown tucked between Tris' brows. "I heard rumbles today that Roberta's back in town." The two women looked at each other. Not needing to voice their thoughts. "So what are you going to do?"

"I'm going to listen to Grady's calm, reasonable approach and I'm calling the Warringtons at 5:01p.m. Friday, because the weekend begins as soon as work ends."

CHAPTER SEVENTEEN

"Maybe Madame is right."

April had wrestled with that thought all through dinner.

"About?" Hunter's gesture stopped her from leaving the portico at the back entry.

"The tree."

He looked at her. "Then why is Rupert bringing around the car for this expedition?"

"Oh, I mean a real tree. We'll still have a tree. But an artificial one might be better."

"The king seemed set on you getting what you wanted."

"I know." With King Jozef being so generous, it was only right to make the tree in the living quarters as convenient as possible. Yet, she also wanted a warm, relaxed Christmas for him. For Hunter, too, if he would accept it.

He was looking at her, she felt it. If she turned, they'd be almost as close together as last night as he'd helped her over the ice.

But the ice was all melted now. Too warm for their breath to show today. No mingling, no connection.

"Giving King Jozef what he wants is the whole point," he said.

He was reminding her that, far from bringing true warmth into the king's life, she also was lying to him. And he was reminding her that his relationship to her was only a product of this charade.

"Of course."

The car glided to a stop in front of them.

Once they were inside, Rupert turned around. "If it's all right with you, Miss, I will drive you to Chalton's Nursery in Maryland. His

Highness had me discover who carries the best live trees in the area."

"I…" She glanced at Hunter. He was looking out his window. "He said that specifically? Live trees?"

"Yes, Miss."

"Then, thank you, Rupert. That will be excellent."

The driver raised the partition as the car rolled forward.

Hunter kept looking out the side window.

"There's something going on between the king and Madame," she said abruptly.

At least that made him look at her instead of out the window.

"The king and Madame." He chuckled. "Your imagination's gotten away from you."

"Maybe not *going on*, but there's something there between them. They both feel it. And it is *not* my imagination. Don't you see the looks?"

"Looks? Are you saying the king and *Madame* are giving each other hot looks?" His tone made it clear which one he thought less likely to engage in such activity, and it wasn't the king.

"Not hot looks. Exactly. But that's because those looks haven't met—not yet, anyway. Mostly they only look directly at each other when they're at odds. Otherwise, he looks at her when she's not looking and she looks at him when he's not looking." She raised her hands to shoulder level then criss-crossed them in front of her, missing the connection. "But if these looks ever do meet—" This time her fingertips met and, still touching, reached skyward before parting in a volcano-eruption-of-emotion gesture. "—look out."

He stared at her another moment. "Impossible."

"Why?"

"Because he is His Royal Highness, Jozef, King of Bariavak and she is Madame," he said, as if that were plenty of explanation.

"So what? Why shouldn't they find love? You're not an age bigot, are you?"

"Age has nothing—"

But she was following another mental track. "You know, I don't think it's finding love, anyway. I think maybe they had something going before. So it's renewing it. Or maybe continuing it."

"*What?* Do you have any idea of the scandal? Any word of such gossip could cost Madame her position."

"I'm not gossiping. I've only told you." Though she wouldn't be surprised if Sharon had an inkling. Maybe Rupert, too.

"Well, for God's sake don't tell anyone else. In fact, don't tell me. It's impossible."

"You keep saying that, but not why it's impossible."

"He's the king."

"There's nothing that says a king can't fall in love."

He shook his head. "Not this king. Some men—some people are equipped to fill a certain job, but not for other aspects of life. It can only lead to disaster if they try to have a family or friends when their only love is their job."

"You're saying it's impossible for the king and Madame to feel anything for each other because his job demands too much of him?"

"That's a simplistic way of putting it, but yes. Now do you understand?"

No, she didn't understand his point. But she thought she was starting to understand him better. Still, she wondered, did he realize that he thought he was describing himself as well as the king?

Picking out a Christmas tree should earn hazard pay.

"What about this one?" he'd asked two feet into the brightly lit lot, when he still had delusions about getting in and out quickly. He had to talk loud to be heard over a tinny rendition of song going on and on about Good Saint Nick being on a rooftop.

She gave him a pitying look and didn't bother to answer.

Then she walked past the first 47,000 trees with "too small," "too big," "not the right color," "don't last long enough," "not the best scent," "those needles can hurt."

"Why are you whispering? Afraid you'll hurt the trees' feelings?"

She chuckled, but said quietly, "I don't want the people picking out those kinds of trees to feel bad."

"They must like them if they're picking them out, so why would they feel bad?"

Pitying look No. 2.

Finally, with that same song playing for at least the fourth time, they came to a section that passed all her tests, judging from her satisfied, "Ah."

But even here she critically examined a half-dozen trees before she said, "Let's look at this one." After a moment, he realized she was looking at him expectantly. "I'd like to see its shape."

Twine wrapped around the tree, holding the branches in. "I'll have to cut the twine. They might not like that."

Pitying look No. 3.

"Anyone who wants to sell trees, expects it. Customers can't make a decision with the tree bundled up," she said.

So he cut the twine, and branches dropped partway.

"Ho, ho, ho, who wouldn't go?" drummed the song. He could answer that question. He had some thoughts on Nell and Will getting their stockings filled, too.

Head tilted, she eyed the now-freed tree critically. "Can you hold the trunk? Out here, so it has room."

He picked up the tree and moved it to the aisle with one hand wrapped around the central trunk. He felt stickiness attach itself to his hand immediately. Grimacing, he extended his arm fully, while she moved around the tree.

"Grady thunks it," she informed him. "To see if needles fall off."

"Why would you want needles to fall off?"

"You really don't know anything about Christmas trees, do you? You don't want the needles to fall off. If they do, it means the tree's not as fresh as you want. So, you thunk the end of the trunk on the ground to see if they fall off. Also—"

He lifted the tree and thunked it. Except he missed the ground and hit his foot.

She sputtered in an effort not to laugh, but at least there was no pitying look. "—uh … It also drops the branches more." She shook her head. "No, not this one."

"Wha—" He looked at the rejected tree. "Why?"

"Too many branches twist, so the color's not even. Let's try this one."

No sense cleaning his hand until they'd finished with the trees, so sap piled on sap, tree after tree.

If Saint Nick didn't get off that rooftop soon, Hunter was going to go haul him down himself.

Finally, after the ninth tree given the full twine-cutting-branch-checking-trunk-thunking-slow-circling treatment, she went back to the seventh tree. "This one."

"Why didn't you say that before?"

"I had to be sure."

He opened his mouth, then shut it when he saw the mischief in her eyes. "Fine. Let's go. Lead the way."

He picked up the tree and started following her. Before they exited this section into the main aisle, they were slowed by a couple doing the same thunking-circling routine. Hunter noticed the guy was wearing a glove on his trunk-holding hand.

Once past the couple, they should have picked up speed again, but April had slowed to a near stop in front of him, her head turned back, looking at the tree the couple was considering.

"Oh, no," he said. He grabbed her hand with his un-sapped left hand and tugged her after him. "Saint Nick is down through the chimney for the last time, and we're done here."

"We still have to get decorations and things in their shop."

"Fine. Fast."

He realized he was still holding her hand only when they spotted Rupert watching them from near the entry to the shop.

He dropped her hand, which Rupert also watched.

At least the shop had a bathroom where he got the top layers of sap off his hand while Rupert stayed with April. And the music in here, while no less tinny, changed from one song to another.

April's cart was full, so this couldn't take much longer. Things were looking up.

As he walked up, Rupert eyed April's cart and said he'd bring the car around to pick up the tree, being prepared now, and purchases.

She added a box to her collection, then focused on something just past him.

"A stand. I wonder … but even if the ambassador's family has one, maybe we shouldn't use theirs. Hunter, could you reach down and get one of those boxes?"

He tried to one-hand it, but the box was too big—judging from the cover because it held a device engineered by the best minds at MIT.

He crouched and reached both hands. That brought him eye-to-eye with a little girl who had half of the straight portion of a candy cane in her mouth and the hooked end gripped in a red-stained hand.

She pulled the candy cane out of her mouth with a sucking sound. "Whatcha doing?" she asked.

Before he could answer or get out of the way, the follow through on her candy cane removal brought it firmly against the side of his thigh, adhering to his wool slacks like glue.

A fact confirmed when the girl released her hold on the curved end and the candy cane remained stuck to his pants leg.

He quelled his first instinct to pull it away, because the thing had to be as sticky as the sap from—

A sound erupted. Training had him reaching for his shoulder holster.

He didn't reach it. Whether that was because his timing was slowed by his hand's residual stickiness or because he recognized the source of the ear-splitting screech as coming from the little girl, he would never know.

"He took my candy cane! The mean man took my candy cane!"

He looked down and saw that the cane, though leaving a clear imprint on his slacks, had dislodged and now rested amid the dirt and pine needles on the floor.

April was around him and crouching down to the girl's level in a breath. "It's okay, it's okay. He didn't mean to. I'm sure he's very sorry."

"I'm sorry all right," he said, standing. How could April stand being that close to the origin of that godawful caterwauling?

"Hunter, tell this poor girl you're sorry, and that you'll get her a new candy cane."

Their eyes met for an instant.

"I'm more sorry than I can say that you lost your candy cane. And I'll get you a new one, as long as you don't open it in my presence," he said grimly. The girl's eyes opened wide and her mouth closed, thank heavens. He added in a mutter, "But if her name is Nell, all bets are off."

April settled in the car with a satisfied sigh. "Didn't you enjoy that?"

"My ears hurt from that stupid song over and over, my hand's permanently sticky, my foot hurts—yes, you can laugh all you want, it does hurt—my pants have a red and white striped stain that makes me smell like cinnamon, and I was accused of trying to steal candy from a baby whose voice can shatter glass. Yeah, I had a ball."

She grinned at him.

And damned if he didn't grin back.

CHAPTER EIGHTEEN

"The king asked to see you when you came in," Derek said before Hunter had his coat off.

He'd made sure Derek was on hand, then went to the office before the rest of the household was up. When Sharon arrived, he'd told her a few details not in his official report.

"So things are going great," she'd said.

He frowned. "He treats April as if she might really be his granddaughter, yet I don't see any sign he's checking her out."

"Maybe he's checking her out so discreetly you don't see it." He gave her a look and she chuckled. "It's possible."

"He's up to something."

But what? Why would King Jozef have her staying at the embassy, spending all this time with her if he didn't think she might be his granddaughter? But if he thought she was truly his granddaughter, wouldn't he be taking some steps to acknowledge her. That's what kept chewing at him.

Sharon's only response had been a shrug. "Does it matter?"

"It will to April," he said grimly.

"Let's see what the next couple weeks bring," Sharon had said.

Now he knocked on the door of the king's office, was told to enter, and did.

"Ah, Hunter. Good morning."

He nodded.

"You and April procured a lovely tree yesterday."

So the king had said last night after they'd put the tree in its stand in the library. April had said it needed to "rest" overnight before being decorated.

They'd then watched an old black and white movie called *Miracle on 34th Street.* At the beginning, the character who believed he was Kris Kringle stopped at a store and corrected the lineup of reindeer in the display.

April turned and looked at him with significance.

He kept his face neutral. But he knew what she was saying with the look. That she was certain he knew about the moment she'd stopped in front of the jewelry store with a similar display the first day he'd talked to her.

Because she was certain she knew he'd been tailing her then.

She couldn't have.

The king's voice brought him back to the present.

"April said at breakfast that she intends to decorate the tree today, before we must depart for the lighting of this country's National Christmas Tree." That was one of the optional events April selected. "I would help her if my duties did not preclude that. Though, surely she would benefit from assistance by someone more adept with a ladder than I am."

"You want me to help her decorate a Christmas tree."

Although it wasn't a question, the king said, "Yes."

Hunter lowered his head in acknowledgment of the order. He was at the door when the king added, "I suggest you change into appropriate clothing first, however. I understand the suit you wore yesterday was, ah, somewhat abused."

He looked back at the king and saw a twinkle in his eyes and a curve of his lips.

April did that.

He didn't know where the thought came from. Or why he gave a quick smile back as he said, "It was. Good idea about changing."

The library door opened, and April turned to see Hunter entering, dressed in a faded pale blue shirt and jeans a slightly richer color.

She'd grouped the boxes—those she'd brought and those they'd bought yesterday—but hadn't gotten any farther.

She'd never decorated a tree alone. With Melly, there'd been no tree, unless they were in a hotel with one in the lobby. With Leslie and Grady or Great-Grandma Beatrice, it was a family activity.

"You're in time to help," she said. "Or … Will you help?"

"That's why I'm here." He didn't sound entirely happy. He approached her array of decorations.

"I promise, no half-eaten candy canes. Though I can't promise there won't be any sap."

"I'm prepared this time." He took a work glove from his back pocket and tapped it against his other hand. He frowned. "Do you have a heavy duty extension cord?"

"I'm sure they have extension cords."

"Heavy duty?"

She shrugged. "The branches have come down well overnight and I refilled the water reservoir, so it's ready for the lights."

"No it's not. Do you have timers?" She shook her head. "Alarms?"

"Alarms? That seems excessive."

"Worth being excessive to avoid an international incident because you burned down Bariavak's embassy. Don't start on the tree. Don't leave the embassy. I'll be back soon."

From the library doorway, he saw the strings of lights were out of their packages and tumbled into messy piles.

"What happened here?"

"Testing the lights. See if all the bulbs are good like Grady does."

He could see only her back, but from her voice, either she'd caught a cold while he'd made the quick shopping trip or something had happened.

Advancing into the library, he placed the hardware store bag on the floor. With her head away from him, she scrubbed the sleeve of her sweater across her eyes.

"Tangling lights is making you … unhappy."

She might have intended a chuckle, but it emerged as a snuffle.

"Not the lights." She gestured to a Campbell's Soup box labeled "Family Ornaments" that he remembered transporting from her storage space to the suite, then the suite to here. "Just remembering."

He sat on the couch. "It won't take long to take the tree down and put the boxes back."

She twisted from her waist to look over her shoulder at him. Her eyes were red and puffy. So was the tip of her nose. "Take it down? It's not up yet."

"That makes it easier."

"Why do you dislike Christmas?" She snapped that, then immediately softened. "Oh. I should have thought—is it against your religion or—?"

"It's not against my religion. I have no feelings about it one way or the other."

Lifting her knees she pivoted to face him completely. "But you must have … I know some people don't like the holidays. And there are all those articles about the stress and everything. But … I mean, your family must have had traditions, if not Christmas, then another holiday. That's one of the things I like so much, with Kwanza and Ramadan and Hanukah and Winter Solstice, it's like everybody's observing a special time."

He shook his head.

Her eyes on him were clearly searching, yet he wondered if she knew how much they revealed. He saw sympathy and questions. But she didn't press her sympathy on him. Nor did she ask the questions.

"I think my very first memory is of Christmas lights," she said. "I remember the colors. But mostly I didn't like Christmas as a kid. I used to hate it, in fact. Everyone else celebrating … But now, it's my favorite time of the year. Leslie and Grady did that for me. Great-Grandma Beatrice, too, but mostly Leslie and Grady, their kids, Sandy and Jake, and all the others. Paul and Bette have two girls and a boy, Michael and Tris had a boy first then twins—a boy and a girl. Paul's sister Judi has a step-daughter, then she and Thomas had a boy and she's expecting again. It's a madhouse when we're all together."

She offered her memories, as if the telling of them would give him some right to share them.

He heard about baking and decorating, movies and songs, presents and surprises. And a lot of laughter.

But her laughter had faded. She looked up, either examining the top of the tree or trying to hold back tears.

She was regretting not being with all those people she loved.

He picked up a strand of lights. It brought two other strands with it. He pushed aside one overlapping string and slid the one in his right hand through an unrelated loop. The result was nearly two feet of unencumbered light string. He neatly folded it back on itself, leaving the lights bunched on either side of his fist.

He disentangled first one, then the next string, winding them into loops. He placed two of them on the coffee table. The third one he held, extending the loose end toward her.

"Okay, so where do we start?"

She looked at him, but he kept his focus on the light he held. Finally, she rose from her cross-legged seat, took the offered end of the light string and headed for the tree.

"It's one of the greatest debates in the history of Christmas trees. Top or bottom? I say start at the top."

The actual lighting of the national Christmas tree took a fraction of a second.

If only security issues were limited to that moment.

Hunter had coordinated with other agencies as usual, and had the king's detail on their toes.

For the lighting of the national Christmas tree, the King and April had seats in the VIP section of President's Park, just south of the White House. That meant they had to be there well ahead of time. And Washington traffic meant they had to leave the embassy even earlier.

Before the ceremony, Hunter stood behind them as fellow VIPs, especially those from the diplomatic corps, came by to pay their respects to King Jozef. Most cloaked their curiosity about his companion, but several didn't cloak their appreciation of her.

Hunter rehearsed a few comments for Maurice about the coat he'd provided, which following her curves too damned faithfully. But he knew he'd never speak them. Maurice would enjoy it too much.

The king presented April to only those with whom he exchanged more than a few brief words. "May I introduce April Gareaux," he would say, sliding right past her identity to add, "April, meet Stegan Longrabaghi, who will be joining us for dinner tomorrow night" or some other phrase.

Finally, organizers shooed them away to have everyone in place before the televised show began. Hunter retreated to steps behind the platform. Out of sight, but within reach.

After the first musical number, the President and the first family came out briefly for the actual lighting.

Musicians came and went on stage. Most made April smile. Which made more of the men in the VIP section focus on her. Some of the younger men downright goggled.

The first family and president returned for the finale, then left the stage almost immediately afterward. *Almost* because the President detoured to shake hands and say hello to King Jozef, leaving the Secret Service, TV cameras, and Hunter to adjust on the fly.

With that over, more VIPs came up to King Jozef.

But at last, the king stood. Without turning around, he said, "Hunter."

He stepped forward, never taking his eyes off the crowd beyond the platform.

"April has expressed a desire to tour the individual trees. I find myself too tired to desire anything more than a chair by the fire."

"I'll come with you," April said to the king. "I can see the trees another time. They'll be here for weeks. We'll go back to the embassy, and Madame can make you a hot drink and—"

"Nonsense, my dear. You are here now and there is no reason for you to postpone your pleasure in seeing these trees. I will not have you adjusting your outings to accommodate my old bones. I am certain Hunter won't mind escorting you and returning you safely to the embassy."

He waited a beat too long to respond.

"No, no there's no need for that, sir," April said. "I'll take a quick tour, then catch a cab and I'll be back at the embassy before you know it."

Hunter met the king's look. "I will escort Ms. Gareaux, who will *not* catch a cab."

King Jozef's mouth eased toward a smile as he nodded acknowledgment, possibly thanks.

The king's security detail encircled him and started off with such efficiency that April hadn't even finished her protest before they were out of earshot.

"Ms. Gareaux," He gestured for her to descend the stairs.

"I'm sorry," she said over her shoulder.

"There is nothing to apologize for."

"I know you didn't want to do this." She spread her long fingers in a gesture that seemed to include her, the trees, the night, and possibly the universe. "It's not really your job."

A stream of people coming the opposite direction buffeted her. He stepped up beside her, slipping his right shoulder slightly in front.

"My job covers a lot of things."

"Fine. It's your job." She sounded a bit sharp, then it eased. "But I know it's not your idea of fun. You hate Christmas."

"I don't hate Christmas. I have no feeling about it one way or the other." She was watching him, so she didn't see the child-laden stroller a woman in a blue parka seemed to be incapable of steering straight.

He hooked his hand around her upper arm and tugged her toward him, Unbalanced, she stumbled, and he put both arms around her.

She looked up.

His arms tightened.

He forced them to relax. "Stroller," he said.

She blinked, then looked around as the woman behind her yelped in pain from contact with that rolling weapon.

"Oh, yes. Of course. Thank you." April straightened, smoothing down the front of her coat. He watched the motion.

"You're welcome."

A few yards more and they reached the backlog of people trying to funnel into a narrow opening to a circular walkway. Everyone seemed in the best of spirits, with children's voices breaking into a piece of a Christmas song. But the physics of more bodies than there was space meant the jostling intensified. He blocked April from it the best he could, then took her arm to be sure they weren't separated. She seemed to understand the necessity, because she didn't protest.

Maybe she was too busy to protest. There were nearly sixty trees— one from each state, plus territories, and the District of Columbia— and she was studying them one by one.

"Oh, look at that." "Which state is that?" "I love the simplicity."

She repeatedly let families step in front of them so the kids could see, which slowed the process even more.

As they waited for the latest to clear out so she could view a tree, she hummed along with the music being broadcast. "I'm glad we're doing this. We used to bring the little kids most years, and it always put me in the Christmas spirit."

"We?"

"Leslie, Grady and me. Sometimes with Tris and Michael and their kids. A couple years Paul and Bette brought their family, too. It was so much fun seeing the magic through the kids' eyes. At least it was once I got old enough to appreciate it myself." With the way clear now, she dropped her voice. "Okay, that one is downright weird."

He surprised himself by chuckling.

She looked around at him, her face so close, the way it had been the other night, the two of them, alone, outside the embassy...

A sound behind him reminded him they were decidedly not alone now. Using the grip on her arm he steered her on. "I think you're going to like Virginia's."

With his height advantage, he'd spotted it through a break in the crowd. "Really? Let's—"

"Oh, no." He kept her from breaking out of line. "You said in order. No cheating."

She looked up again, her head practically on his shoulder from the press of other people. Something flickered in her eyes. He felt a response of heat, a growing heaviness.

She blinked, and even before she spoke, he knew she was going to pass it off. "Who knew you'd turn out to be such a Christmas stickler."

"Just following orders, Ma'am." He was relieved. Had to be relieved.

"You're happier giving than following orders."

That sounded like Sharon. He nodded toward the next tree. "Here's the one from Virginia."

"Oh. It's lovely." She smiled.

Then he saw tears in her eyes. Over a Christmas tree, for heaven's sake.

Leslie picked up the phone before the first ring ended.

"Hello."

"It's me. Tris. What's wrong?" Of course Tris knew something was wrong from her *Hello.*

"She's not there. April. At the Warringtons. I called at five, and that butler of theirs said April wasn't there. Not Reese or Lois, either. I asked to have them call me back. Nothing. I tried again at eight. They still weren't in—at least that's what that butler said. I waited almost three more hours, and this time I asked where they were, and he said I would have to ask them—"

"Leslie."

"—as if I could when they aren't *there,* for pity's sake. I know it's his job to protect his employers' privacy but—"

"I know where April is."

"What?"

"At least I know where she was earlier this evening. Are you watching the news?"

"No. Why? Oh, *God*—"

"No, she's fine. Fine. Looks great as a matter of fact. And happy. I'm sending you the clip right now. It should put your mind at ease."

CHAPTER NINETEEN

Leslie Craig Roberts replayed the clip Tris had sent to her, repeating the sequence she'd gone through several times last night.

In fact, she'd stopped last night's repetitions only because Grady was coming to bed and would want to know what she was watching. With her immediate concerns relieved, she didn't want Grady thinking she was overreacting … or, worse, to have him overreact. Because Grady with a full head of steam in protection of one of those he loved was not an easy freight train to stop, slow, or steer.

It certainly was April in the news clip. She'd known that on the first play last night, when April's smiling face had relieved fears she could only acknowledge now that they were dismissed. Even then, a particular unfamiliar figure had caught her attention.

But she took things in order. So, the next viewing last night had been to see if she'd missed Reese somehow. No.

This third time she'd focused on the interaction between April and—inexplicably—the aging monarch of a little-known but strategically vital country, according to Tris' note this morning. That background information came from Tris' husband, Michael Dickinson, the chief of staff for Illinois' senior senator.

As if the thought produced her, the phone rang now, identifying Tris on the other end.

"What do you think?" her friend asked without preliminaries. "I mean, beyond that she's obviously safe, looks terrific, and seems to be having fun. You agree with all that, right?"

"Oh, yes."

"Good. Bette thinks so, too." Bette Monroe was the wife of Tris' cousin, Paul, who was close friends with Grady and Michael. "So, so you think it's a replay of Littrell?"

"I never thought there was anything—"

"I know you didn't. I tend to agree with you. But Reese Warrington? There must be some father-figure seeking in that. And this guy's a king for heaven's sake."

"Father-figure seeking?" Slowly Leslie said, "I don't think that's it."

"It would be natural with her dad dying when she was so young, but you're thinking because she has Grady? Okay." Still, there was doubt in the word. "Putting aside the father-figure question, though, raises the other issue."

"No. I'm as sure as I was with Littrell. Absolutely no on her part, and almost the same on his. Hard to be certain without knowing this man, but I see great fondness. And … sadness."

"Problem is, even though *we* know there's nothing going on, it could be like with Littrell. Other people thought so and that scared off eligibles."

"Do not speak to me of eligible." Her native Virginia accent deepened on the words.

Tris chuckled. "Whatever we think of Reese Warrington, he *is* socially eligible. What do you think about his not being there?"

"I don't know what to think." She hit replay once more. Watching a different player this time. "But what with her adopting a dog…"

"Les, something I wanted to tell you—Roberta's definitely back in town. But she's gone very quiet, which makes me uneasy."

Leslie tucked her inner lip between her teeth. Between his mother and his ex, Reese had no backbone. Trying to help him grow one was the Herculean task April had taken on. If Roberta decided to take him back…?

April would be out. Leslie couldn't mourn that, but she did worry. "She hasn't called or been in touch since Thanksgiving, and that call was so strange. If the engagement's over, why hasn't she told us? And if she's not at the Warringtons' where is she?"

"According to what I've heard, possibly at the Bariavakian embassy."

Leslie had half expected that answer. "If so, how'd she go from the Warringtons' to there? And why? Why hasn't she told us anything? There's something else, too."

"You mean *someone* else?" Tris said. "The guy in the background. The one with the face that looks like it came off Mount Rushmore? The one who looks at April like he's trying his damnedest not to look at her, because he's doing his damnedest not to feel what he feels when he looks at her? That someone else?"

Despite her concerns, Leslie chuckled. "Yes, that one."

"Think he's the colleague she mentioned at Thanksgiving?"

"I have no idea. Though I've met most of the people she works with, and believe me, I would have remembered him. Plus, I called the Vegetable Consortium without identifying myself, and all I got was that April Gareaux was not available. But the third time I tried, the person who answered was clearly a fill-in and she said April was on leave until after the first of the year."

"*Leave*? To hang out with the King of Bariavak? And what's Mr. Mount Rushmore have to do with it? Any idea who he is?"

"Looks like security of some sort. But whose? And why?"

"And what does he mean to our April?"

"Yes. That's the question."

Leslie also talked with Bette Monroe that morning. Bette's questions were less direct than Tris', her concern about April just as genuine.

The other woman kept the call brief, ending it by saying, "If there's anything I can do or Paul can do, or if you want to change the plans to come here for Christmas … Dad Monroe's leg might let him travel by then."

"Not comfortably, the poor man. Thank you, Bette, but I don't see us changing the plans. Seeing that clip, April looks so wonderful, I can't imagine there's anything seriously wrong. I do wish she'd talk to me about whatever's happening. But if she *does* need help, I know you'll both be there for her. So does she."

She felt reassured by the call. Bette had that effect on people.

The next call had a different effect.

"What is April Craig Gareaux doing with a monarch of some country I have never heard of?" demanded her grandmother, in full Grande Dame mode.

Leslie stifled an urge to chuckle at Beatrice Craig making it sound as if Bariavak had committed a crime by not previously having come to her attention. Chuckling was not advisable when Beatrice was on a high horse that would make a Clydesdale look puny.

"I don't know. You should ask April that question directly."

There was a pause. "She has not yet returned my call."

"Nor mine."

"Hmph." Beatrice's high horse shrank to pony size. "What is that girl *thinking?*"

"I don't know that, either," she said evenly.

"And no opportunity to ask her, since she's not coming tomorrow for the Craig Christmas. All because of that upstart Warrington woman and her son. As if coming here would be lowering themselves. Yet they send April off cozying up to a mere king. *Upstarts.*"

Leslie was almost certain her grandmother's last phrase was aimed at the Warringtons, not Bariavak's royal family. But rather than risk asking for clarification, she merely assured her grandmother that her branch of the Craig clan would be in Charlottesville for the festivities the next day.

April watched Hunter return to the reception room Saturday night.

This is where she had met King Jozef's guests for what he'd described as a small, informal dinner.

Clearly, he'd never had dinner with Leslie, Grady, and the rest if he thought this was informal. Even accustomed to the crowds at their family gatherings, she wouldn't call twenty-two people sitting down for dinner at a table that easily accommodated them *small.* Especially not with the dinner catered and served under Madame's iron supervision. Now they had returned here for coffee, liqueurs, and conversation.

Even with the confidence of wearing one of Maurice's dresses, at times April had felt like she was in a riptide, about to go under.

Each time, she'd held on to her calm, calling on her experience as Beatrice Craig's great-granddaughter, Grady Roberts' de facto daughter, part of their circle of family and friends, and, yes, her lessons from Hunter.

As he entered, he scanned the room. There was minimal movement of his head, but his eyes took in everything.

Their looks held for an instant then Hunter Pierce slowly winked at her.

"You did very well, my dear," King Jozef said to April. "Did she not, Madame Sabdoka?"

He added the last as Madame returned to the room after escorting out the last guest.

Madame inclined her head, a gesture that managed both to acknowledge the king's words and to dismiss April's achievement.

"Ah, Hunter agrees with me, do you not?" the king said, prompting both women to turn toward him.

"Yes," he said. Because she had. She had been herself without bumping against any of the sharp edges of protocol.

But he'd seen the toll on her.

Back in this room for the after-dinner drinks, he'd seen that she was flagging. He didn't know where the wink had come from, but he'd seen her surprise. And that the surprise had given her new energy.

"Come, sit with us for a moment, Madame," the king said. "Let us coze a bit about our friends and enemies who were here tonight."

"I have a great deal to oversee in the kitchen. The wait staff and caterers that were hired—"

"Did a magnificent job. You chose well."

"Thank you." She bowed her head. "However, they require supervision now, as they have throughout the day."

She stood, waiting for him to dismiss her, yet with something in her almost of defiance.

The king looked back at her. "Very well. Return to your work as you wish. For now."

For another instant their look held.

Maybe there *was* something in April's theory that there was something between King Jozef and Madame. The earlier debate about a live tree and his possible allergies had indicated a mutual history. And this look…

Hunter met April's gaze for an instant and saw a flicker of *Told You So* there. He stifled a grin.

CHAPTER TWENTY

April placed the cards, stamps, address book, and pen on the library's large table.

It gave her a great view of the Christmas tree, which she looked at now with pleasure and a little sadness.

The pleasure came because not only did the tree look good, but it had been the magnet that had the king, Hunter, and her eating meals in this room now. She hoped they'd spend the evening here tonight, too. A relaxed, quiet antidote to last night's *small* dinner party.

The sadness came because it reminded her that she was missing the Craig Christmas today for the first time since she was thirteen.

Reese had said it was about time she separated from her family. God, how had she swallowed that? He'd never separated from his mother, not the least little bit.

She propped her chin on her hands and faced the truth.

She wasn't going to shed any tears over Reese Warrington. Not now, not ever.

Reese was weak, but he wasn't a totally bad guy. He'd been kind to her in his way, especially before she moved in. She'd liked the idea of his strong roots, of his family home. Heck, she'd even looked forward to moving in. Two generations sharing a home had appealed to her … until she got to know Mrs. Warrington.

Even with her preventing it from being a true home, it was a great house. Unlike Gerard Littrell's, which had been cluttered, messy, and dirty when she'd gotten there. But in the end it shined. She was glad Gerard had been able to enjoy it the last years of his life the way she'd known it could be the first time she went there.

Oh.

The click in her head was almost physical. Had she been drawn to those two very different men because they had homes that had been in their families for generations? A reaction to her years wandering with Melly? Some instinct to recreate the Craig family home in Charlottesville?

She'd have to think about that. If she was developing a pattern … Although Hunter certainly didn't match—not that there was anything between her and Hunter or … well, anything.

She looked down at the table in front of her.

Enough of this.

These Christmas cards weren't going to get done on their own.

He knew where she'd be. Where she was most of the time now, in the library with the Christmas tree.

He held his laptop in one hand as he slowly turned the knob with the other. Might as well keep an eye on her while he did his other work.

The door eased open silently—Madame would not tolerate any squeaks.

April sat at the table, her head bent, concentrating on what she wrote.

Sunlight dipped strands of her hair in gold and red. It was nice, but he'd liked the more subtle sheen of her pre-Etienne hair, too.

As he watched her, a glow stole up her throat and into her cheeks. Not the bright color when she'd been angry at Madame, not the color when she was embarrassed … He veered off from defining what emotion she might have been experiencing when that color had brightened her cheeks, and made the color of her eyes deepen and soften, making a man feel as if he could fall into them and…

No. His disciplined mind closed the door on that thought, too, though it took some effort. He wasn't accustomed to meeting so much resistance from the other side of these closed doors.

Her head came up. She looked straight ahead an instant, as if steeling herself, then whipped her head around.

"Oh." It wasn't a sound so much as the shape of her mouth. "I knew it was you."

She couldn't have known anybody was there. He hadn't made a sound, or let his reflection be caught, or made a move that could have disturbed the airflow around her.

Her eyes, those honest eyes, though, said she believed what she'd said. That could explain the rising color. She'd been aware of someone nearby.

His heart jammed against his ribs, as if he'd been running. Not someone. Him. *I knew it was you.*

No. It wasn't logical. She couldn't have sensed it was him.

You were following me ... From the Willard.

Not when Derek was on surveillance, only when he came on.

"Are you all right, Hunter?"

His mind shoved those thoughts, too, into the room behind that closed door—*getting crowded in there*—and dealt with the issue in front of him.

April Gareaux.

He called up a reassuring smile. "I'm fine."

"Did you need me for something or does the king—"

He dropped a hand to her shoulder to stop her from rising. It stopped her all right. Froze her solid in that half motion, then her muscles seemed to give out, because she dropped back to the chair. He refused to let his hand follow her shoulder down.

"Everything's fine. I wondered what you're doing. Didn't mean to interrupt you."

"You're *wondering*? What I'm doing?

It was the sort of thing he'd ignored for years coming from Sharon—although April's seemed genuine astonishment rather than sarcasm. Maybe that's why it jabbed under his skin like a splinter that stung. Stung a lot.

He picked up a stack of hand-addressed envelopes. There were addresses in California, Ohio, Louisiana, Arizona, Florida, Minnesota, Georgia.

"What are these?"

"Christmas cards."

"I know that." He did receive a few cards every year. The dry cleaner, office of the Secretary of State, his landlord, a few co-workers like Sharon not deterred by the fact he didn't reciprocate. "Who are all these people?"

She picked up an envelope addressed to Cincinnati, Ohio. "The Mastersons were terrific to me. When I was about ten and they were newly married, I thought they were the most sophisticated, romantic people I'd ever seen." She chuckled. "They, bless them, were beyond patient. Now they have four kids, with the oldest at Ohio State."

"These were all neighbors?"

"No. This is to a former teacher."

"So most of these people were closer to your parents' age than yours?"

"Their age doesn't matter. It's important to remember the people we think of fondly. They were all kind to me."

Did she realize what she gave away in the wistful spaces between her words? Her mother had been so wrapped up in herself that she'd uprooted her daughter time after time with little opportunity to do more than gather addresses for sending Christmas cards a couple decades later.

He would have liked to take Melly Gareaux by the back of the collar and shake her ... if that weren't such a ludicrous thought. Hunter Pierce didn't get involved with other people's lives—especially not when one of them was dead.

"I like to let them know I'm doing fine now. And, no, I'm not telling anyone about *this*." Her sweeping hand took in the room as well as both of them.

What would she write if she were to write about him?

Of all the stupid questions....

"I'm not," April insisted.

It took him a moment to realize he'd shaken his head—at himself—and she'd interpreted it to mean he hadn't believed her. "You want to keep in touch, I understand."

Her eyes widened. "You do?"

He shrugged. "Bother you if I work in here a while?"

"Not at all," she said politely, then added, "But I'm not changing the music."

For the first time he realized Christmas carols were playing softly. "As long as Saint Nick's not on any rooftops."

She chuckled, and turned back to her task.

He picked up one of the cards. It had a wreath with a red velvet bow, dusted with snow. A perfect rendition of what she wanted Christmas to be.

He put it down and got to work.

CHAPTER TWENTY-ONE

"Would you care to join us, Madame?" April asked.

The king looked up from the calendar he was consulting after breakfast, surprise quickly smoothing over to neutrality. So quickly that she couldn't gauge if he was pleased or not.

Madame left no such doubt. She drew herself up and her mouth was so firm that the words came from her like steam from a pipe. "Most certainly not. That would be entirely inappropriate."

She turned on her heel and marched out—no, not marched, that would be too graceless. She glided out, head high and back straight, as always.

They planned to go to a candlelight tour of Mount Vernon tonight, another of April's picks.

"I'm sorry, sir," she said when the door closed behind Madame. "I shouldn't have acted on impulse."

"Do not concern yourself, child. You sought to include her from the best of intentions."

She sighed. "Adding another layer of pavement to you-know-where."

"No, I do not know where."

"It's an expression: the road to hell is paved with good intentions," said Hunter to the king, adding a phrase in Bariavakian. Then he said, "Excuse me," got up from the table, going to the far side of the room as he took out his phone.

"I beg your pardon, sir. Sometimes I forget—you're so easy to talk to—and I fall into colloquial English."

"Not at all, my child. But I would speak to you of this encounter with Madame. It would have resolved itself as you wish if you had ordered, rather than asked."

"But how could an order make her *want* to join us?"

"You have a very kind heart, my child." His smile faded, and his gaze shifted to Hunter, standing with his back to them. "Nevertheless, I maintain that, at times, an order is required."

April and Rufus both appeared content and happy as they entered the embassy grounds after their walk.

Hunter, who'd been with them, wasn't.

He'd long ago perfected the ability to filter out the personal conversation of his charges, all but what might pertain to their safety—where they were going, who they expected to meet, how long they planned to stay. Yet when he should have been tuning out April, responding only if absolutely necessary, he'd instead discussed Rufus' amazing progress in his training.

And now that they'd returned to the embassy grounds, where Rupert was tending two cars with rubbing cloths, he was fully aware of each syllable she exchanged with the man, including that she was now on a first-name basis with him.

"Are you enjoying your stay, Miss?"

"It's an amazing place, Rupert. I've never stayed anywhere quite like it before. Am I correct that Madame holds the reins here?"

"You are correct." A thread of amusement filtered through the bland voice. "Ambassadors and their wives might come and go, but Madame endures. Though I believe she would tell you the current situation does not meet her standards."

"Really? Everything's so perfect."

"She is not pleased that His Highness instructed that only a skeleton staff be kept over the holidays. Most of the household staff, as well as embassy personnel returned to Bariavak with the ambassador and his wife on a chartered flight. Madame has expressed herself quite forcefully in the belief that details are being overlooked as a result."

"What a wonderful thing for the king to do."

"He is a generous ruler." He smiled slightly. "He has overruled Madame, allowing me to attend an event tomorrow when everyone sings the Hallelujah Chorus from the Messiah. I have never done that before."

"Oh, you'll love it, Rupert. I did one of those a couple years ago. It's amazing how wonderful all the voices sound together. And to be part of it … But why didn't you go to Bariavak?"

"I have no family left in Bariavak. My only living sister lives now in Baltimore."

"You're not married?"

"My wife died some years ago."

"I'm so sorry."

"Thank you, Miss."

"Rupert, I have a friend named Zoe I think you should meet. She's ver—"

"No," Hunter said, tugging her away. Which proved what he'd been thinking—he listened too damned closely to her.

"But—"

When they were nearly to the door, he said, "You are not going to play matchmaker with the staff of the Bariavakian embassy. Is that understood?"

She looked mutinous for a moment, then relented. "Okay. I see your point."

He opened the door. "Besides, Rupert and Zoe Holland would be awful together."

She spurted a surprised chuckle at that.

The king, saying he was tired, begged off going to Mount Vernon for the candlelight tour, but insisted April go, accompanied by Hunter.

Hunter clearly took it as a work assignment. They did not talk on the drive across the Potomac River into Virginia, and then south along the river.

Tour guides played the role of Martha and other members of the household, pointing out historic details of the house as well as authentic decorations. There was singing and dancing. Hunter lurked at her side as if the ghost of George and Martha Washington might jump out and tackle her.

By the time they reached the kitchen she was genuinely smiling despite the dark cloud at her shoulder. She listened to the description of cooking methods and menus from the times. Including that Martha Washington's recipe for "Great Cake" called for 40 eggs.

Hunter did apparently like the cake and cider.

Outside, she headed toward a candlelit garden path that stretched down to the river. The sound of caroling came to them from a distance.

An uneven surface caught her foot. His hand gripped her arm before she got even halfway through the stumble.

"Thank you." It was the first thing she'd said to him since they left the embassy.

They walked a minute or two in further silence.

"Looks like one of your Christmas cards," he said.

She suspected he meant that it wasn't real. But she responded with, "It *is* beautiful."

The wind's bite had turned her cheeks red during their brief walk. She seemed to relax as the warmth of the car surrounded them for the return trip to the embassy.

He wished he could relax.

There'd been something in Jozef's expression when he announced that he wasn't joining this outing, "but you two have an enjoyable evening." Then he'd repeated the phrase roughly translated into Bariavakian. Very roughly, because there were connotations of a couple in his translation for "two" and "an enjoyable evening" edged toward the English "date."

Then Rupert had grinned and promptly raised the smoked partition when they got in the car at the embassy.

That should have given Hunter plenty to think over as they moved through the rooms of George Washington's home. He'd been here enough with various dignitaries to know it well by now so it hadn't occupied a lot of his attention.

But the rooms weren't usually softly lit by flickering light that gleamed in a woman's eyes. Plus, the Christmas crowds and April's tendency to want to be in the middle, had packed him up against her, where her hair kept brushing against his chin and her scent kept spilling into his brain.

He'd done no thinking at all.

So, this was the time to recall the nuances of King Jozef's words and behavior, to assess if he'd imagined—

"You didn't even try," April said suddenly.

"Try what?"

He *had* tried—his damnedest—not to let her know the effect she had on him, not to touch her the way he'd wanted to.

"Worse." She swung around in the seat and faced him. "You actively resist any chance that you might enjoy Christmas. Or is it me?"

That startled him into addressing the less alarming part of her speech, "The cake was good."

With a peremptory wave of her hand that would have done any royalty proud, she said, "Cake and cookies that's all you like. I thought with the tree … But now you're back to dismissing everything but the *food.* Yes, that garden in the candlelight looks like one of my Christmas cards. That's a *good* thing. Not something to make fun of."

She had him feeling defensive. He didn't like it. "I didn't—"

"And you could send cards if you want to. You must have someone to send cards to."

"Like family?"

"Yes or—

"My family's dead." He'd set her up to turn the momentum with those words, and it worked. He was off the defensive, which should have made him feel better than he did. His words had punished her.

He saw it in her eyes, and he couldn't look away.

"Everyone? But—"

"Everyone."

"I'm so sorry, Hunter."

He shrugged, fighting against sinking into the softness in her eyes. "No reason for you to be sorry. You didn't kill them. Besides, you're in the same position. Just took longer for you to get there."

"I have family," she said, "but I've also lost family, and that's all the more reason to value those who remember you and your family. Don't you have anyone like that?"

"No."

"What about the people who helped you when you came to this country?"

"How do you know—? Sharon."

"Foster families or—"

"No foster families." He could shut down this conversation. Easy. By punishing her more. "I didn't want that. The first two years I was in a resettlement home run by a church. Then I boarded, like I told you. Maurice, Etienne, and me. Stayed there year-round."

"No one—"

"Helped me? Sure. This country—its people were generous to me. I don't have to send a card to remember that. Donating so another kid can be helped makes a hell of a lot more sense than a Christmas card to a committee."

"Didn't anyone take you home for the holidays or—"

"I didn't want that. I said no."

"You shut yourself off? You refused to let anyone—"

"I let plenty of people help me."

"I was going to say love you."

He met that with the silence it deserved.

"What about the family of your soldier?"

Sharon again. Damn her.

His jaw throbbed. He made his muscles loosen. No sense denying, and this time silence wouldn't work either. He knew April well enough now to know she wouldn't let this go.

"Have you ever contacted them?" she asked.

"No."

"You could let them know how much he did for you. You must have a name—"

"I was a kid, not exactly in a position to exchange business cards with these guys. I knew him as Scotty, I didn't need any last name."

"That's all you remember?" Tears welled in her eyes, not falling.

He shrugged. "Listen, April, This is not one of your Currier and Ives moments. It wasn't sentimental and it wasn't pretty. I was a starving runt they picked up to keep me from falling over at their feet. Not all of them were for it. I knew them as Scotty and Mac and Raz and Bomber and Memphis and LA, the names they called each other. The Army doesn't keep records listed that way."

"But if you *could* find them, his family I mean, you could write them a Christmas card and let them know how much he meant to you, how—"

"No."

That last *no* told her she'd pushed him to the limit, past his limit.

For now.

She could find the family of Hunter's savior. She was almost sure she could.

One of the things Zoe had taught her about lobbying was to be aware of what resources she had available, And in this case she had several.

First, her own ability to dig on the Internet. And then a few government connections she'd made through the job, who would be so glad she wasn't nudging them about Brussels sprouts that they would help as much as they could. Then she had Zoe and Sharon. Finally, her ace in the hole, His Royal Highness, King Jozef.

Yeah, she could find the family of the soldier who had rescued a frightened, starving refugee.

But what would Hunter do if she did?

Would it open him to people, to his own goodness? Or would it close him down for good?

CHAPTER TWENTY-TWO

"…and I thought I'd go shopping this afternoon," April said at breakfast Tuesday.

"Thought you and Sharon wiped out the stores online," Hunter muttered.

She said with great dignity, "I have a few additional things to get. What are you going to give Sharon for Christmas?"

He drank more coffee. "Nothing."

"Don't you have any ideas for her yet?"

"Haven't given it a thought because I don't give Sharon a gift."

"But you're friends." Before he could dispute that, she added, "And she gives you something, so I thought—"

"No, she doesn't."

She frowned at him. "Cookies."

The king coughed. Hunter looked at him suspiciously, but April was intent on her questions.

"I hoped you can give me suggestions for Sharon. Don't you have any ideas?"

His mind was blank. Utterly blank.

How many thousands of ads had shoved their gift suggestions down his throat from placards, magazines, TV, newspapers, the Internet and radio these past weeks? He couldn't recall a single one. He didn't let them past his mental spam blocker because he had no use for the information. Presents? He knew nothing about them.

"Perhaps perfume?" suggested the king.

"Perfume is lovely, but that's something her husband should give her," April said. "I'll have to think about this more. A tin of Christmas cookies that she's made herself is a thoughtful gift, something she's put herself into. That's the sort of thing. Maybe I'll get an idea this afternoon."

Madame entered the room with the printout of the daily digest of overnight reports.

"Madame is going shopping for some presents this afternoon. You may go with her."

"Your Majesty," Madame began, with reproach echoing from each formal syllable.

"You said earlier this morning that you had a number of items to purchase to supplement what was ordered by the embassy staff. It is a perfect solution."

Hunter felt a surprising tug at his mouth. A perfect solution for the king, who did not want to go shopping, even in the company of April.

"It would be lovely to accompany, Madame—" Ah, yes, April had learned her princess lessons. "—however, I'm sure Madame has a full list of specific items, while I am hoping to get ideas. Window-shopping, wandering—I would slow her down."

"Nonsense. You can wander and look while she purchases. A fine solution."

The women eyed each other with misgiving, but neither was willing to directly contradict the king.

"Hunter, of course, will accompany you for security," the king added.

Great. Not only did he have an afternoon of shopping ahead of him, but an afternoon of Madame.

Madame walked out with Hunter practically on her heels. The duplicate body language expressed displeasure times two.

"And yet he was of quite a sunny disposition as a boy."

The king's words took an extra beat to sink in.

"You knew him when he was a boy? But ... how?"

"Have you never wondered how he came to know Bariavak's language?"

"I thought … The State Department…"

He lifted an eyebrow at her fumbling. She'd been a pretty good liar as an adolescent, but hadn't called on the skill much since. The rust showed. "The translators are professional, of course, but the rest? Bah. No, Hunter knows the language as only those who are born to it do."

"He's a native of Bariavak, and you knew him as a boy," she said, as if recapping. "But … I don't understand."

"Hunter's father was on my staff. One of my best—and most loyal—aides. The rebels' attack threatened the palace. For me to be killed would have been given them victory immediately. Hunter's father led the defense, repulsing the rebels."

Hunter's voice echoed in her head. *My family's dead.*

Dread rose as a yawning gap between her heart and her throat. "He was killed."

The king nodded slowly.

"But you said he'd led the defense that repulsed the rebels."

"He did more." He said simply. "It took great skill, and great courage. But the capital was in chaos, and not even skill and courage were enough."

Anger rose up in her. Anger at Hunter's father, who had died for his king. And, yes, anger at her father, who had left her. Maybe it wasn't fair, but they'd been children, she and Hunter. "He left his son."

"He fulfilled his duty."

April focused on the gorgeous things surrounding her, determined to set aside her earlier mood.

Beautiful arrangements of holiday music played discreetly in the background, the red and silver decorations were festive, the tree in the corner was real and sharing its scent generously, and the items in this tiny antique jewelry store off Connecticut Avenue were gorgeous. And Hunter—

He was like a stone pillar standing there. Except stone pillar's eyes didn't scan the area constantly looking for danger. Or pretending to so he didn't have to interact with her.

It wasn't like she expected to have any true impact on him, not when the Genghis Khan of romance had failed to storm his battlements. No, she just wanted him to loosen up a little. Like Sharon, she wanted to chip away at him enough so he would allow himself to have friends. Like her. A friend.

She moved from a case of Art Deco brooches to a smaller case with tiny, ornate boxes.

If she could get him off-balance. Maybe it would open him up enough to—

"You have found something you would like to purchase?" There was both curiosity and a hint of censure in Madame's voice.

"What?"

"Your focus indicates you have found something that pleases you."

"An excellent choice, an excellent choice," enthused the gnome-like clerk.

April looked more closely at the tiny boxes in the case. Not one of them had a price tag. Not a good sign.

"Which one has caught your interest?" Madame's words seemed to have an unspoken, yet surely exasperated *finally* hidden among them.

Without saying a word about it, she had made clear that she considered April's aimless wandering around the establishments they had stopped at so far a dead weight. But really, none of the places Madame had taken them were what April had in mind. So what could she do, while she waited for her turn to select where they would go, other than idly look at these elegant extravagances? The ones with price tags had her turning away. The ones without, she didn't even want to think about.

"Ah," breathed the clerk, drawing a gem-encrusted square from the center of the case. "I am sure the young madame's excellent taste has drawn her to the spectacular example of fifteenth century Florentine craftsmanship."

He held it out to her, and what could she do but accept it? The gold that formed the box glowed and the gems decorating it winked their varied colors under the artful spotlight above.

Fifteenth century? That was *antique* as in lots of zeroes at the opposite end from the dollar sign. April's muscles clamped around a sour ball in her stomach.

This was why she stayed on the outside of the windows when she looked—it was so much safer, and you never had to tell the hopeful clerk that no, you weren't going to buy his fifteenth century Florentine example of—of what? A pillbox? Stamp box?

"Whom are you considering purchasing it for?" Madame asked. A frown drew down her brows, "His Highness appreciates fine pieces, but I am not at all sure that a snuff box—"

"Snuff box?"

Her voice had skidded up, but now she saw the lifeline and grabbed it with both hands.

"I'm sorry, but that won't do at all." She extended the box toward the clerk. He did not take it, as if thinking that as long as she held it she would have to purchase it. She raised one eyebrow *a la* Madame, and he took it. "No, nothing related to tobacco. His Highness is concerned about the health of his countrymen and would not set such an example. Thank you for showing it to me. It is quite extraordinary." If gaudy. "If you don't mind, I will wait in the car while you complete your purchases, Madame."

Madame inclined her head the smallest amount to indicate acceptance, and April fled.

If it could be considered fleeing with Hunter doing his me-first-into-the-line-of-fire routine at the shop door, escorting her to the car, holding the back door for her, then going around to the driver's door. With Rupert off today, he was driving as well as escorting.

Their eyes met in the rearview mirror. Only because he was looking around for lurking threats and happened to choose that instant to check the mirror. As for why she was looking at the mirror...

"You handled that well," he said.

"Thank you. I'm not sure Madame would agree."

"Don't let her get you down."

On that unexpected bit of advice, he got out of the car again to open the door for Madame.

Back in the driver's seat, Hunter said, "Ready to return to the embassy?"

"I have completed my purchases," said Madame, with extra starch in her voice. "Miss Gareaux, however, might have additional stops she wishes to make."

April sat up straighter. "Yes, I do. If you would rather not come, since you've finished your shopping, we could drop you at the embassy. In fact there's no need for Hunter—"

"I'm driving you wherever you're going," he interrupted.

"His Highness expressed his wish that we be paired for this outing." Clearly, as far as Madame was concerned, that settled that.

"Okay. Let's go to Tysons Corner."

She saw Hunter's jaw working as if he were going to say something, but before he could, Madame turned her whole torso toward her. "That is a *mall*. You intend to shop at this mall? This Tysons Corner?"

"Oh, no," April assured her. "I scout at the regular malls, then go to the outlet malls to buy."

"Outlet?" Madame's voice climbed toward the heavens. "The guest of the King of Bariavak does not shop at an outlet!"

"April—"

She ignored Hunter's warning from the front seat. "I'm buying presents for my friends, not King Jozef's, so I'm spending my money. But if you want my opinion, he has better things to do with Bariavak's money than pay full price."

CHAPTER TWENTY-THREE

King Jozef came down the back stairway as they entered, as if he had been waiting for them.

"A successful afternoon of shopping?"

"If you will excuse me, sir, I have duties to fulfill in my office," Madame said, descending the stairway to her basement command center.

"If you will excuse me, sir, I have things I need to do in my room," April said, climbing the stairs past him.

King Jozef looked toward Hunter, as he hung his coat in the back closet.

"You were longer than I expected. A successful afternoon of shopping?" he asked again.

"Some things were bought, but I wouldn't say it was particularly successful, no. Have you ever watched those nature shows where two Big Horn sheep run at each other, lock horns and butt heads? Let's just say, it's behavior not restricted to the males in some species."

"Ah," the king said. It held a wealth of comprehension.

For a moment, they shared the amusement, tinged with a hint of terror.

Then the moment was gone.

"Come into my office, Hunter."

He would have preferred not to. But his preferences weren't the issue.

The king took the seat by the fireplace he'd occupied the first time they came here, and gestured for Hunter to sit across from him.

"I have been receiving the extension of the flyover agreement. You wish that I sign?" King Jozef asked.

"Yes. Having access to that airspace will allow the United States government to maximize its air bases to reach trouble spots. It cuts hundreds of miles off flights, reducing risks for the crews and personnel they carry."

"Why is it important to you that I sign this agreement, Hunter?"

"I've told you—"

"No, you've told me why it is important to your government and why it is important to your military. Why is it important to *you*?"

"I am a servant of my government."

The king simply looked at him.

"Faster air support." He wasn't sure why those words had come out of him.

The king looked at him for a long moment then nodded slowly. "To support troops on the ground. To come to the rescue of those on the ground who might be under attack."

"Yes." The one word came grudging and sharp.

"To protect soldiers you don't know in a war you're not part of, because of the one soldier who died. Ah, Hunter, you are more Bariavakian than you know. The past rides on your coattails."

Hunter, even more withdrawn than usual, escorted them to the row that held their seats for the concert at the Washington Cathedral that evening.

Them included Madame, who apparently had received an order.

"Hunter, you will sit with us," the king said.

"Your Majesty, that—"

"It is what I wish."

The older man leveled a look at Hunter she had not seen him use before, and the order behind the wish was clear. If she had needed a reminder, considering Madame's presence, of the power of a king, this provided it. Until today she had seen the man, not the sovereign.

Hunter's jaw tightened, but he dropped his head in a curt nod. "I sit on the aisle," he said grimly.

"But of course," the king agreed, smiling.

Then, the king took her wrist, holding her back. He gestured for Madame to go in first, followed her, then drew April along after him. His maneuver left her nothing to do but sit one seat in from the aisle, with Hunter beside her.

The king tipped his head and spoke very quietly to her alone.

"Ah, you see, my dear, you must agree that at times, an order is much more efficient than a request."

Madame issued formal thanks, then disappeared before the rest of them had their coats off.

The king asked her, "Did you enjoy that magnificent music, April?"

"It was magnificent, wasn't it? It was so kind of you to secure the tickets for us, sir."

"To instruct Madame to secure the tickets," he corrected with a chuckle. But you have not answered my question concerning your enjoyment of the music. Is it, perhaps, that you did not care for those moments of whispering, followed by an explosion of sound?"

"Why do they do that? Get so quiet and then shout at you?" She chuckled. "It's like they're testing to see if you're awake—but first they put you to sleep. And it always makes me jump, even though I *have* been listening."

"So it was this method that induces guilt that prevented you from fully enjoying the music?"

Hunter cut across whatever tactful response she'd been formulating. "She wanted to sing."

"Indeed? You harbor an ambition to perform musically, my dear?"

"No! No, I—I don't know what he—"

"She wanted everybody to sing." Let her try to deny that.

When she didn't, the king said, "Ah."

She glared at Hunter. He looked back at her.

"All right, yes. It seems a shame to have everyone sit there when we could all be participating—yes, singing—" She shot at him, as if it were a high caliber retort. "Everyone knows the words and the songs are so beautiful when voices simply come together. Plus, if the idea is to get people into the spirit of the season, having them participate does a lot more than making everyone sit there being sung at."

Her crescendo of belligerence—which had grown as she'd stared at him—fell off a cliff of good manners when she looked back at the king. "Not that it wasn't beautiful singing. I don't—"

"Do not apologize for having an opinion, April."

Hunter saw April studying the King's face at breakfast Wednesday.

When Madame came in with the daily digest, he watched with a good deal of surprise as April caught the older woman's eye, raised her brows and tipped her head slightly toward the king. The surprise deepened when Madame, after surveying the king under the guise of rearranging the plate of toast, gave a brief nod.

"This evening is the open house at—"

"Sir," April interrupted. "Would you mind if we skipped that tonight? I want to do a bit more shopping this morning, but beyond that I could use a quiet day. If you don't mind?"

The king looked over his reading glasses at her. "Whatever you wish. You're not feeling poorly, are you?"

"Not at all. But I could use a laidback day." She flashed a look toward Hunter that he didn't understand, but that put him on alert. "Especially because I do have one more thing I would like to do this week. I thought of it yesterday while we were out shopping—a personal holiday tradition that I've done every year since I was little, no matter where we were living. May I fulfill my tradition Friday night, since we have no social obligations then?"

What was she going to inflict on him now? Her holiday traditions were ending up as holiday tortures.

"Of course, my dear," the king said. "May I inquire what it is?"

She smiled. "Ice skating at the Mall."

CHAPTER TWENTY-FOUR

"I don't know, Sharon. It's awfully … uh…"

Hunter heard April's voice through the open doorway of the Periwinkle Room. He could see in, but neither she nor Sharon seemed to know he was there.

April's face was turned away, while her figure was in profile to him.

He heard Maurice's voice in his head. Chin, throat, chest, to your bosom. Yes, you have a fine, high bosom.

She wore a floor length dress in a reddish color. It dropped straight over her hips with a subtle flare at the bottom so her movement wouldn't be restricted, say, if she were dancing.

"That's exactly the point," Sharon said. "Sometimes you need a dress that's awfully 'uh.' Sometimes you need dynamite to blast through granite. Or an ice jam."

"Granite?" Her voice went up. "I'm not trying to blast through granite. Why would you think—"

"You don't believe me? Here's Hunter, let's see what he thinks."

April pivoted to face him through the doorway, her right hand holding a wrap in the same material over her left shoulder. "Hunter. What are you doing here?"

Good question. "I don't remember this dress."

"I'll return it. I wasn't sure—"

Sharon overrode April's words. "Tonya from Maurice's delivered it with those that needed additional alterations" And that explained the three tea cups on the coffee table. No doubt April had insisted they all sit down and chat. Probably ate cookies. "Along with a note from Maurice de Chartier saying he'd come across it after you left the shop last week and he's convinced it's perfect for April. I agree, but she won't listen."

"It's a beautiful dress, but…" April looked down at the skirt. Uncertainty resided right beside fragile exultation. "We didn't order it, but Tonya and Sharon say … And Maurice sent it and they say Maurice has the best taste in Washington. I don't know."

"It looks very nice on you."

"Without the wrap," Sharon said from the loveseat beneath the window.

The smirk in her voice warned him. It didn't matter. April released her hold on the wrap, it slid off her shoulder, and then it could have burst into flame as far as he knew. All he saw was what it revealed.

A flow of creamy skin from April's throat, over her delicately carved collarbone, and down, to the rising curve of her breasts. Then the dress curved in, defining the line between her breasts, cupping their smooth curves like a lover's hands would cup them in the second before his mouth—

"It's too low."

The words came too fast, but his voice sounded normal. That was a damned miracle.

Sharon made a sound that might have been an aborted chuckle, but he didn't look her way. He made himself look up, to meet April's eyes.

Uncertainty had surged to the lead in her expression, leaving the exultation trampled in the dust.

Then she sighed.

You would think a man with any sort of discipline would have no trouble surviving one single intake and output of air by a woman. Hell, all he had to do was look somewhere else. The ceiling, his shoes, out the window. Anywhere.

Instead, he saw her lips part for the inhalation and his gaze dropped to her chest. Her breasts rose, micro-millimeter by micro-millimeter. The fabric rose, too, but not at the same rate. Einstein should have had a formula to show how a low-cut dress and a deep sigh could bring a man to his knees. Her breasts seemed to fight for freedom with that breath, gaining territory an atom at a time. He wanted the battle to go faster, to be over, to know the result and have it behind him. He wanted to slow it so it lasted a lifetime.

Stillness. Absolute stillness. No sound, no movement. The smooth flesh's curve pushed above the slight restriction of material. He could feel the smoothness of that flesh in the tingle of his fingertips, taste its sweetness in the dryness of his mouth, smell its musk in the flare of his nostrils.

And then the slow release of April's breath, the slow retreat of her breasts back into the cover of the clinging material.

Those precious micro-millimeters out of sight, though God knew not out of his mind. Not out of his body, either.

It was as if the release of that pent-up air from her body had entered his, expanding and swelling his groin until it hurt.

"I'm sorry you don't like it." She squared her shoulders and replaced the wrap over her shoulder. "But I'm going to keep it. I might never have a chance to have another dress like this, and I'm going to keep it. I'll pay for it. I wonder if Maurice has a lay-away plan? Or—"

"We'll pay," Sharon said. "You need something for the White House party."

"Oh, God. The White House."

"Relax, April. It's a party—a big party, but just a party. First say you'll keep the dress."

But April wasn't listening. She was turning toward him, and as she did, the wrap slid off her shoulder again.

He had to get out of here. Now. Before his body reacted—Oh, hell! Before she or Sharon spotted his body's reaction.

"But ... Are you sure it's okay, Hunter? If you think it's too low...?"

He didn't answer. He grabbed the doorknob and pulled it after him.

Before the door closed, he heard Sharon's chuckle behind him, along with something that sounded like "Ka-*boom*!"

He could hear Maurice's voice.

Yes, you have a fine, high bosom, and we shall show that off.

But it was what he kept seeing behind his closed eyelids that was driving the bus at the moment.

April blushing. The slow rise and fall of her breasts. Her head tipped back as if waiting for a kiss. Her hair mussed from pulling a sweater over her head, the way she would look if she were peeling her clothes off … for a man.

He shifted against the cold, stone seat of the bench in the small garden by the embassy's back entry, and he knew it wasn't the cold or the stone that made him uncomfortable.

CHAPTER TWENTY-FIVE

April put her own coat and gloves on first, took his jacket from the peg by the back door, and outside, going directly up to him. "You should be ashamed of yourself."

His head came up at that.

"Put this on," she ordered.

And he did.

"If you didn't bite other people's heads off and if you weren't so hard-headed yourself, you wouldn't be out here freezing with no jacket on."

His mouth quirked. "*That's* why you think I should be ashamed of myself?"

"Of course. You shouldn't have come out here without a jacket, and then everybody was too afraid of you getting on their case to bring a jacket out to you. It'll be your own darned fault if you get sick from freezing out here."

"I've been colder." He tilted his head, watching her as she sat beside him. "You weren't afraid to bring my jacket to me."

"No, I wasn't." She turned toward him. "I'm not."

They looked at each other for a long moment.

She thought … but she'd thought before that they'd moved past some of his walls, only to have them reappear in time for her to walk right into them.

Then he said in a low, even voice, "Okay, April. Go ahead. Ask."

She expelled a long breath, still holding his gaze. She wanted to ask everything. That would never work. "Tell me about the soldiers. Tell me what you remember."

Pain flashed deep in his eyes before he looked down at his hands.

Just as she'd decided he wasn't going to, he spoke.

"The first thing I remember with clarity is lying in low weeds beside a road, and seeing a truck with an emblem painted on it. Red and white and blue. The truck was dirty, but someone had swiped clean where that flag was and it seemed to dazzle my eyes. I wanted to touch it. I got up and went to the truck."

Half a heartbeat's hesitation before those words *got up* told her what that effort had cost him all those years ago.

His mouth twisted. "I don't know if I succeeded. If my fingers did touch where that flag was painted. I see my fingers stretched out, and then blackness. The next thing I remember is the motion of the truck, someone holding up my head and giving me sips of water, while voices argued over my head. I would have died that week if they hadn't picked me up."

She saw him assess his statement, weighing its accuracy.

"Maybe the next week," he said.

Tears pressured for release. She blinked them back.

"There was no one to turn me over to or I'm sure they would have. One said to leave me there, but the others said no. I didn't understand their words, but I could tell that from their faces. They gave me food and clothes. They gave me a name.

"They called him Scotty. I stuck with him for … I don't know how long. Four, five months or more. It had been winter when they picked me up, and it was warm when they turned me over to the humanitarian unit. That was after Scotty was killed. A sniper. Their officer said the rest couldn't afford to be distracted by me like Scotty was."

A thousand questions pressed against her lips. What had Scotty been like? Where was he from? Did he know anything about Scotty's family? Had he been there when Scotty was killed? Had anyone comforted the little boy who had lost his protector and friend?

"Memphis—he'd been Scotty's best friend—took me to a nurse he knew at the humanitarian unit. She looked out for me in the refugee camp most of the time I was there. She got one of the volunteer doctors to look at my leg, where I'd been hit by shrapnel. Her tour ended so she left soon after that, but eventually the doctor got me to a hospital in the States.

"One of the rehab therapists took me in for a while. Then I got a scholarship to the school in Virginia. More scholarships helped me through college. Got my citizenship when I was old enough. After I graduated, I looked at the military, but special forces were out because of my leg. I found out about DS—State's Bureau of Diplomatic Security—and here I am."

She thought she knew the answer, but she asked anyway. "Military? State Department? Did you ever consider anything else? Anything in the private sector?"

"This country fed me, clothed me, repaired me, and educated me. The least I could do was give something back."

He had been taken in by people, but they had died, left, changed. What had been stable for him, from the time he'd seen that flag, was that all those people belonged to one country. That was what had endured. But what of *people* staying in his life? What of his family? What of the father King Jozef had spoken of?

"You don't remember anything before the soldiers picked you up?"

His lips parted, then closed on a silence she feared might become permanent. Finally he said, "What's there to remember?"

His mother was the pale woman with the sweet voice who had gone away so long ago.

His father was the tall, strong man who had come for him later. Taken him somewhere strange. Then left him, never returning.

April and Sharon double-teamed Madame about baking cookies in the embassy's impressive kitchen.

"Look at this marble counter, it's made for rolling out cutout cookies," Sharon said.

"And this table—" April contributed, patting the wooden surface of the table that stretched nearly the length of the room. "—is made for cooling racks and putting together baskets."

"No. Making cookies is a duty for the kitchen staff."

"But as you've mentioned, Madam, the kitchen is understaffed now. And I enjoy making cookies. So why not—"

"No. It is not seemly."

It was the closest she'd come to accepting April's status. It almost was a shame not to simply accept that advance and let the cookies go.

Almost.

"Perhaps we could go to your house and make them there." April said to Sharon, but with the corner of her eye focused on Madame.

"Absolutely. A great idea. I'd love to have you come out to the house. Of course King Jozef has said he'd like to watch us baking cookies. Oh," Sharon added with a glint. "We'll invite him, too. I bet he'd enjoy decorating the cutout cookies. You know, the cookies shaped like bells and trees and Santas that you slather with colored frosting and shake the different colored decorations on."

She paused, and April wished the Academy Awards nominating committee could see this performance. Meryl, Halle, and Nicole would be eating Sharon's dust.

"The kids can get a little wild with the frosting and shake cans, but I'll explain that the king's off limits for putting sprinkles in his hair. They'll listen to that." She frowned. "I'm sure they'll listen this time."

Madam sucked in an audible breath.

"His Highness is not going to the kitchen of a common house in the suburbs—" She pronounced that word as if it were a curse. "—to be subjected to colored frosting and sprinkles or for any other reason as long as I have breath in my body."

April faced her, arching her brows. "The only alternative is to make the cookies here."

"Very well."

"Thank you. Will Tuesday suit you, Sharon?"

"Perfectly."

"Is that satisfactory, Madam?"

"I shall see that it is."

Madam exited with her back so straight and her head so high that guilt pinched at April.

"Mission accomplished," Sharon said. "You did great. I think you're getting the hang of this royal edict thing."

April couldn't help grinning at her. "And you are wicked."

"Aren't I just? It's why you like me." Her tone changed. "And why I don't let up on Hunter."

April cut the older woman a look, but said nothing.

"Can't let up on him. For his own good."

It was as if Sharon had heard all the doubts and second-guessing scratching at April's heart from the inside. Had she pushed him too far? Did she have any right to push him at all? What if he was right to forget the past? How could she be sure—

"The man makes a clam look like a motor mouth," Sharon continued. "In our business it's not all bad to be able to keep your mouth shut. But it's way beyond that with Hunter. Some days I think all the pressure's going to build up inside and the man's going to blow. Other days I worry he's gotten so good at letting nothing out that before much longer there won't be anything left to let out."

CHAPTER TWENTY-SIX

"I don't see how ice-skating on the National Mall can be some childhood tradition when you didn't live here as a kid."

Hunter was grumbling, and he knew it. Why didn't he keep his mouth shut and stoically get through this? Sure it was chilly, but he'd stood for hours in bone-chilling cold without complaining. And it wasn't as mind-numbing as a lot of assignments he'd withstood as a rookie. He even had enjoyable things to watch—the crowd, he meant, not her.

Her.

That was the core of his discontent. April was up to something. That had to be why he didn't like this outing ... not because it was the two of them. Or because of that outfit she was wearing.

The leggings molded to the sleek curves of her legs. The fleecy tunic didn't mold. It flirted, swinging with her slightest motion to reveal the swell of her breast or the rounded shape of her rear end. He couldn't even blame Maurice. She'd said these were part of her regular wardrobe. She shouldn't be allowed on the streets in those things.

Still, it wasn't any of that. It was that glint in her eyes he didn't trust.

He stared down as if he could read her thoughts through the back of her head, which was all he could see as she bent over to put on her rented skates.

"Done," she announced standing and pulling on gloves. She had a pair of earmuffs looped around the tunic's turtleneck, ready for use. "Well?"

The skates put her closer to his height, so he could see the glint in her eyes more clearly than ever. He returned his most forbidding stare.

It didn't dim the glint and it didn't stop her words. "Aren't you going to put skates on?"

"No."

"Don't you know how to skate?"

He made a neutral sound.

"Then you'll have to let me teach you, won't you?"

"No."

"Afraid to admit there's something I can teach you? Afraid you can't keep up with me when it comes to learning something new, huh? Huh?"

She looked about eight. Too bad his body didn't think so.

"Yes."

"So, you're going to have me go out there alone?"

"This was your idea, not mine."

"It's been my idea to go several places and you haven't let me go alone. With that let-the-bullets-hit-me-first business of going out the door first, but now you're going to let me go other there in a spotlight where any assassin could target me?"

"You're being melodramatic."

"Me! After these weeks of—" She bit it off. "Okay. Fine. In fact, great." She produced a smile he didn't quite buy. "It will be a pleasure to be alone out there, amid all these strangers, with the chance that one might ask me a question and I could answer the wrong thing and—*poof!*—everyone would know."

He knew a threat when he heard one. Why she was making the threat, he had no idea. But it wasn't his job to understand, which was a damned good thing because he hadn't understood much about April Gareaux. It *was* his job to prevent disasters, and that he was good at.

"Okay. Don't move."

"Yes, sir."

She was getting a smart mouth. Smarter mouth.

He leveled a look at her to be sure she knew he meant business. She smiled back.

He kept an eye on her as he stood in line for the rental skates.

He hoped he could stand up in them. From the standpoint of protecting her he'd be better off in shoes. But this mission wasn't really about protection. And he'd grimly accepted that whatever this particular outing was about was known only in April's mind.

With both skates on, he bent over to begin tightening the laces…

Bent at the waist like this, his field of vision narrowed to his hands and the skate laces.

The hands he saw changed. They were broad, long-fingered. Older. A scar across the back of two. Strong.

With accustomed ease they tightened the laces of small, brown skates, badly scuffed. Handed down, but treasured. Starting closest to the toe of the skate … always the toe … always…

Always start at the start, my boy. And go on from there.

The deep voice patient, while Hunter's whole body thrummed with eagerness and excitement. Cold nibbled at the tips of his fingers inside his mittens, so he curled them into a fist. Skating, he was going skating. And today Papa had promised to teach him how to spin.

That is how you get on in this world. Always start at the start.

He'd done that. He'd learned to stand and skate forward and make turns. He'd been practicing and practicing skating backward the way Papa had taught him, and he would show him how well he'd learned that, and then Papa would teach him to spin.

"Hunter?"

Her voice reached him. She crouched in front of him, touched his calf, and it warmed him through the denim of his jeans.

"I'll do the laces. I guess you really don't know how to skate, huh?"

The hands from another life faded. Hers were there now. Long and narrow, the skin soft and white, the short nails gently curved.

"I'll do it." He took the ends of the laces from her before she could strain those delicate hands by trying to draw them tight.

She started tightening his other skate. He finished that one up, too. He stood, stiff and awkward. The unbalanced sensation of standing on a narrow blade wasn't the only reason.

Belatedly, he realized the memories of a moment ago had not come to him in English.

She shot him a questioning look, but he wasn't in the mood to give any answers.

"You wanted to skate, so let's go."

She looked solid and confident on the skates. Nothing fancy, really, but moving easily enough to flit around him.

"Isn't it beautiful?" she said. "I love how the lights loop around the whole rink. Like Christmas lights."

That was a poke at him. He knew it even before he looked up from watching where he was going to the challenge in her eyes.

He grunted.

"Look at that, the way the rounded tops of the bare trees look like a garland all around us. And the way all the buildings are lit up. Archives, the National Gallery, and over there the Natural History Museum. So festive. You know this is a fountain during the summer? And they have free concerts here. Grady brought Leslie and me a lot when they first got married."

He felt the rhythm, the balance, the flow.

"You're really good. Must be from being a natural athlete."

He shifted his weight to one leg, following some long-forgotten motion.

"That's great, Hunter. You're almost skating backward."

Another move, the next element to complete the shift—no, it was gone. He stalled. And she was too small to guide him into it. It worked better when the teacher was big and the student small, like—

"Let me go on my own."

He pushed off, and that did it, without his thinking. He was going backward, pumping his legs to move away from her, checking over his shoulder that it was clear. He found the balance for the straight-line glide. Then pumped again for more power.

"That's great, Hunter!" She was smiling, as he put distance between them. But she skated toward him, closing the gap. She had more speed. She swooped around him as he let his momentum fade to stillness. "You're a natural. I bet you could spin."

"No."

"Sure you can. An easy move to get the feel … Here, take my hands."

His hands clasped hers before he could tell his body no. Her tug on his hands turned him as the axis of the circle she skated around him.

"No, don't look at me, Hunter. That will make you dizzy. Spot on something stationary, and keep coming back to it."

How could he not look at her? Even though he was getting dizzy. But was it from their surroundings blurring as only her face stayed in focus? Or was it something different?

"Okay, now this is what you do." She released his hands. With her skates shoulder-width apart, she twisted her body. She released the twist, and rotated smoothly, gradually drawing her arms in, increasing her speed. "Now you do it. Focus on one stationary object."

He mimicked her motion. The blur before his eyes raced to a flow of colors. Now she was his stationary object, her face the one certainty in a blur.

"Great. You're doing it, Hunter."

"Excellent, my son," said another voice in another language.

"No."

He put one skate out to catch the ice with the tip, halting the spin abruptly. He half stumbled out of the motion.

"Hunter? Hunter, are you all right?"

She was right in front of him, a hand fisted into the material of each sleeve of his bulky sweater. He tried to twist away, she glided along with.

"Hunter."

Her voice made him realize, the sympathy, the worry, the compassion. Yes, her voice told him before his own body realized that tears threatened.

There was only one way to hide his weakness, only one escape.

He grasped her shoulders and pulled her to him, dropping his mouth onto hers.

"I want to walk," April said.

He didn't look at her. He hadn't since that kiss. Brief, comprehensive, and incomprehensible. His mouth firm and complete on hers. Caught by surprise, her lips had parted. His had, too. Their breaths mingled again. One more instant and—

He'd backed away from her immediately. Then he'd looked around as if searching for danger.

To her, it felt like the danger came from him.

She skated several more minutes, circling with the other skaters, ignoring his presence behind her, calming her mind.

When they announced it was time to clean the ice, she was done and exchanged skates for her boots.

She didn't wait for his permission to begin walking, but headed to the center of the Mall. Turning one way, she saw the Washington Monument rising tall and straight with the Lincoln Memorial beyond it and the swelling rises of Arlington Cemetery across the river. Then she pivoted and looked toward the Capitol. In that instant, wandering snowflakes began to sift down.

She smiled and tipped her head back, opening her mouth to catch a slow-moving flake.

One finally dropped into her mouth, melting before it even reached her tongue. She straightened.

Hunter was right there. So close.

He was going to kiss her again. She saw it in his eyes.

Her lips parted, she looked up at him.

He leaned closer…

He straightened and turned away. "Time to get back."

CHAPTER TWENTY-SEVEN

Hunter watched her return with Rufus and Derek to the embassy grounds after their walk Saturday morning.

Keeping out of sight, he heard her tell the king she was going to finish her Christmas cards in the library.

She was lying.

He didn't question his certainty, but kept watch.

Yes, there she went. Slipping out with a quick look around. He followed on foot. She went straight to the nearest Metro stop. When she made the first transfer, with him trailing behind, he was as sure of where she was going as he had been that she was lying.

At the animal shelter, he asked to see a puppy that the woman at the front desk said had a waiting list for adoption. Through a window in the introduction cubicle, he watched April sit on the floor of the main area, cuddling Dragon and feeding him treats.

The puppy chewed on the edge of his shoe. He reached down and detached the puppy's mouth, offering it a toy from a basket. But he never took his eyes from the window.

So he saw the moment she began to cry.

He caught Sharon on her way out of the embassy, after she'd spent half an hour with April.

They'd dispensed with the professional on Sharon's way in. Now he asked her, "You've got a house and kids, right?"

She narrowed her eyes at him. "Don't tell me you've actually listened to things I've said about my personal life all these years."

Of course he had. It was important to know who you were work-ing with so you could anticipate their weaknesses and bring out their strengths.

"Three kids—two boys and a girl." Maybe he was showing off a little.

"Be still my heart! If you know their names, I'll faint dead away."

He didn't. Which was just as well, since he was the only one around to pick her up. Besides, their names didn't figure in to this. "Kids should have a dog. It's … it's good for their character. Teaches them responsibility. And, uh, loyalty and … and about social structure and interactions."

"If you say so, Hunter. You do know I have a husband, too, don't you? You've met him, oh, five, six times."

Hunter waved off the existence of a man he remembered vaguely as stocky and with a wide grin. Why did she keep straying from the subject? She was as bad as April, with these detours.

"A dog," he said. "Your family needs another dog. One for each kid. I know just the dog. Housetrained, good with kids and other animals. He—"

"Hold on there, Dr. Doolittle. If we get another dog our commu-nity says we have to declare ourselves a kennel and get a special license. I already have a zoo—no way am I going to add a kennel. Why don't you keep him yourself?"

"Me? What would I do with a dog? I'm…. I'm a professional."

"You don't think I'm a professional?" Her voice was even, but she jammed her hands on her hips. "I've got, as you've said, a house and kids and a husband and—yes—dogs. So that makes me not capable of doing my job professionally?"

Hunter knew the ice had thinned under his feet in the last few seconds. Damn. Why'd he have to think of ice. And skating. And kissing—

"You're not only capable. You always do your job professionally. If you did not, I would ask for another assignment."

Her posture relaxed. "Ah, you silver-tongued charmer, you," she murmured. "As for what you would do with a dog, you would love it and play with it and let it look at you adoringly. Oh, yeah, and let it chew up some of your shoes. So why do you have it in your head that this job means you can't have a dog?"

He glanced at his shoes, as if they could protest against hypothetically being chewed. "For you, this job is a place to work. For me, it is…" He backed away from that and started again. "If someone came to you with the offer of another job, a good job, you would consider it. Because this job doesn't … You do it well," he continued quickly, "but still it is only a part of your life. Maybe not the most important part."

"Your *maybe* is right. It shouldn't be for you, either, Hunter."

He said nothing.

She shook her head at him, then said in a tone she had never used to him before, "You can be a professional without pulling down all the shades and pretending there's nobody home inside your life, Hunter."

They went to a performance of the Messiah at the Kennedy Center that night. With Madame.

She unbent enough during the drive back to the embassy to express pleasure at the music.

April was quieter than usual and heavy-eyed.

The king gave Hunter a sharp look, as if suspecting he was the cause. Nope. A four-legged scruffy, old dog.

CHAPTER TWENTY-EIGHT

Where the hell was the king?

He usually kept April right by his side. But now, when a royal presence—a disapproving royal presence—could do some real good, he was … Hunter checked that King Jozef was still talking to the British Ambassador in the State Dining Room, beside the fireplace under the portrait of Abraham Lincoln.

The British Ambassador had added his government's pleas to the Americans' that the king extend the flyover agreement. And Hunter knew an unofficial conversation at a function like this often achieved more than a formal exchange.

But, dammit, the man had an obligation to keep April from getting out of her depth.

Which was exactly where she was at the moment, and judging by the way she was smiling up at the slick chief of staff to a certain rising senator, she didn't even realize her feet couldn't touch bottom anymore.

This First Lady's well-known passion for ballroom dancing had led to the Family Dining Room being cleared of most of its furniture, festooned with garlands, outfitted with a quartet from the Marine Band adding dance rhythms to carols, and a portion of the guests dancing happily.

The dancing wasn't the problem. In fact April's dancing was so effortless, that unlike when they'd practiced in the hotel suite, she had plenty of attention left over to chat away while looking directly into the eyes of her partner.

That was the problem. Her partner.

For the fourth time tonight.

The man known among many Washington women as Nine-Handed Neil, because he was beyond an octopus. That's what Sharon had said when they'd crossed paths with this guy before.

The man also had sat next to April at the dinner for a few dozen select guests in the Diplomatic Reception Room before the party. From his distant view, as befitted someone at the bottom of the social pecking order for this event, Hunter had obtained only glimpses of her talking and smiling at her tablemates, especially the senator from Missouri's chief of staff. And then he'd watched her go from dance to dance, with one eager partner after another.

But while the others who asked her to dance were satisfied with one song, this particular partner had come back again. And again. And again.

The music ended, the dancers applauded, and April's gaze went toward the doorway. She shifted, clearly trying for a sight-line to the King through the crowd and intervening decorations. Hunter breathed a little easier.

Then Nine-Handed Neil leaned closer, as if whispering in her ear were the only way to make himself heard. She glanced in the direction of the king again, that giveaway tuck of concentration between her brows. It smoothed out as she nodded, then smiled up at Nine-Handed.

The man put his palm to the small of her back.

A snarl clawed at the back of Hunter's throat.

Only because she was letting herself be directed through the momentarily still dancers, *away* from this doorway where he stood. *Away* from the king.

She should be at the king's side, adding her support to whatever the British Ambassador was saying.

That's why he was so frustrated.

A thought flickered at the back of Hunter's head. He shot it down.

Not that kind of frustrated. Professionally frustrated. About the mission. Getting the agreement extended.

Where was Nine-Handed Neil steering her? As if she couldn't find her way across that room without his hand on her back. Did the jerk think she was stupid? Asses like that wouldn't care if she was, wouldn't notice that she wasn't. Asses like that only looked at the way that de Chartier dress clung to her curves, at the swing Etienne had given her hair, at the heels, and manicure.

Nine-Handed Neil didn't care about the woman who visited animals she couldn't save, who made friends with every soul in a hotel, who made muffins for one of the best known men in D.C., who had to find the perfect Christmas tree for a king she barely knew, who had come down the back stairs at the embassy earlier with a fluttering smile and uncertain eyes.

Hunter saw where Nine-Handed Neil had her headed now.

The Ushers' room that connected the Family Dining Room and the Entrance Hall. Probably told her it would be quicker to go that way than through the crowds. Right.

Hunter headed toward the Entrance Hall side of the Ushers' room with as much speed as he could without attracting attention.

He pulled the doors closed behind him as he entered, noting the corresponding doors to the Family Dining Room were already closed. Long drapes covered a slightly recessed window to his right, the space beyond it dim.

Still, plenty of light to spot the sweep of April's dress there, partially obscured by the curtains, and how the man was crowding her deeper into the shallow window alcove.

"No, Neil—"

Hunter was there before she finished the second word.

The space was cozy for two. With three it was downright crowded. Especially with the distance April had put between her and Nine-Handed Neil. She had both palms planted on his chest, and her elbows locked.

The man wasn't called Nine-Handed for nothing, however. He was palming the points of her bare shoulders, murmuring something about her being a "babe."

Hunter yanked him back. April stumbled sidewise at the release of the resistance to her stiff-arm. The other man swung around on Hunter—literally.

Hunter sidestepped at the same time he blocked the ineffectual punch with one forearm. Neil stumbled into the curtain, seemed to get all nine hands tangled momentarily.

"You all right?" Hunter demanded of April.

"I'm fine. What on earth are—"

But he'd turned back to the other man, who was nearly free from the curtain.

"The senator's looking for you."

"What?" It was like magic. Or like the man's brain had suddenly retaken control after being hijacked by regions significantly farther south. "Where?"

"Got back through the Family Dining Room. You'll see him."

Straightening and smoothing clothes and hair as he went, Neil was out through those double doors in an instant, leaving Hunter alone with April.

"You okay?" She looked okay. Hardly mussed at all.

"If you're waiting for me to thank you, you can forget it." She sounded irked. "I didn't need you bursting in here like that."

"The curtains were closed." Why had he said that? Of all the inane comments.

"So we could see the Christmas lights better. We couldn't see them with the drapes open because of the inside lights."

"He wasn't looking at any Christmas lights when I saw him."

"I was handling it."

"You don't know about men like this, April."

"How do you know what I know—Oh, of course, your file on me. I hadn't realized it had gone to such detail. But your research wasn't foolproof, Hunter. Just because you thought I was an ugly duckling before you transformed me, don't be so damned sure I don't know about men like Neil."

"Ugly duck—I don't..."

He felt a kinship with Nine-Handed Neil he never would have expected. In the closed off area, the warm scent of her twined around him like steam after coming in from the cold. Her cheeks were rosy, her eyes glowed and her lips ... her lips were moist and surely as soft as they looked.

Hunter Pierce was suddenly angry.

"What the hell were you doing going with him to a spot like this if you know about men like him?" His arm jabbed at the sliver of space between them. "When all a man has to do is—"

He slid his right hand around the back of her neck, then up, to cup the base of her skull, tilting it back.

Her lips parted.

He looked down at her.

Somewhere a voice told him this was his last chance. His very last chance.

He told the voice to go to hell, and kissed her.

CHAPTER TWENTY-NINE

Her mouth opened under his. He slid his tongue into her warmth, seeking. Their tongues met.

She made a soft sound, and it drove him deeper, fuller. Wanting the source of that sound, the source of that warmth. Her palm slid along his jaw line, thumb stroking his cheek. Trying to soothe?

There was no soothing this.

He stroked into her mouth, the rhythm certain and powerful. Her hands came around to the back of his neck. Holding on. Opening.

They had been kissing for a heartbeat. They had been kissing forever.

He didn't know. Only wanted to keep on.

She gave a small gasp. He felt it more than heard it. Gave up her mouth, instantly.

He looked into her eyes, almost too close to see. They both dragged in air, ragged with the need—for oxygen, for more.

If he took her mouth again now … no…

He kissed the corner of her mouth. Her eyes drifted closed. His mouth slid down, over the curve of her chin, down her throat.

He wanted to keep going, to find the edge of the dress, then under it to her breast. To take her nipple in his mouth, to feel it smooth and hard—

He jerked his head to the side. But could not force himself to end the connection.

Never lifting his head, he kissed along her bare shoulder, the skin so smooth, so warm. He put his mouth over delicate flesh covering the bone and sucked on it. She dropped her head back, pressing herself against him. The rhythm took hold again. Something only they knew. His arm across her back supported her as she arched and he covered the curve of her body with his own.

Felt the soft pulse of her breasts against his chest, knew the heat he would discover as his leg found a place between hers despite her dress.

One hand spread across the fabric below her hip, then closed, drawing the material up. Then again.

Once more and he'd feel her skin. Be so close to—

He spread his fingers, feeling the fabric slide away from him, back to covering her. He jerked himself straight, bringing her with him.

He grasped her shoulders, holding her away. Keeping himself away.

He breathed hard. Wanting to—.

No. If he thought of what he wanted to do, he'd do it. Here. Now.

Her hair was tumbling, her mouth was swollen, her skin was flushed from the rub of his skin.

A surge so strong it was painful pulsed through him. The desire, the need—

"No. This can't—We have to get back. *You* have to get back. King Jozef will be looking for you."

She looked at him for a long moment. Her eyes so clear, yet he had no idea what she was thinking.

"I shouldn't have—" he started.

She slid out of his hold, as if he'd never had a hold on her at all. Turned so he had only her profile as she reached up, her fingers tucking tendrils of hair.

The motion raised her breasts, brought them tighter against the dress. Another few inches and—

"I'm not naïve, Hunter." Her voice was almost even. Almost in control. "I know what—"

"Like hell. If you weren't naïve, you wouldn't have been maneuvered into this alcove with him in the first place and you wouldn't have stayed here after…." After he'd entered and couldn't control himself. God, she had to be the most naïve woman on the face of the planet not to see the desire revving through him. "Because you would have known what could happen."

She started toward the doors to the Entrance Hall. He turned with her movement, as if he couldn't keep his eyes off of her. With a hand on the doorknob she paused. "I would have if I wanted that to happen."

She flicked a final look at him over her shoulder—dear God, a shoulder with a faint redness still showing. From his mouth or his hands?—swung open the door and swished through the opening, back into the party.

If she'd wanted it to happen?

Which *it*? Nine-handed Neil? Had he intruded on an interlude she'd wanted?

Perhaps hinted or flirted into happening? But that wasn't like April. That wasn't her way.

So … She'd wanted what happened between *them* to happen?

Something surged up through him, hot and thick. It rose higher, threatening to swamp his brain. *Think. Analyze.*

She was a woman. He was a man. He wanted her. Okay. Lust was one element of the potent brew he felt. He could deal with that. But the rest of it? What *was* that?

But then his analytical brain, holding out against the onslaught of this surge, found an ally. A response he knew well flowed down over him. The cool, deliberate mantle of duty.

Whatever April had meant, he would protect her—from Nine-handed Neil or from himself.

"Your Majesty."

"Please, sit down, Hunter."

"I prefer to stand."

"I prefer you to sit."

The impasse last another twenty seconds before the younger man sat stiffly in the chair opposite his at the small table by the window.

"You asked to speak with me before I retired, Hunter?"

Jozef, King of Bariavak, congratulated himself for such diplomacy. Hunter Pierce had barely waited for April to be out of earshot on her way to her room to demand this audience, even at such an unusual time as immediately upon their return from the White House.

The drive from the White House to the embassy would have told him, of course, that something had occurred. Hunter's grim silence. April's over-bright cheerfulness in recounting her pleasure for the party. Neither looking at the other.

But he already knew.

So many years of ruling his country. So many connections. So many unofficial and very willing spies.

"Yes. I request leave to speak bluntly rather than as a diplomat would, in the interests of time."

"You have observed many diplomats, Hunter, so you should be aware that the best diplomats never waste the time of others. It is one of your qualities that would serve you well in diplomacy."

Only the slightest hesitation betrayed the younger man's temptation to set the record straight that he would die to protect diplomats, but he had no interest in becoming one.

With some amusement, the king wondered if Hunter decided not to pursue that red herring because he didn't want to disagree with a king, or because he didn't want to waste time. Jozef suspected the later. His amusement deepened.

Ah, the introduction of April Gareaux into his life was a blessing indeed.

He nodded, both hiding the twitching of his lips and indicating Hunter should proceed.

"It's about Ms. Gareaux."

Jozef stilled inside, waiting for what came next. "Yes."

"She is a very intelligent young woman—"

"She is." As he'd intended, Jozef's prompt agreement stopped Hunter's set speech. When he resumed, he sounded less like a robot.

"But she is not experienced in..." He cleared his throat. "You have undertaken to entertain her during her stay here. That entails responsibility. The circles that you have introduced her to are not what she's accustomed to. She doesn't have the experience rebuffing the advances of certain kinds of—"

"Perhaps my information is faulty," Jozef interrupted smoothly, "but I understood that it was not the senator's staff member that she kissed, but you."

Hunter stood. "I will tell my supervisor that you require someone else to take my place immediately, Your Majesty. My resignation—."

"You will do no such thing, but you will sit down." The younger man remained standing "Sit down, Hunter."

He did.

"You will most certainly not resign. You will not tell your supervisor. And you will not leave this assignment."

"But—"

"Do not interrupt a king who is insisting you keep your job." King Jozef did not let the touch of humor undercut the iron in his order.

Hunter's mouth tightened.

His staying silent satisfied King Jozef, so he proceeded. "Perhaps you think that because I have lived my life as a royal that I am the one to instruct April in the dangers that she might encounter in this world. Instead, I am the last person to do so. This life is too engrained in me, the dangers too familiar for me to even see them. I sidestep them without thinking. So how could I warn anyone else of them? I could not. No, what would benefit April is someone who has knowledge of both the world she has come from and this new world she has entered, for however long that might be, and can point out to her the differences—and the dangers. Someone, in addition, whom she trusts. Someone who cares about her. That person is you."

"Sir, there—"

"You do care about her, don't you, Hunter?"

His mouth clamped closed an instant before he responded, "That is immaterial to my job."

"It's very material to your kissing her."

The younger man's face went still, his eyes cool. Some might say blank. But Jozef knew better. He knew the emotions that could, and no doubt did, roil beneath such a façade.

He thought of the report on Hunter Pierce he had revisited shortly before this interview. The facts there softened his voice.

"A job is not a man, Hunter. Not even *this* job," he tipped his head toward the painting of his ancestor. "Love defines a man, and gives him a life. Family."

He cleared his full throat, unashamed. "That is what I have learned. I tried for a time—too long—to persuade myself otherwise. But I know now that I have wasted a great deal of time. All these years of so cautiously seeking my granddaughter because I feared being hurt again, I should have been seeking to build other love into my life. Not to replace the loved ones I had lost, but to honor them by practicing what they had taught me—love and life and family. Do you understand?"

"Your Majesty."

The straight, taut line of the shoulders told him Hunter had braced himself against truly hearing the message of the words. He sighed.

Perhaps he should not have spoken so soon.

"You are forgiven." The tiny muscles at the corners of the younger man's eyes twitched. He wanted so to point out that he had not asked forgiveness. But he was well-trained, perhaps more by his life than by his profession. "And now you understand that it is my wish, as King of Bariavak, that you remain in your position. Indeed, I have a commission for you, beginning immediately."

He outlined that commission, watching Hunter closely.

He saw the protest before it reached Hunter's lips, and short-circuited it. "I have, of course, vetted this through your supervisors. They agree. When you check with your office, you will find arrangements are in process. You shall start immediately."

He waved a hand of dismissal.

But he didn't start humming a jaunty little Bariavakian folk tune until the door had closed behind the straight back of Hunter Pierce.

He was still humming when Madame entered almost immediately upon the sound of her knock.

"I have come to see if you require anything before retiring, sir. And to enquire if you have a preference for breakfast."

Madame Sabdoka never made such a check on him, nor gave him a choice in menu.

"I should like coffee, please." He'd left today's tea—herbal, decaffeinated, and otherwise robbed of taste—untouched.

"No, Your Majesty. The surgery is in two weeks, and the doctors said no caffeine for two weeks."

"They advised it, they did not order. And even so, the two weeks do not start until Thursday, so I shall have coffee tomorrow."

"No, Your Majesty. And I do hope your interview with that American has not upset you. The doctors said—"

"If 'the doctors said' is going to be the extent of your conversation, Madame, I shall banish you." She clattered a lamp she was adjusting but made no other comment. "As for my conversation, rather than upset me, it intrigued me. An interesting young man. With an excellent head on his shoulders and the heart of a lion."

Madame snorted, if such a word could be used for one so dignified. Ah, but he remembered a time when she had not been so dignified.

When they had both been young and wild, and not yet reined in to the duties that awaited them.

He had fared better in that regard than Marusha. He had come to love his wife dearly. And he had had, for a time, a family as loving and normal as any monarch could hope for. Marusha's arranged marriage had not been as successful.

Her sole child, too, had died during that damnable uprising. Months later, her husband died unexpectedly, not having had quite enough time to finish the job of gambling away both their fortunes.

She had refused the offer of a post as ambassador to a country where the title would be mostly ceremonial. She intended to earn her living, she had announced. So she had come here, and for nearly thirty years she had served her country by running this most important embassy far more than any ambassador could.

"Yes, an excellent head and the heart of a lion. But he lets the one rule too strongly and does not trust the other." He tapped a finger to his chin. "Not yet."

"That young man does not show you the proper respect. And the young lady is not at all conversant with royal protocol."

"You are, as always, absolutely correct, Madame Sabdoka." He settled back and smiled. "Isn't it refreshing? There is much the young can teach us, and yet, I do believe there is much I can teach them. That young man, especially—"

"You are not going to get involved with the personal life of some young American—"

Their gazes met.

"—Yes. An American, as he has chosen. Or with the romance of this young woman who may—or may not," she added darkly, "be your granddaughter as you could have determined by now many times over. Yet you have chosen not to know for certain because you are indulging in meddling of the most—"

He drew himself up, stopping her words instantly. "In your king it is not meddling. It is ruling." He relaxed. "Ah, truly, this is by far the most fun I have had in a very, very long time. Let us enjoy this holiday."

He smiled at her. For an instant, he saw the laughing face of a girl, her hair frothed wild by the wind. Then Madame Sabdoka returned.

"Yes, Your Majesty."

CHAPTER THIRTY

On the drive to the first stop of his commission, Hunter analyzed the conversation with the king from every angle. It always came out the same.

He'd gone in there to urge Jozef to be a stricter chaperone to April. His unprofessional behavior in kissing her had come out and made it blindingly clear he not only shouldn't be on this job but probably should resign.

And yet here he was, not only still on the job, but with orders that would take him even deeper into April Gareaux's life.

Both Jameel and Maria remembered him and were inclined to be friendly until he started asking questions about April. They clammed up, and stayed clammed up.

Mandy Roteen hadn't been as reticent. But most of what she had to say was either already in the report or consisted of how much more ready for fun Mandy was than April.

"Michael? It's Grady. Are you alone?"

"Just a minute." The sound of a door closing came through the line, cutting off background voices. "What's up?"

"Have you seen that footage from last night's White House party?"

"Yeah."

"I'm downplaying it to Leslie, but that guy behind April—same one from the tree lighting clip I sent you."

"Yeah."

"I want to know who he is. Any chance—?"

"I'm on it."

"No reason to worry Leslie or Tris with this."

"No," Michael agreed, though he sounded less sure. "I'll get back to you as soon as I know something."

The percussion of the knock on her door somehow transferred to April's heart. "Come in."

The door opened.

"Oh, Derek." She tried to keep her reaction out of her voice. Though what that reaction was … Relief. Yes, certainly relief. It would be awkward when she saw Hunter next. Wouldn't it?

"Hi, April. Wanted to check in, see what you've got planned to-day?"

"It's pretty much a day of rest. No outings. A nice, quiet Sunday." She produced a smile and he smiled back. "Wrapping, thank-you notes."

Including one for the party at the White House. Hunter's mouth on hers. Dizziness that spun not just her head, but her whole body…

"Good. Then I can ease into it."

"Ease into it?"

"Taking over for Hunter."

"What?" Her lungs burned, as if she'd drawn in heated air. "Where is he?"

"Don't know. Other than gone."

"Why?"

"Don't know that, either. Got the call to get over here right away, and that I'd be lead for you. As long as you're not going anywhere right away, I'll get settled. Come get me for Rufus' walk."

He closed the door, leaving her with thoughts swirling through her head.

The man who'd answered the door brought Reese Warrington back with him.

"Thank you, Barton." The man departed again. "What is this about," Reese tried in the blustering tone of the ineffectual. He was holding Hunter's business card, so he knew some of what it was about.

"I have a few questions about your relationship with a woman named April Gareaux."

"So it *was* April at that party last night." His eyes lit up, but Hunter put it down to curiosity.

Barton reappeared. "Excuse me sir, but Mrs. Warrington requires that you bring the gentleman into the drawing room."

Reese grimaced, but gestured for Hunter to follow Barton.

"What is all this about," the older woman of two in the room demanded immediately with authority. "Who are you?"

Reese performed the introductions to his mother and wife, ending with, "He's here to see me, Mother."

"About what?" she demanded of Hunter. He looked back at her without speaking.

She glared at him, then turned to her son, who said immediately. "It's about April, actually."

"April?" scoffed his wife, taking a long drink of what appeared to be a cocktail. "What about her?"

"You were engaged to Ms. Gareaux, Mr. Warrington?"

"Yes, yes I was. I told you that was April with that king on the news last night," he said to the women.

Neither seemed to hear him.

"Engaged?" said Roberta Warrington. "Hardly. She latched onto him, until I came back and put an end to that nonsense."

"It was being handled," her mother-in-law said.

"For four months," Reese Warrington said to Hunter.

"How did you meet Ms. Gareaux, Mr. Warrington?"

His mother said, "She picked him up. Not part of our circle, of course.”

Reese waited for her to finish before he said, “We started talking when I attended the sale of Gerard Littrell’s library. He had some remarkable first editions of classic science fiction.”

The women made a dismissive sound in unison.

“She was so open, so kind. But tell me, *is* she the granddaughter of this king? That’s the rumor I heard.”

“Ridiculous. She’s a nobody. A non-entity,” the younger Mrs. Warrington said.

“I’ll speak to your staff now. In the kitchen,” Hunter said.

“You’ve hardly asked us anything,” Reese protested.

Yet they’d answered plenty.

Hunter stood. “I’ll speak to your staff now.”

“My staff? Absolutely not,” Lois Warrington said.

Hunter looked down at the woman.

“Mother, please,” Reese said.

“Really.” Roberta Warrington flung one hand wide. “What can it matter?”

Lois Warrington broke the look first. “Fine.” As Hunter walked out, she added, “Just don’t let it hold up our dinner.”

As he left the Warrington estate forty-five minutes later, Hunter called Sharon Johnson.

The message he left on her cell was succinct. “Rumors are starting. See what you can do.”

“Sir, I must talk with you—please.”

“Of course, April.” He gestured her to come into the office.

For an instant it reminded her of that first day. Two weeks ago. Was that all it was? Two weeks?

The king rose, coming around the desk, taking her hand and leading her to the sofa before the fireplace, sitting beside her, and ending any similarity to that first meeting.

She drew in a breath.

"I am not your granddaughter."

She said that slowly and distinctly, looking into his eyes.

"Ah."

Her calm precision disappeared in a rush of words. "I am so sorry. So terribly, terribly sorry. And I know you have no reason to believe me when I tell you how deeply fond of you I am, when you're thinking that if I really were I would have waited until after the operation to tell you—or that I wouldn't have pretended at all. I wanted to help my country, yes, I absolutely did, and I do hope you will sign that extension. But, truly, sir, I thought I could make your holidays happier, too. I know what it's like to feel alone because that's how I felt a lot growing up, and it's especially hard around the holidays. I thought … I thought I could let you go on thinking—but I can't. I can't do this. If I were stronger, I would have waited until after your surgery, but to let you go on thinking you'd found your granddaughter—your *family*— and to know all the time that it was a lie. I can't."

"Have you told Hunter that you can't continue this?"

She blinked against sudden heat in her eyes. She would not cry. She would not.

"No." He handed her a handkerchief. White and soft and spotless. "You're the one I've been lying to, so I had to tell you—" She sucked in a breath, refusing to allow it to become a sob. "First."

She twisted the handkerchief. He placed his hand on hers, stilling the restless motion. Then he slowly settled back against the sofa cushion.

"Ah. You thought that once I knew that you believe yourself not to be my granddaughter that I would throw you out, saving you from any need of telling Hunter that you have confided in me."

"I, uh—"

"Or perhaps you thought I would throw you both out. Which would mean—"

"Oh, no. I'm sorry for interrupting, but you have no reason to throw Hunter out. This is all my doing. All my—"

She bit off her words under the double-barreled impact of his raised brows and a dismissive wave of one hand.

"April, my dear, I will save you from returning yourself to a position that seems to cause you discomfort—lying to me. I know how it came about that you were presented as my possible granddaughter. I did not know it all at the beginning, but I made it my business to find out in these past weeks. Hunter came to you, persuaded you to this role. Not the other way around."

"He never persuaded me. He gave me the facts. Never pushed me to agree. This whole thing wasn't his idea. He hates it—he doesn't say it, but I can tell. From what Sha—other people say, he argued against it."

He chuckled. "My dear, never, never become a spy. *Sha—other people* are correct that this brainstorm was not of Hunter's making. Although I did not find that out immediately, either. I will admit that, initially, I was quite disappointed in young Mr. Pierce."

She remembered that first meeting again. The way the king had looked at Hunter for so long before even turning to her. She had wondered why he hadn't focused immediately on the woman he'd been told might be his granddaughter. It almost seemed as if he was disappointed in Hunter, calling him to account for...

But that would mean...

"You *knew*. You knew all along that I'm not your granddaughter."

He dropped his head in a slow nod. "I knew all along who you are."

"But ... But why?"

"Why did I know? Because my staff is quite dependable and professional, and your resemblance to the royal family has not gone unnoticed. I believe you lived in Cincinnati the first time a report on you came across my desk."

"Cincinnati? We only lived there a short time. I was in elementary school."

"Yes."

That simple word convinced her. His Royal Highness, King Jozef of Bariavak had been tracking her since her childhood.

"So as soon as Hunter said *April Gareaux*, you knew…"

"Before then, to be precise. My agents had heard word of Hunter's activities. He made so little attempt to hide them that one could almost wonder if he hoped that they would be discovered beforehand."

That wasn't true. Look at all the times Hunter had scolded her in the hotel about not telling anyone, the times he had shielded her in those trips in and out of cars.

She shook her head. "When I ask *why*, I meant why did you go along with it? Why didn't you denounce me right that moment as a cruel imposter?"

His eyebrows arched again. This time with what she read as genuine surprise. "Is that how you see yourself? As a cruel imposter? I do not. I see you as a charming young woman." His mouth lifted in a faint smile. "Which provides the answer to your question. My holidays stretched before me lonely and dull, with only the strictures of the doctors and the surgery next month to look forward to. Instead, I have been having a delightful time. My best holidays in decades. And I very much hope I shall persuade you to remain without having to call upon your government to add its voice."

She couldn't help smiling at him, but started a protest, "Sir—"

He held up a hand to stop her words. "There was also an old man's sentimental desire to see what a granddaughter lost so very long ago might have looked like as a grown woman. To see what she might have become. I would be proud if she were like you, April." He placed his hand over hers again. "There is also…" He cleared his throat.

"What?"

"I hesitate to venture on this subject. But as you have mentioned, your early upbringing was not tied strongly to any one place for a long period of time. Your parents were even more peripatetic at the time of your birth."

She nodded. "I see what you're saying. There might still be a small possibility? Because with all the wildness Melly—my mother—showed you couldn't be certain she didn't pick me up somewhere like a hot diamond necklace. A hot kidnapped princess. And there's no denying that would have appealed to her. But we *can* be sure she didn't—those of us who knew her, I mean.

"Because there was one thing Melly could never do, and that was keep a secret. Especially if it were a good story. She wouldn't have been able to stop herself. And that goes for whether she knew she'd been given a stolen baby princess or whether she picked up a baby somewhere. So, you see, Hunter had no reason to be certain all along that I'm a fake, but I did. I'm the one who's lied to you."

"Ah." He sat back. "Tell me, are you aware that Hunter has left us?"

She hitched forward on the seat, "But there's no need for him to lea—"

"There is every need. The work he does for me now requires travel."

"The work he does for you?" she repeated, at a loss.

"With the approval of his employer, of course."

"You ... You haven't sent him away for good?

"Not at all. For a few days only."

She felt as if she'd been suffocating and now she could breathe again.

"When he returns," the king went on, "it would only confuse matters if we confided to him—or anyone—what you have told me. It will be better to go on as before and see where this background information he gathers leads us."

"Background on me? But I've told you, there's no need for that any longer."

"There is every need, my dear."

He would tell her no more than that.

In the end, she agreed to his request to keep what she had told him about her identity between them alone.

CHAPTER THIRTY-ONE

Tris and Leslie met at the door going into their offices Monday morning.

"Leslie, did Grady call Michael yesterday?"

"I think so. He hasn't said anything about it, but he disappeared for a while and Jake said he was talking to Uncle Michael."

"I thought so. Michael answered a call, then disappeared into the garage. Then he was out there later making calls."

They looked at each other, then Tris said, "I think the four of us should have dinner tonight, don't you?"

"Oh, yes. Grady's put Michael on to finding out what's going on. Bless his heart," Leslie said, with a small smile. "He thinks I'm too delicate to be worried about any of this. When what was really bothering me was that he was all laid-back and casual about it. It was so unlike him that it made me really nervous. Tonight we'll find out what's really going on."

Charlottesville, Va.

Tact didn't get far with Beatrice Craig. She knew exactly what he was asking beneath the politeness.

"April Craig Gareaux is my great-granddaughter, young man."

"Yes, Ma'am, but—"

"She is the daughter of Melanie Craig Gatwick Gareaux, who was the daughter of my elder daughter Doria. That's Doria Halifax Craig Gatwick for your records. Doria died when Melly was twenty-two."

"Yes, Ma'am. What—"

"I'm speaking, young man."

He shut up. It was the *young man* that did it, he thought.

He'd driven last night, stayed at a chain motel outside Charlottesville and had breakfast before arriving here.

She'd been inclined to turn him away at the door before he began his explanation that the Department of State hoped for some background on a family member who had connections with a foreign government. Then she'd looked at him sharply, still with the chain on the door, and demanded he hand his identification to her.

She took the ID, closed the door on him and left him standing there for several minutes. If he'd been a gambler, he'd have laid a bet she was calling State at that very minute. It must run in the family. He started to smile.

The door opened and he wiped away the smile. She still gave him a suspicious look.

She'd led him through a house that had been in the family for generations judging from paintings and photos that showed it in previous centuries. Its furnishings respected that history without giving up comfort.

Here in a room at the back enclosed by glass on three sides, the emphasis was on comfort. He'd glimpsed one Christmas tree in a front room. A second stood here. April would approve of both trees.

He pushed aside the thought and got to work, eliciting details around the time of April's birth, and beyond.

"Jeff's death was the more difficult for the child." A sigh escaped the woman. Hunter couldn't imagine many did. In fact, he didn't imagine much escaped her—in either sense of the phrase. "I'd like to think it was because by the time Melly died, April had matured, and more importantly had connected with Leslie and Grady, as well the rest of the family. Also the Craigs."

That confused him—the Craigs *were* the family—but he wasn't going to stop her now.

"I suspect it was also because Jeff was her true parent. Oh, not that he was a paragon, mind you. Some say he was maturing rapidly, becoming more responsible. I will concede that he took a true interest in April. Spent time with her. In addition, Leslie maintains that I am too harsh in my judgment and that Melly was better when Jeff was alive. Less erratic." Her features sharpened and she sat even straighter. "Impossible for her to have been more erratic."

"April's mother died of—?" The official report said pneumonia.

The woman met his gaze unflinchingly. "Hard living."

"And her father?"

"Idiocy."

He coughed. Good Lord, the woman had almost made him laugh during an interview.

"I understand he was mountain climbing with his wife…"

"What could be more idiotic than going to a mountain for the express purpose of climbing it? If one needed to climb one in order to get where one needed to be, yes. Otherwise, idiocy. And, further, to have Melly as his companion and, presumably, his safeguard. I have wondered … but the State Department does not care about the musings of a senior citizen."

He did. But he didn't know how to say it.

"What happened to April after her parents died?"

The woman paused, studying him. He was certain she'd say that information was not germane to his inquiry. She was right.

"After Melly's death, life went on for April as it had been for several years. She finished high school here, then attended college. In that way, there was little material change in her circumstances. Melly had been absent more and more."

"What about earlier, after her father died?"

"That was different. Both April and Melly were heartbroken. They expressed it in very different ways. Melly became ever more restless, ever more flighty. April drew in. The more wild Melly became, the more April withdrew. It wasn't until she was thirteen, and with Melly more and more inclined to fail in her duties as a mother, that Leslie and dear Grady came into her life. For the first time, April became a true Craig."

He suspected that wasn't how counselors or most people would express it, but he recognized it as the highest praise from Beatrice Craig.

"And you're positive that April is the biological daughter of Melly and Jeff?"

"I beg your pardon, young man." He had never felt more like begging pardon himself.

And then he wanted to grin. April would look like this, and she'd act like this when she needed to. She already had this backbone, and this heart. Not yet honed as sharply by the forces of nature and time. But she'd protect her family as fiercely as this woman did now.

"I have to make sure, Ma'am."

"You can be entirely sure that April is a member of the Craig family. There is no shred of doubt about that."

"You said a while ago that April became close to the family as well as the Craigs…?"

"Ah. I wasn't sure you were listening, young man. Yes, April *is* a Craig. She also has wide and deep support from a close-knit group that includes my granddaughter Leslie and her husband Grady."

She studied him.

He remained at ease under the survey. Until an odd notion struck him—these eyes were the kind that would sense being followed, and April had these eyes.

"Yes, I see," she said, making him shift on the seat. "Bless your heart, young man, you believe you know about these people. You do not. As you will discover one way or the other. You would be well-advised to make sure that you do not discover it by hurting our April."

He was dismissed shortly after that.

As he began the return trip to Washington to catch a flight to New York that would get him there before the close of business, he thought over what Beatrice Craig had said.

One element kept coming to the front.

He'd read the report. He'd known her father had died when she was six, but her mother had lived another ten years, and by then April had already transition to the care of her cousin and great-grandmother.

What he hadn't realized was that she'd been an emotional orphan in those years with Melly after Jeff's death.

He and April had more in common than he'd known.

New York

"You just missed her." The receptionist pointed to double glass doors still swinging from the force of the push by the woman who'd blown past Hunter. "You can wait—"

He'd already pivoted and grabbed the door on its latest backswing. He wasn't waiting.

The agent for Gerard Littrell's literary estate was partway down the hall, past the elevators, apparently heading for the door at the far end. He gained ground with every step, but not as much as he would have expected. Below the hem of her straight dress, the bulging muscles in the back of her calves operated like pistons.

"Marlene Pagenter?"

"What?" She snapped it, but impossible to tell if that was because she was in a hurry—she barely turned her head and she didn't slow down—or from habit.

"I called from Washington, D.C. Hunter Pierce."

"Yeah?" No sign of recognition.

"About Gerard Littrell."

She stopped with a grip on the handle of the far door. He had the notion that if she'd gotten through it there would have been no reaching her.

"About April," she said. It was a correction.

"About their association."

She snorted. "Let's see your ID."

He showed her. She took her time with it.

When she was done, she said "Sit," and retreated four feet to a bench across from the elevators. "What's this about?"

He sat after she did. The bench was almost as uncomfortable as it looked.

"As I said on the phone, it's about April Gareaux's association with Gerard Littrell. And your observations of that association."

"Really?" She did sarcasm well. He was guessing she'd had a lot of practice. "The State Department's security branch has an interest in dead science fiction authors, does it? Or could it be that April appears to have become the protégé of a certain monarch who's useful to this country's interests? Never mind, don't answer. I don't have time for your diplomatic lies and a bald-faced one would piss me off."

She crossed her legs.

"Okay. You want to know if there was something untoward going on between April and Gerard? No. I'm as sure of that as anyone can be who's not with them 24/7. You want to know if she was milking him for money or angling for a big inheritance? No way. She didn't get more than a pittance, so she'd either have to be incompetent—and she's not—or honest."

He'd known both assessments of her relationship with Littrell before they'd ever approached her. The money was Background 101. An affair had been a more delicate matter. Everyone they checked with said the same thing: No.

Although, as Marlene Pagenter said, there was no way of knowing for sure without being with the couple every minute of the day.

Except he did know.

April had told him.

He knew.

"Then what was their rela—association."

She squinted at him, as if he might not be in good focus. "Friend-ship. Gratitude. Caring. Generosity. And she was one hell of an assistant. It's a fact that he wrote four books in the final years of his life that would not have existed without April. She protected his time and his creativity, kept him on track, and smoothed every bump out of his way." She smiled suddenly. "Except for the bumps that did him good. Can't have it perfectly smooth, or a writer'll slide right into sloth. Especially a man. Delicate creatures men."

He met her gaze without looking away or reacting.

"What sort of assistant duties?"

"Mail. Fans. Helped with proofs. Errands. Interview requests. Scheduling. Making sure he had tea at the right time and the right temperature. Buying supplies. Talking him out of what he shouldn't do, into what he should. Only thing she never could talk him into was getting a dog from that shelter she went to all the time. Her sole failure. Probably would have kept the old curmudgeon going another couple of years." She shook her head. "What did April do? What any good assistant does—everything that needs to be done before it needs to be done. Offered her a job myself after he died. She didn't want to leave her family in D.C. Pity."

"She seemed close to her family?"

"Sure."

"Ever meet them?"

"Most of them, one time or another."

"Who did you meet?"

The squint was back. "Unh-unh. I don't know what you're looking for, but that question wasn't for your job." She stood. "If that's all the questions—the official questions—I have work to do."

CHAPTER THIRTY-TWO

"I don't know, Grandma Beatrice."

"Well, I do, Leslie Aurelia. You and your family go ahead and go to Illinois today to begin your Christmas as you planned. April will be fine."

"I wish she'd call me. I also wish I knew what in the world is going on."

"You said Michael Dickinson gave you information."

"He did. Grady and I had dinner with him and Tris last night, and the guys came clean about trying to find out more about this man who's been in two video clips with April. His name is Hunter Pierce. He's with State's Bureau of Diplomatic Security. Has an exemplary record, very highly regarded, not a smudge on his record. But what is he doing with April? That's what I want to know. And that's where Michael ran into a wall."

"No curiosity about this king? Apparently his family shares the characteristic of the Craig hand." In Beatrice's hierarchy the Bariavaks clearly came second to the Craigs.

"Well, of course, but—"

"Exactly, so. It's as plain as when I first saw you and Grady together. What you must learn, Leslie, is that sometimes you have to have faith in the people you love and let them make their own choices."

Leslie nearly choked. As if her grandmother hadn't always thought she would be better at guiding Leslie's life than Leslie had been.

"Besides," Beatrice Craig added, "I have now met the young man, and I approve of him."

"You—You've met him? How? Where?"

"He came to call on me, of course."

"Came to—? He was at your house? I don't … Please, Grandma Beatrice, just tell me what happened."

Leslie listened closely, trying to sort through the coloring that her grandmother's strong personality cast over most facts. It sounded as if Hunter Pierce had been conducting a background interview.

But, why? If the King of Bariavak truly thought April might be his granddaughter wouldn't he have his own people conducting such interviews? For heaven's sake, wouldn't he have DNA tests done?

And the points about April's difficult upbringing … Didn't they sound like someone looking at how she'd become the adult she was now, rather than if she could possibly have been a princess at birth?

"Now, this has taken quite enough of my day," her grandmother started.

"Grandma Beatrice, tell me one more thing. This man. This Hunter Pierce, is he…"

"What?"

"Do you think he's one of April's lame ducks?"

Beatrice Craig was still chuckling when they ended the call.

Hunter rubbed his forehead.

He'd hoped to return to D.C. to deal with the next interviews.

The office relayed a message from Sharon that, instead, his next stop was going to be Chicago.

But not until tomorrow, because the East Coast was socked in by weather.

This got better and better.

"Leslie."

"*April.* It's wonderful to hear from you, but we're actually on the airplane, about to take off for Chicago."

"Sorry. I won't keep you—"

"Damn. I so want to talk to you."

April heard Leslie's son Jake crow in the background, "Mom said a bad word," his sister Sandy say, "You are so obnoxious," and Grady trying to restore order.

"I can't really talk, Leslie. Not for a while yet."

"For a while yet?"

"I'm sorry. I've promised … But I did want to tell you—and I can, because it's part of my personal life, not—Reese and I aren't engaged any more. We're not anything anymore. I gave back the ring, moved out. It's over."

Again, Leslie repeated part of what she'd said, "Moved out?"

"Yes, but I'm fine. Truly. I'm with some, uh, friends. You can reach me on my cell. And I'll try to be better about calling."

"April—"

The flight attendant's robotic announcement overrode whatever Leslie had been about to say.

"I've got to go now, Leslie. Give Sandy and Jake and Grady hugs from me. Give my love to everyone. I promise, we'll talk after the holidays."

The days seemed quieter with Hunter gone. Less full. Less fun.

Which was nonsense, of course, considering what a Grinch he was about the holidays.

Derek was much more likely to tap his foot along when carolers came to the door. And he hadn't objected at all to another shopping trip. He'd even joined her in a wrapping session. And when Sharon spelled him, as she was doing this afternoon, it should be even more festive.

Except festive wasn't exactly the mood at the moment.

Sharon had brought her two younger children to join them in baking cookies in the embassy kitchen.

Madame watched their every move from a stool she'd set against the far wall, having a dampening effect on the mood of all the bakers, except for three-year-old Ben, who was enchanted by Rufus. It was a good thing he ignored the cookies as well as Madame, because his hands were soon coated with dog hair.

Five-year-old Kyana kept shooting wary looks toward Madame.

To distract her, April quickly mixed dough for another cookie while Sharon finished up a batch of chocolate chip cookies.

"Now, you're going to do the most important part, Kyana," April said, placing a cookie sheet in front of her, along with a spoon and the bowl of batter. "You're going to make these into the shape of an acorn. You press it gently to the cookie sheet, then pinch here so it will look like the top of an acorn. There, now you try. Yes—exactly like that."

The girl had completed the first row when Madame came and looked over her work. Kyana looked up at her with wide eyes.

Madame said in her usual stern tone, "Very good, Kyana. The last one is particularly good."

Then she moved to where April had made the dough, picking up the recipe card.

"My grandmother made a very similar cookie," she said. "Though, when they are cooled, she dipped them in caramel rather than chocolate before the coating of nuts."

"I like chocolate," Ben announced.

"I like caramel," Kyana said immediately.

"Chocolate!"

"Maybe we can try some in each when we're ready to dip," April said.

"Caramel!"

"Or neither," Sharon said. The dispute ended.

"That is not your handwriting," Madame said to April.

"No. That's my grandmother's handwriting. My father's mother. Mom had the recipe from her. It's one of the few things I have from that side of my family, because my father's parents died before I was born. I had copies made several years ago so we could put the original away for safekeeping. The story is my grandmother had the recipe from her mother."

"Indeed."

"I never knew my grandmother. Do you remember yours?"

"Very clearly." Her voice softened.

"I used to make cookies with my grandmother at Christmastime," Sharon said softly. "I remember the smells, and the warmth…"

There was a pause. April held her breath, waiting to see if Madame would pick up the fragile thread.

She said, "The fineness of the flour through my fingers. And her hand over mine, guiding it, shaping these cookies."

"Like this?" Kyana asked. "Is this a good one?"

Madame stepped over to the little girl, considered the cookie gravely. "Exactly like that. That is excellent."

Lake Forest, Ill.

The older woman who answered the door looked at him with warm, interested eyes.

"Yes?"

"Leslie Craig Roberts, please?"

"Who shall I say is here to see her?"

"If you'd ask her to come to the do——?"

"I'm Leslie Craig Roberts, may I help you?"

Still outside, he held up his opened ID as he watched her come down the last steps of a substantial staircase. "Ms. Roberts, my name is Hunter Pierce. I'd like to speak with you."

"State?" she said, resting a hand on Mrs. Monroe's shoulder. She must have good eyes to have read that on the ID from that distance.

"Why don't you take him into the living room, dear? I'll help them settle in upstairs," the older woman said, opening the door to him.

"We've just arrived from the airport for a visit," Leslie Craig Roberts explained, leading him to a large, comfortable, well-furnished room. The scent of the real Christmas tree greeted him as she gestured for him to sit on the couch. She took a chair nearby. She and April didn't look like each other exactly, but there was a way of walk, of holding themselves ... a connection that came through. "It will be marvelous chaos from now through New Year's. Now, what on earth has driven you from Washington to here simply to talk to me?"

"I am doing background at the behest of the United States government—"

"What's this about April?"

A tall, good-looking man strode into the room. His tone was both protective and confident of having his question answered.

Interesting. Grady Roberts' source of information must have been Mrs. Monroe. Yet April's name had not been mentioned.

Without taking her gaze from him, Leslie said to her husband, "It's all right, Grady. He's been to see Grandma Beatrice."

"Has he? Ah." The older man smiled. Hunter saw satisfaction in the smile. Was that also sympathy? "Then she set him straight."

"I would imagine so," Leslie said lightly. To him she continued, "Yet you have come all this way to discover more, Hunter? Do you mind my calling you Hunter? I feel as if I know you."

"April—"

"No, April has not told us anything about you."

Grady's frown returned. He seemed about to say something, but Leslie reached up and took his hand, causing him to look at her. He moved behind her chair without speaking.

Leslie turned to him again. "We have gathered from news reports that she appears to be spending time in the company of the King of Bariavak. I can only assume that is how you and she have come to know each other."

He tried to recapture the lead. "Your grandmother said that April is definitely the daughter of her granddaughter, Melly Gareaux."

She looked at him for a long moment, head slightly tipped as she studied him. These Craig women were going to be the death of him.

"Leslie?" Grady said, a note of concern in his voice.

She stared a beat longer, then smiled. Hunter thought the stare had been easier to stand up under than that smile. "Yes."

As much as he wanted to retreat, he knew his duty. "Yes? You're confirming that she is the biological daughter of your late cousin?"

"I am definitely confirming that Melly brought her home after one of her more peripatetic spells, which, if I recall correctly, had lasted more than two years, and presented April as her fourteen-month-old baby."

As a definitive statement, that made great Swiss cheese.

"I'd like to pin this down."

She touched his arm and smiled again. "I know you would, Hunter."

"Ms. Craig—Mrs. Roberts—"

"Please, call me Leslie."

"Ma'am. But—"

Another four people came into the room.

"Oh, good. Hunter, this is Bette Monroe and her husband Paul. This is Mr. Monroe, Paul's dad, and you've met Mrs. M. Everyone, this is Hunter Pierce. He's here about April."

"What about April?" Mr. Monroe asked.

"Does this have to do with that jerk fian—" Paul started. His wife stepped on his foot, possibly accidentally as she helped her father-in-law, who had a stiff leg, to settle on the couch cushion beside Hunter.

"Hunter's with the Department of State's Bureau of Diplomatic Security. He's in from Washington to talk to us. I'm a shade unclear exactly what it has to do with," Leslie said. She turned toward him, and so did all the others. Clearly inviting—more accurately, demanding— an explanation.

"I am not at liberty to disclose more than I have."

"Oh, aren't you?" This time it was Grady who was stopped by his wife. Though Leslie Craig Roberts simply placed a hand on his arm.

She then faced him.

"Hunter, we would not consider asking you to jeopardize your career as an employee of the United States government. We thank you for serving it and our country. We hope you'll stay and have some cookies and egg nog with us. Do you prefer it with or without nutmeg? Since you are driving, it is without any, shall we say, other embellishments."

"Leslie?" Paul Monroe said. "You sure?"

His mother said, "Leslie's absolutely right to offer Mr. Pierce some holiday cheer."

"Do get comfortable, Hunter. If you want to know about April, this is going to take a while." Leslie exchanged a look with Nancy Monroe, then added, "It's a shame our friends Tris and Michael Dickinson and their family aren't here yet. They're coming in from Washington, too, as a matter of fact. Perhaps you've met them already? No? Ah, but Washington's such a small town in so many ways, I'm confident you will meet them before long."

Was he paranoid for thinking that had a thread of threat to it?

"You could meet them if you could return tomorrow evening," Bette Monroe said.

"I have a flight overseas tomorrow evening."

"What a shame," Nancy Monroe said.

From the corner of his eye, Hunter caught her daughter-in-law, son, and husband looking at her quickly. Grady Roberts was watching his wife.

The older woman went on, "But how lovely that you can stay with us until tomorrow afternoon, so we can help you truly get to know April."

He stood. "That's not—"

"Plenty of room for you, and we insist, don't we, everyone? We can take you to the airport when we go to pick up Michael and Tris and everyone. Now, nutmeg or no nutmeg on your egg nog? Never mind, we'll bring some of each. You sit back down there, though I think you'd better move to the other side of Mr. M—you'll thank me. I do believe I hear the children coming. Step over James' leg. Careful now."

"That won't—"

He could swear the woman pushed him into the seat. "Yes, his cast is off at last, but his poor leg is still quite stiff. Tell him all about it, dear. And Paul, if you'll move up a chair for Bette. Excellent. I'll get the egg nog."

He was neatly penned in.

O'Hare Airport's rushing crowds felt like a respite to Hunter.

At least none of them stared at him and asked if he was the mean man who wasn't letting April have Christmas.

The first kid who asked him that it had taken an extra half beat to realize they meant Reese Warrington. Because the description fit him, too, didn't it?

And, damned if he didn't catch Leslie Craig Roberts giving him a knowing look after that hesitation.

That first questioner had been the youngest of Paul and Bette Monroe's three. Cassie, he thought they'd said. But he hadn't been any too popular with Sandy or Jake Roberts, either.

By the end, he would have preferred another couple go-rounds with the candy cane screecher to the reproachful stares. Guess he should consider himself lucky the Dickinson kids hadn't been around yet.

But he had learned more about April. A lot more. Including that she was loved by people who didn't need to be related to be a clan.

What he hadn't learned was anything that applied to her parentage.

Now he had another trip to make. The longest. The hardest.

CHAPTER THIRTY-THREE

King Jozef put the report he had been reading on the cushion beside him and removed his glasses, rubbing his eyes.

Hunter was on an airplane, returning from Bariavak to Washington. It had been, he knew, Hunter's first trip there since he had left as a boy. A boy with a different name, a different life.

Had sending him back done any good? Might it have done harm?

And was he a wise judge for which was which? He was an old man. Should he be meddling? Should he—?

A knock sounded on the office door.

"Enter."

Marusha came in with her usual grace, closed the door behind her, and waited for his acknowledgement of her presence, thus granting her permission to speak. He had seldom felt such impatience with the old ways.

"Yes."

"I wish to speak with you, sir, about April."

"I have expressed my wishes, and I expect—"

Her formality fell away. "No, Jozef, you misunderstand. I am not here to renew my objections and concerns."

His heart jolted.

Before April came into his life and Hunter reentered it, he might have told himself the jolt was satisfaction that the most stubborn woman he knew had finally come around to his way of thinking. He knew better now.

He had not been addressed simply by his name in years. It must be since Dmitry, his long-time prime minister, had died. And those instances had been rare. Before that…? his cousin Rafka, he supposed.

And yet that also was not the full reason for the jolt of his heart.

Marusha calling him Jozef.

The voice of the girl that had often whispered his name in his dreams. She was no more a girl now than he was a boy. They were old, there was no other way to call it. And yet, it was his name on her lips that caused that jolt.

Ah, maybe not so old after all.

"Come beside me here, Marusha." He patted the couch beside him. He had made this invitation before. She had never accepted. That was no reason to quit, as April would say. "And tell me what is on your mind, then."

She surprised him first by doing as he asked and his heart gave another leap. Then she astonished him by adding, "What exactly do you know of April Gareaux's heart, Jozef?"

Sharon called him as he walked past her door.

"What is it?" Damn. He'd been sure she wouldn't be in her office the Saturday before Christmas. Especially not this early.

Her eyebrow quirked up. "You look awful. Haven't seen you look this bad since we pulled those three red-eyes in a row."

He grunted as he sank into a chair across the desk from her. "That about covers it."

"Don't get too comfortable in that chair, Pierce. Heard you're just back from Bariavak."

"And New York and Charlottesville and Chicago. So if you'd please tell me what you want so I can go sleep, I'd appreciate it,"

"Thank God you're in security and not on the diplomatic side."

"You've never wanted diplomacy before."

"Not me." She thumped down a folder, flipping it open to show a number of letters on official letterhead, plus a flurry of phone message reports. "The U.S. Senate."

"The Senate? I didn't talk to anybody in the Senate."

"Close enough. This is from the senior senator from Wyoming, expressing concern over Diplomatic Security's inquiry into the background of a U.S. citizen."

"Wyoming?"

"Need to do more background, Pierce. Nancy and James Monroe's daughter—that's Paul Monroe's sister, and through him friends with Leslie and Grady Roberts—is married to a Wyoming rancher."

"Good grief."

"These," she took out more letters, "are from both senators from the state of Virginia. As far as I know this is the first thing they've ever agreed on, but they happen to both hold a woman named Beatrice Craig of Charlottesville in the highest esteem possible. And they will be distressed if she is distressed by unwarranted intrusions into her family's privacy." Another letter joined the pile. "Ah, yes, and this note from a Congressman is thrown in for good measure, but that's hardly worth worrying about."

He looked up, knowing there was more, facing it head-on.

"Because," she said, "this is the one that's really worth worrying about."

She placed a final letter on the top of the pile. It was considerably briefer than the others. "It's from Senator Bradon of Illinois, requesting a meeting with the Assistant Secretary of State for Diplomatic Security and the Director of the Diplomatic Security Service. Senator Bradon's chief of staff is Michael Dickinson. Perhaps you've heard of him. Yes, I see by your wince that you have."

"Met him," he said.

She raised her brows.

"At O'Hare Airport on Tuesday, no, Wednesday. One of those quiet types who can chop you off at the knees with a word."

She nodded. "So you already know he's another friend of Leslie and Grady Roberts. And this—" She held a final paper from the folder over the accumulated pile on her desk. "—is the Director's order that you and I report to him as soon as you return to Washington."

She stood. "I said not to get too comfortable in that chair. Let's go,

Pierce."

Once you went from the frying pan to the fire, what was the next step?

Because that's where he was headed as he followed Madame's stiff back to the king's office.

King Jozef said all the right things in welcoming his return, hoping his journey was not too arduous or uncomfortable, then he finished with "Report."

"I am a federal agent for the United States. I have reported to my supervisors. If they choose to share—"

"I shall hear your travels directly from you. I shall wait while you call Ms. Johnson."

He didn't call, because he'd already had his instructions. Why he'd resisted made no sense to himself.

When he finished, King Jozef remained staring at the tips of his fingers, steepled in front of him.

"You talked to those few who said they saw the man leaving the palace with a baby. What do you think of their accounts?"

"They believe what they are saying. Whether it *is* true or not, it is impossible to say this long after the events."

Slowly, the king nodded. "You went, also, to meet your father's cousins who had cared for you after you mother's death?"

Hunter felt his muscles tightening. But this, too, was a professional question. Not one that truly touched on him personally, no matter how those strangers had insisted that he was family. "Yes. The last time they saw him, he said nothing to them that might shed light on who might have taken your granddaughter."

The king bowed his head. "The last time they saw him." He looked up without raising his head. "That was when he collected you, to bring you to the palace."

"That is what they said."

"Your father, who gave his life for our country, as—"

"For you. Not for a country, for *you*."

"I *was* the country to him. King, country, impossible to separate. And he sacrificed his life in its service, as I have devoted my life to it. And because of that, my family and your family suffered greatly. Perhaps if Laurentz and I had known what would happen to our families … perhaps we would have make different choices. What of you, Hunter? What choice will you make?"

"Me? My choices are made."

"You are too intelligent a man to lie to yourself, Hunter. You have many choices. The most important being about April, and what you will do with your love for her and hers for you."

"She doesn't—"

"Don't be a fool as well as a liar, Hunter. She does. But to claim her love, you must ask her for it, and you must ask her to accept yours."

"That is not—"

"*Go.* Out of my sight, before I lose my temper with someone so blind."

Six days after the White House party, April opened the library door as Hunter reached to knock on it.

She recoiled, and he watched the pulse in her throat jolt.

"You're back," she said.

"Yes."

"For—for how long?"

"The rest of the time."

"Oh. You look tired."

"I am."

He watched her studying him.

Hunter said, "You look … good."

Her eyes flicked to his then away. "I am."

He could think of nothing else to say. Or perhaps he was afraid that if he started talking he would never stop.

After a pause long enough to grow awkward, she started down the hall past him. But after a step, she stopped and turned her head toward him. "Hunter. May I ask you a question?"

He felt wariness. He was too tired, too awash in memories, impressions and other people's emotions. If her question unbottled all that now…

She clearly read his reluctance. A frown squeezed her forehead. He wanted to put his fingertips to those lines and massage them to smoothness. He clenched his hand against the desire. And it made his response come out harsher than he'd intended. "What's your question?"

The frown tightened, but she didn't back off. "I would like you to translate a word for me." She spoke six syllables in careful concentration. "If you know it."

He relaxed. The syllables sounded familiar, but didn't sort themselves into words immediately. Something wasn't quite right. He murmured them to himself, giving them the Bariavakian rhythm, and then he had it. A muscle at the corner of his mouth tugged. Oh yes, he knew it.

"It's a phrase, rather than a single word," he told her. "Along the lines of a child fathered by Satan, but not that literal. More like Devil Child."

"Oh." Clearly, she didn't know how to react.

"It's often a term of affection, a little along the lines of *you rascal.*" He had never doubted the love in his mother's voice the many times she had applied the phrase to him, even at her most exasperated.

But April appeared doubtful. "Oh, I think she meant it literally."

He didn't need to ask, so he made it a statement: "Madame."

She nodded dolefully. "I don't know if she meant Sharon's kids or me."

He laughed.

She startled. He tried to pull it back, but there was something about crusty Madam using a phrase he associated with affection to April that brought out the reaction.

He laughed more.

She tried to be indignant, but she was smiling. ... Then he saw tears shining in her eyes.

"April—" He took half a step toward her.

"You better get some rest," she said hurriedly. "Before you fall over."

"Let's be sure we're all on the same page," Sharon said at noon Sunday in the king's office. "With Christmas only two days away—"

"Security doesn't stop because it's December the twenty-fifth," Hunter said. At least he felt human now, after sleeping through a night for the first time since the night before the White House party.

"I—we—go nowhere Christmas or its Eve," King Jozef said. "April and I discussed this, and decided, no engagements until the Receiving Hours on the twenty-sixth. That evening, I will take April to a restaurant the ambassador recommends most highly. Until then, we shall stay snug in the embassy. So you will not have duty those days. The staff will be dismissed as they complete their duties on Christmas Eve day, then be free through Christmas night."

"Great. I can drive up to Delaware, and..." Derek's enthusiasm trailed off as he turned toward Hunter.

"Security doesn't stop because they stay inside, either."

"Hunter is correct, of course. So I request, Sharon, that he be assigned close security for those days. With us every minute." The king might have been having a hard time keeping a straight face. "But you, Derek, and of course Sharon are at liberty."

"Only until the night of the twenty-sixth," Sharon said to Derek. "I'll help cover the Receiving Hours in the afternoon. Then you plan on working straight through, giving Hunter a break the next day. We go back to normal schedule then."

From behind his desk, King Jozef nodded. "Until a week from Thursday."

The day of his surgery.

April was up to something.

Getting phone calls, huddling with Sharon. Her eyes bright when she got those phone calls she wasn't talking about. Could it be Reese? Not Nine-Handed Neil. It couldn't be.

Not that it was really his business. Unless it interfered with the mission.

"What are you two up to?" he asked as he entered the kitchen and they headed for the back stairs toward April's room.

April froze. Not Sharon.

"Hey, it's like I tell my kids," she said. "If you weasel around and find out about what's supposed to be a surprise, then you don't get the present."

"I don't want presents or surprises, so go ahead and tell me."

"No, Sharon's right," April said, no longer frozen. "You're not supposed to ask things like that at this time of year. You'll have to put up with the suspense for once instead of always trying to control everything around you."

He threw his hands up. "Fine. Don't tell me."

"I won't," she said cheerfully.

Just before he closed the door, he thought he heard Sharon say, "That was impressive. You are *good.*"

"Go on, go on," April said, shooing him and the King of Bariavak out of the kitchen.

She'd said she and Madame had work to do.

She and *Madame.* Maybe this was what they meant about this being the season of miracles.

"Come into my office," the king said. Not quite a command. Then he amended it to "No, let us go into the library."

Seated across from each other, the ruler of Bariavak cleared his throat. "I hope you are not offended by the personal nature of this inquiry," he began with a formality that fell apart as he finished his question, "but I must ask: What are you going to give Sharon for Christmas? Since it is now clear that you will, indeed, be giving Sharon a gift."

Hunter kept the curse ricocheting around his head from reaching his lips only by the greatest will power.

"I have no idea."

"Perhaps I could help you. I am not unacquainted with what women would like to receive as gifts."

"She's a co-worker," he reminded the king.

The man drew himself up, but the twinkle in his eyes didn't diminish. "Not all my associations with women were amorous. I counted a number of them as friends … eventually."

Hunter gave in. He would need any help he could get. "I would appreciate it, sir. I guess, with all those cookies…"

"Ah, yes, her cookies are excellent. I will help you acquire an appropriate gift for Ms. Sharon, your friend, co-worker, and baker of excellent cookies."

"Thank you."

"You are welcome. And in return—" Ah, here it came. He should have known the king wanted something. "I ask for your help."

"I don't know what I could—"

"Listen to the request before you search ways to refuse it, Hunter."

As quiet as the words were, the reproach flicked a nerve that said the king was right. "Your Majesty."

"Sir," he corrected.

"Sir."

The king's gesture accepted the implicit apology. "Humility does not suit you. But beware of arrogance. Now, as I was saying, April has determined that gifts should be *restrained*. I had planned … but she refuses to have even the least jewel from me. What can I give her? Do you have any idea what she might like for Christmas?"

Hunter opened his mouth to deliver the words his brain had lined up—"No, sir, I have no idea."—in the tone that indicated it wasn't any part of his duties to speculate, either.

What came out instead was, "Yeah, I think I do. If you're willing to have Madame be royally ticked at you."

The king's eyes lit up. "What could be better? A present for April that will raise Madame Sabdoka's ire."

CHAPTER THIRTY-FOUR

The day before the day before Christmas, April hardly saw Hunter. It was almost as if he were still gone. Except she kept expecting to see him around every corner.

Derek said, with some bemusement, that Hunter had said he had errands to run for Christmas.

King Jozef had told him at breakfast this morning about the decision made in his absence: They would not exchange presents beyond a few items in the stockings April had purchased.

So, he certainly wasn't out getting Christmas gifts for them, and he'd been quite clear he didn't exchange them with anyone else.

Christmas Eve Day, and April was in her element.

Oddly, so was Madame.

Sharon had swung by first thing in the morning, delivering a bounty of cookies. April gave her a seasonally wrapped box that she opened immediately. It held cookie cutters and a certificate for a Mommy and Me baking class.

"I figure it's really for the whole family, since Ross, Caleb, and Ben will benefit from what you make," April said.

"It's perfect." Sharon hugged her.

As she was leaving, Hunter quietly gave her an envelope. She stopped in her tracks. "What is this?"

"Open it later."

"No way." She tore it open. Read quickly, then beamed at Hunter. "Thank you."

She hugged him, and he thumped her on the back twice. "Santa's little helper."

With her gone, he turned back and found April staring at him.

"You have to tell us," April said.

"A donation in her name to a scholarship fund she supports."

April looked at him for a long moment, then slowly smiled. "I think you're getting the hang of this, Hunter Pierce."

Now, the long table in the kitchen was lined with baskets despite Rupert having made one trip already. His next trip would be the big one, with most of the baskets destined for the homeless shelter, plus a few baskets and many treat bags for the animal shelter.

While Rupert delivered those, Hunter would drive her to drop off baskets for Etienne and Maurice. Rupert already had the basket he would take with him when he left this afternoon for his sister's home in Baltimore.

Madame had it organized to the last second.

From his first round, Rupert had already relayed appreciation from Corrinda and Harlan at the Warringtons.

"At the hotel, all were delighted. Manny and Vanessa particularly asked to be remembered to you and to thank you for remembering him," Rupert said.

She beamed.

"Ms. Holland also said to wish you the best of holidays, and that she was delighted by your present to Jason."

The others looked perplexed. Hunter frowned. "The jerk at your office? The one who told everybody at the Willard that you skipped the Brussels sprouts? You gave that guy a present?"

She smiled. Not her usual open, bright smile. Instead it held mischief. "A basket of Brussels sprouts."

Hunter laughed.

There was an extra beat, then the king and Rupert joined in, along with April.

Madame, however said, "You do not care for Brussels sprouts? I shall prepare them so you will."

There was no arguing with that tone.

"Great, now we're going to have to eat them," Hunter complained in a low voice as they took the next set of baskets out to his car.

After Christmas breakfast at the sunfilled table in the kitchen, the king, April, Hunter, and Madame, under royal order, repaired to the library to open their stockings.

"But, first, there is a present for you, April, that will not wait. Hunter?"

He reached his room, started back at a good clip, saying out loud, "This better work."

April's view of his entrance was blocked by the large chair the king occupied, but Rufus almost ruined the surprise, alerting instantly. Hunter raised a commanding hand to him, and he stayed where he was.

April, sitting on the ottoman, was thanking King Jozef for giving her the Christmas she'd asked for when she stopped in mid-sentence.

"Dragon."

Her voice shook.

Hunter dropped the leash and the dog went directly to her.

He thought that was good, then he heard her sob.

"April?"

She didn't raise her head from where she had it buried on the animal's neck, but gave a sort of fluttering wave with one hand that left him no less mystified.

He could have sworn … Hell, he *had* sworn to King Jozef that she would be overjoyed at this present.

"If there was another dog you would rather have," started the king.

A simultaneous tongue click from Madame and muffled sound from April stopped him. She lifted her face, showing tears tracking down from red eyes in twin tracks framing her red nose. She opened her mouth, but before she could say anything, Dragon turned his head and slurped her cheek in a canine kiss.

April started laughing. Hunter and King looked at each other.

Rufus bounced over to join the fun, but failed to oust Dragon from the prime spot.

Hunter recognized what he saw in the King's eyes, because it was what he felt, too. Relief overlapping a residue of unabashed horror. That moment when she started crying and he was sure they both thought, *Oh sh*—... well, maybe the King of Bariavak didn't express himself that way, but the emotion was still the same. Here they'd been thinking they'd pulled off the perfect present, and the woman burst into tears.

Dragon saved the moment with that kiss.

Hell, if he'd known that kissing her was the answer to … No, better not go there.

"Of all the dogs at the shelter … Oh, this is a wonderful present. Wonderful!" She turned to Hunter. "When you followed me to the shelter—"

"What?" he said stupidly.

"That morning a couple weeks ago. I knew you were behind me."

"You couldn't have."

She smiled at him over the dogs' heads with tears still hanging on her lashes.

Protesting more would be useless.

"But I had no idea you meant to get me Dragon—both of you." She beamed at him, then the king.

"He's the king's present to you."

"I would not have known to make the present without Hunter."

"But how did you do it? They usually don't allow adoptions right before Christmas, because too many people change their minds after the holiday."

"I have some small measure of influence," the king said with dignified hauteur.

Hunter met April's look for a moment, seeing their shared amusement at the idea of King Jozef of Bariavak using his royal influence to secure Dragon.

"You've had him groomed, too."

"I should hope so," murmured Madame.

"Rupert took care of that Monday after we picked him up," Hunter said. "And took care of him during the day yesterday."

"While Hunter has tended Dragon in his room the past two nights."

Her eyes widened. "Really?"

"Really," the king confirmed solemnly, but Hunter heard the amusement underneath it, so he was prepared. "In his bed according to what Madame was told."

He shifted, but faced her directly. "Had to keep him from barking. It would have given everything away."

Madame emitted a disbelieving, "Huh."

But April wasn't looking at him. She was looking down to where Dragon had backed up against Hunter's leg, while he absently scratched the animal's flank.

Her eyes welled again, while her mouth smiled.

Hunter went back out and brought several more gaily wrapped packages, setting them in front of her.

"But we said only a few small things in the stockings," she protested.

"These are not for you." King Jozef sounded affronted that she would question his adhering to the agreement. "They are for Dragon."

Laughing, she opened a new dog bed—which Rufus promptly appropriated—water and food dishes, and several dog toys.

"Now the stockings," she declared.

She took each down from the mantel, handing it to the correct recipient. All were overflowing. They hadn't been nearly this full after she'd put her purchases in before going to bed. There had been other Santas at work last night.

They each had some chocolates, nuts, and change. King Jozef pulled three quarters from his stocking.

"To get yourself a little treat," she said straight-faced. Then she shrugged and added, "It's a tradition in my family."

"A delightful one. I shall find a vending machine in which to spend my Christmas booty."

April opened a package and found a small book of Bariavakian cookie recipes. She looked up, smiling, saw from their expressions that neither King Jozef nor Hunter had thought of this, then met Madame's eyes. The older woman had opened the packet of laminated recipe cards of the cookies they made last week that April had given her.

She held the woman's gaze, smiled, then nodded her thanks as well as an acknowledgment of a connection forged.

With delight, King Jozef immediately delved into a volume of "strange Americanisms and where they came from" he unwrapped. April grinned at Hunter's sudden absorption in Dragon.

The king's reaction to his family photos April had put into a flip stand that could accompany him to the hospital dampened his eyes.

There were complementary leashes for Rufus and Dragon in the royal colors of Bariavak, a photo of a mountainside that clearly had significance to both Madame and King Jozef that neither of them divulged, a top-quality lint (and dog hair) catcher for Hunter that had them all chuckling, a pair of tickets to a basketball game for Hunter.

Then the final item in April's stocking. A square box that fit in the palm of her hand.

She pulled the paper away and found a plain cardboard box inside. Tape slowed the opening, but then she had the top flipped back, pulled some cushioning paper back and pulled out a snow globe.

She glanced at King Jozef. He gave a tiny shake of his head. Surely not from Madame.

Then she held up the snow globe, and looked at what it held inside.

CHAPTER THIRTY-FIVE

Madame complained the meal would get cold, but King Jozef insisted they eat Christmas dinner in the library, With the tree and a fire in the fireplace, it was as if nothing existed beyond this room.

And so the four of them ate goose with apple, cranberry and potato stuffing, a green salad, mashed potatoes, and … Brussels sprouts.

King Jozef dug right into his. April and Hunter exchanged a commiserating look, then each speared a sprout.

April's eyes widened. "These … these are *good*."

"It requires care not to overcook them, which makes them bitter," Madame said with great dignity.

"But … it's more than that, isn't it?"

Madame's attempt to stifle a smile turned it closer to a smirk. "A great deal of butter and brown sugar. My mother said always that anything was good if you applied sufficient butter and brown sugar."

His Royal Highness, King Jozef of Bariavak, snored lightly as he dozed in the big chair angled to one side of the fire.

She and Hunter sat on cushions on the floor, with Rufus on his back, balanced against the side of her thigh. Dragon had been stretched between her and Hunter until Hunter got up to add another log to dwindling blaze.

Dragon circled three times, then sank down with a sigh, resting his head on Hunter's thigh.

"I have something for you that isn't quite … ready. I hope to give it to you tomorrow," she said quietly.

"No need—"

"Not need. Want. Just as I want to say, thank you, Hunter."

"No problem."

"For the fire. For the tree. For helping Madame. For your kind-nesses to the king. For Dragon." The dog's ears perked at his name, or perhaps at her voice shaking, but didn't move his head. "For my present."

The snow globe showed a view of the Capitol.

The view they had seen together as snowflakes began to fall on the National Mall after they had been ice skating. The view that captured the moment after he had kissed her the first time, and when he had almost kissed her again.

She didn't know all the meanings that small, round of glass held for him—not even for herself. She knew there were many. For right now, right here, that was more than enough.

"For today." She leaned forward, kissed him lightly on the cheek. "Merry Christmas, Hunter."

CHAPTER THIRTY-SIX

Muscles ached that April hadn't known she possessed.

Her cheeks from smiling, her hands from shaking, her back and shoulders from maintaining her posture and most of all her brain from thinking about what she said before she said it. No, not just thinking. Assessing, projecting, balancing Princess muscles.

She sat in the nearest chair the moment the doors closed behind the last guest from the Receiving Hours.

King Jozef, already seated, said, "You sit as well, Madame. No, put down that dish. That is for the staff. Sharon, Hunter, you sit, as well. Let us rest. Appreciate the quiet."

Even Madame seemed worn. She had every right. She'd been up since before dawn supervising the staff and extra help hired to prepare for the open house from three to five p.m. Bariavakians had streamed through, greeting the king, consuming cookies and punch, snapping photos, and taking video.

"Never have so many attended Receiving Hours," Madame declared.

"I am gratified," said King Jozef.

Madame looked at the king, then at April. April nodded, yes, she also noticed he'd seemed to flag in the waning minutes.

"You are tired," Madame said.

"Nonsense," he replied, but without his usual vigor or opening his eyes.

April said, "We'll stay in. You can read or rest—."

"We have a reservation—"

"We'll cancel it."

"No. Hunter, you shall take her."

"I don't want—" April tried.

"No more argumentation," commanded Madame. "His Highness is tired."

And that was the final word on the situation. King Jozef was tired, and he had asked this of her, and commanded this of Hunter.

April tried to rouse herself with cold water on her face, fixed her makeup, fluffed her hair, changed into a silk de Chartier dress, and trudged back downstairs.

In Hunter's car, she had her eyes closed, her head back before they were out of the embassy gates.

"Do you want to go to this restaurant, April?"

"No, but the king wants me to, so…"

He grunted, hit a button on his phone. Said, "Sharon" and in a moment April heard the other woman's voice answer. She opened her eyes.

"Sharon. Know that reservation in the name Sabdoka? If you and Ross can get there in time, it's yours."

He hung up on her questions.

April rolled her head to look at him.

He didn't return the look, but said, "Can't go back to the embassy for a while without a lot of explanations. Where do you want to go?"

"I guess you can't take me home, since I don't have a home. Not really. If Leslie and Grady were in town … But they're not." She sighted. "I want to be ordinary. Let's go to McDonald's or a movie or the mall or … or bowling."

He glanced over at her.

It was more solid than the fiercest refusal.

"Please, Hunter. I want to be myself. Ordinary. Just for a little while."

He turned right onto a side street off Connecticut Ave., then right again almost immediately and down to an underground garage.

He used a card to get in, parked in a spot he seemed to know would be open, turned off the car, and only then looked at her.

"You really want ordinary? This is it."

His home. Or at least where he lived.

She pushed back too many thoughts, too many questions.

"Perfect. Let's go."

Like most apartment building hallways it was narrow and anonymous. But as they walked she saw that each door had some individualizing mark—some had a year-round decorative "Welcome" sign or a family name on a plaque, others had a wreath of metal jingle bells, a small basket with mini-candy canes, a framed child's drawing of a Menorah, a spray of evergreens wrapped with a red bow. Only one door was entirely bare except for the apartment number, and that was the one Hunter opened.

He let her step in first, but held her arm to keep her from going too far in while he reset the alarm—surely not standard equipment in this building—locked the door behind them, then made a quick survey of the main room before disappearing into an adjoining room.

She barely had time to take in the bare bones décor of the room before he returned.

"Okay." He held out one hand. "Your coat."

While he hung it up, she looked around her. Bare bones was right. There was nothing on the walls, no photos or decorative touches on any of the other surfaces. A solitary stool sat by the counter that divided a Spartan kitchen from the living room. A large-screen TV with components around it that made Reese's look like a tinker toy dominated one side of the room. Another wall held a row of neatly filled miss matched bookshelves interrupted only by a door, presumably to the bedroom. Steel gray blinds covered the wide windows. A long black leather couch and a heathered gray and black rug covering part of the hardwood floor were the closest things to a softening touch.

"What do you want on your pizza?"

"What?" She turned around to find him holding a phone.

"You wanted ordinary—what's more ordinary than ordering pizza? What kind of toppings do you want?"

She had a crazy urge to say anchovies to see his response. Except she didn't really want anchovies. "Sausage, black olives and extra cheese."

As he punched in numbers he clearly knew by heart, she looked around at what little there was to see.

As he hung up, she began studying the titles held by the bookshelves. He remained silent behind her. Watching, she knew.

A broad mix. Classic fiction, nonfiction on history, security, politics. A whole shelf of books on Washington area landmarks, including Mount Vernon. Research for his job? Or interest?

She crossed to the other bookcase, this one with shelves closer together because it held mostly paperbacks. Some of the same mix, but with more added.

"Taking inventory?" he asked as she tipped out one title, then another because the spines were so creased it was hard to read titles.

"I don't have a dossier on you or resources for a detailed report, so I make do."

He made a sound. She liked that sound. The beginning of a chuckle. Even when he cut it short, it meant he'd found amusement. It meant she'd found what amused him.

"Ah." She pulled out a thick book, and turned to him, brows raised. "*Very* interesting. Background or—? No, this is too old, too worn, too loved."

He shrugged. "Millions have read Gerard Littrell. Great action."

"You really think you're going to get that past me?" She shook her head. "Not one of his big sellers, precisely because it didn't have as much action. More of a cult favorite among those who found the character growth of the protagonist compelling."

He shrugged again. "So shoot me."

"I've been tempted."

His mouth slanted with a suppressed grin. "Done with your new form of background investigation?"

"Medicine cabinets are nearly as revealing."

"That so?"

She nodded.

"What did Reese's medicine cabinet tell you?"

She grimaced. "It told me I should have known better. Everything in it was chosen by his mother."

He chuckled along with her, then he nodded toward the half-open door. "Bathroom's through there."

That was as close as she'd get to an invitation to explore the rest of his apartment. It meant a lot that he'd come that close. For Hunter Pierce it was practically baring his soul.

The bedroom was more of a computer room. A large L-shaped desk, with filing cabinets underneath, state-of-the-art computer equipment on top, and an ergonomic chair. The bed, covered with a black duvet—what did the man have against color?—was pushed into a corner as if it were an afterthought.

Black and white tile in the bathroom made her wonder if that was why he'd rented the place. He'd followed through on the theme with black towels and a white shower curtain.

She caught a glimpse of deep bright blue in the mirror and spun around. It took her an instant to realize it was the sleeve of her dress.

She looked down at the de Chartier dress and thought about pizza sauce.

Something close to recklessness sizzled through her blood. She had requested ordinary, hadn't she?

When she returned to the main room, she had the pleasure of seeing Hunter Pierce taken by surprise.

"I hope you don't mind…" She gestured down at his State De partment t-shirt and black boxer shorts she now wore.

"Mind…?" He cleared his throat. He was staring at her legs. "Cold … uh, won't you get cold?"

She pointed one foot, demonstrating it was covered in a thick athletic sock that advanced well up her shin. "These will help."

They stood across the room from each other, and suddenly she was as nervous as she had been that first day when she'd gone into the conference room.

"I didn't want to risk spilling on the dress. I mean, if I got anything on it, how would I explain to Madame? Champagne, foie gras, salmon—those I could explain, but pizza sauce?"

She aimed for a sophisticated chuckle, but it had too many nerves in it.

"April, I didn't bring you here for … with any expectations."

She drew in air slowly. "That's too bad, Hunter."

Standing there, letting him see into her while he absorbed her message was one of the hardest things she'd ever done.

Shivers of nerves were going through her knees before his frown shifted, caught fire.

He took a step toward her.

The buzzer sounded.

They looked at each other.

The buzzer sounded again.

"They couldn't have been late this one damned time?" he muttered.

She giggled. Then covered her mouth for fear she couldn't stop.

He looked at her an instant longer, then wrapped one hand around her upper arm, guided her to a corner of the couch, then left the apartment.

He was back with the pizza before she'd entirely recovered.

He set the box on the coffee table in front of her. Yanked off lengths of paper towel to use as napkins, opened the fridge, placing a bottle of beer on the counter as he asked what she wanted to drink. "I've got beer or water."

"Water, please. I don't care for the taste of beer."

He looked over the top of the open fridge door at her for a suspended instant. Why was he staring—?

Then he returned the beer to the fridge, got out two glasses and filled them with water.

Oh.

How was she going to swallow pizza after that?

She did. Somehow.

He turned on the TV to a basketball game.

"Mind?" he asked.

"No. Though I like football better."

He looked over at her and grinned. "Do you?"

She ate one slice, he had two. They watched. Commented desultorily about the game and about the commentators.

He shifted on the couch. Not coming closer. Yet brushing his leg against hers.

That's all it took.

The game continued. At least she thought it did. She suddenly couldn't hear the announcers.

Her breathing changed. She heard his change, too.

"Done?"

"Yes."

He took the carton and glasses to the kitchen. She was standing when he returned. They looked at each other a long moment. Then he took her hand and led her to the bedroom.

Beside the bed, he unbuttoned his shirt partway, then pulled it over his head.

He looked down at her. "That shirt's never looked better. And I've never wanted to get rid of it more."

She pulled it over her head and dropped it to the floor beside them.

"Lacy." With his index finger he traced the uneven edge of the bra cups. Her breathing also went uneven. "How attached are you to those shorts?"

"Not very." She slid them over her hips and let them drop. Her voice shook a bit, but she got out the next words. "But, Hunter Pierce, if you leave me in these socks, I will never forgive you."

He laughed. Then he slid both hands down one leg, furling the sock, following it with his mouth. She rested a hand on his shoulder to balance as he pulled it off her foot, feeling his motion in the shifting, bunching, and stretching of his muscles.

He repeated the motion, holding her foot up, bending down to place a last kiss on the inside of her ankle.

She could have melted into the bed right then.

But he stood before she could, placing her hands at his zipper, then taking her mouth in a kiss that stroked and rocked, and apparently motivated her hands. Because she was pushing down his pants and his briefs together, feeling his bare, hard skin under her hands.

He kicked away the pants. Drew both straps of her bra down until her breasts were free, bent and covered her with his mouth, drawing on her nipple. She jolted, pressing herself against his erection, feeling it through thin material that was all that covered her.

He tipped her back toward the mattress, holding her with one hand and pulling back the covers with the other.

He unhooked her bra. Both of them were pulling at her panties.

Finally. Finally, they were gone.

He had a bedside drawer open. A condom. She kissed the side of his neck.

Then he was over her. Sliding into her, slowly, carefully.

"Hunter." She tried to draw him in faster.

He held himself back, the tendons in his arms standing out.

"Hunter."

She wiggled sideways and he slid in deeper. He groaned.

"Yes, Hunter. *Yes.*"

He returned to the bed, resting on his side with his head propped on his hand.

The sheet covered most of her. But, as he watched, her nipples pebbled, then peaked, nudging one corner almost enough for him to see that changing center of the breast nearer to him.

"I like that." His voice sounded unfamiliar to him.

She caught her breath, drawing it in. Then as it came out again, he caught the corner of the sheet and lifted it. To see all of her.

"This is what I thought you were saying I should be ashamed of. That day on the bench in the garden. I'd seen you in the dress, and all I could think of was wanting you like this," he said.

She turned her face to him. "No. Never. Because I've wanted you like this even longer."

He entered her again before she'd finished her sentence.

CHAPTER THIRTY-SEVEN

Without either saying it, they knew it was time to return to the embassy. They showered together.

He wrapped her in a towel, then kissed her, deep and slow.

He picked her up, her hair tumbling out of the pins that had protected it from the shower, the towel trailing away.

He laid her on the bed. One knee beside her, he looked down at her.

She saw the struggle in him. Knew it was a deeper struggle than the one he thought he waged.

He cupped the inside of her calf with one hand. Drew it up to her raised knee, then down the slope of her thigh. Down, and inside her.

"What—?" But her body knew what. Knew it immediately. Her eyes went wide. Her internal muscles tightened around his fingers with alacrity.

With his thumb, he gently flicked the nub at her opening, then stroked his fingers deeper inside of her. She arched, pushing her hips toward him, drawing him in more and more.

He pressed against her side, then hooked one foot over her leg, drawing it wide. His fingers delved inside her, his thumb easing and teasing. Over and over. Her hips lifted and he encouraged her. Urged her. Pushed her. Opened her. Touched her.

Released her.

And held her.

She was sinking right through the bed and floor and into the earth several stories below. She was weightless, floating up into the sky with no sense of cold or movement.

She just *was*.

Complete and empty.

Hunter rose from the bed, went to the bathroom, then into the living room. From the faint sounds, he was communicating with someone. She supposed telling Derek they were safe. And not returning.

Whatever might follow from that did not penetrate her haze.

She'd never had this before.

It wasn't that the few other men she'd been with had been selfish lovers—well, maybe a little selfish. So they wanted her to come— expected her to come—at the same time they did. That way they got to prove they were masterful lovers at the same time they reached their own pleasure. No need to expend a lot of energy that didn't directly reward them.

Hunter had given her this.

An orgasm that was all about her.

He came back to the bed. Laid beside her, pulling the covers over the two of them together.

She'd slept. It was deeper night now. Not darker, because of light seeping in from the street, but later.

He was awake.

"My mother died when I was little," he said. "Four, five maybe. I don't know. I remember her a bit. Soft voice. Thin. Guess she was sick by the time I knew her."

She placed her hand on his ribs. Rising and falling with the intake and exhale of his breaths.

"I lived with a family. Some sort of cousin of my father's. When the fighting started, they wanted to leave the city, get to the country where they thought it would be safer. They said my father didn't want me to be that far away. I don't remember that. They told me about it when I was there last week."

He breathed, steady and even.

"They hugged me. The man, his wife, a couple of their kids who were older than me and came running from nearby houses when they heard I was there. They cried. All of them cried. And they hugged me over and over. I don't remember any of them. They said how glad they were to see me, to see with their own eyes what they had been told—that I had grown up to a man, with a fine job. I don't know how they could have known anything about me, have been told anything about me. I asked, but they waved it off—not important. As long as I was safe. ... Safe."

She felt him slip back into memories—of last week's meetings or of longer ago?

After several minutes, he expelled a deep breath.

"I don't remember them. What I remember is my father coming to get me. There were men with guns in the street. Not soldiers, but they must have been loyal to the king, because they let us through. My father brought me to the palace. Told me that my duty was to be brave. Then he was gone again. I don't remember much about the days of fighting except not being allowed outside. And knowing that my father was doing his duty. That was always what he did—his duty to the king and the country.

"I never saw him again."

His hand on her back drew her against him. She reached farther around him, her body covering more of his, as if she could protect him. But the pain was inside him.

"The next memory is the man saying the words that meant he was dead. I knew the words. But I didn't understand—couldn't take in the meaning. He couldn't be dead. My mother was dead, but she'd been small and sick. He was big and strong. I couldn't believe it. Not until I saw that the man held the shoulder belt from my father's uniform and my mother's locket. The next thing I remember is running and running, and knowing I'd already been running a long time. I knew I couldn't run any more. I slept where I'd stopped running. Then I did it again. I have no idea how long. No idea where I ran to or from. Until ... Scotty."

She tightened her arms around him.

They were about to leave in the morning when she said, "Hunter, I have something else for you. Something I only got yesterday."

He looked around, then made a show of looking behind her back. "Can't be a present. No wrapping paper in sight. And you wrap anything that doesn't move."

She tried to smile. From his expression the attempt failed.

She handed him the paper where she had carefully written the numbers and words. Not like her hasty scrawl on the pad she'd been using for notes as she'd advanced layer by layer until she reached these few lines of information.

He read it, flipped the paper over, saw that side was blank and read the front again. Then he looked at her.

"What is it?"

"It's an address and phone number."

They'd lived not half an hour's drive from here all this time.

"I can see that." His mouth started to lift into a grin. Then it stopped. As if he knew.

"It's Scotty's parents," she said.

"I told you—"

"They want to see you."

He swore, short and profane, harsh enough to make her throat hurt in sympathy.

"Did you know his father had been in the foreign service? That he'd even worked in that embassy that was attacked in Africa—Oh, my God. How stupid of me. Of course you knew. That's *why*—why you joined the Diplomatic Security forces. Sharon said you could have gone to any agency, but you chose State."

He looked away from her. That was okay, she didn't need to see his face to know she was right.

"They want to see you," she repeated.

"I don't want to see them. I won't see them."

He thrust the paper toward her. She kept her hands at her side.

He closed his hand into a fist, so tight the tendons in his arm stood out. Then he opened his hand, dropped the crumpled sheet at her feet and walked out.

The drive was silent. Inside the gates of the embassy, he turned off the car, but neither of them got out.

"I'm going to the office, I'll be back this afternoon," he said.

"Hunter, you have to face the past. You have to face his parents. You have to forgive yourself. They expect you today."

She placed the crumpled sheet she'd smoothed out on the console between them. Then she added another sheet. "These are the directions. And their names."

"I'm going to the office," he repeated harshly.

She reached out and stroked the back of his head, down to this neck. "I wish you'd do it for yourself. You deserve that. But if you won't, then you have to do it for them. And for Scotty."

"No—"

"Their names are Pierce and MaryLou Hunter Ascot. He named you after his family."

"Where's Hunter?" Derek asked as soon as she walked in. "I saw his car come in."

"He has an errand to run."

"I'll call him—"

"No. Please." He looked up at her vehemence. That's when she noticed the strain on his face. "Is something wrong?"

"I don't know. There've been a lot of calls … Madame hangs up on them and says the king can't be disturbed."

"What kind of calls?"

"I don't know," he repeated. "She won't tell me. Says it's embassy business."

"Then it probably is." Surely Madame could handle any situation. "I'm going to walk the dogs, then take a shower. After that I'll see if I can find out from Madame what's going on. In the meantime, if you're really worried, call Sharon. But, please, Derek, don't call Hunter. It's important."

The knock on her bedroom door was so perfectly timed April was tempted to believe the knocker somehow knew precisely when she slipped her shoes on and finished drawing a comb through her hair.

She opened the door. Madame stood there.

"I must speak," she said.

"Of course. Is this about the phone calls?"

Ignoring the question, Madame came in, closed the door behind her. "You have sent him to those people. The people of that Scotty."

"The family of the soldier who helped him?" As confused as she was by Madame, she added calmly, "Yes."

The other woman said something that could only be a curse from the tone, though April had no idea what the word was. "He must return to Bariavak when King Jozef goes. Before the surgery, he must know the boy will go with him."

April shook her head. "Hunter won't go to Bariavak. He won't leave here, his job—"

"He will go if you go to Bariavak."

"Me? But … but you know I'm not Princess Josephine-Augusta, I'm not his granddaughter."

Madame made a dismissive sound. "Of course. I have known since before I ever set eyes on you. Yet you paraded as his granddaughter."

"I did not. Besides, he knows—"

"It doesn't matter what he knows. It is what he needs. And he needs that boy with him. He needs a new generation of true men. Not that nephew of his. So you must go to Bariavak so the boy will."

Questions crowded forward. The one that came out was, "Why? Why would King Jozef need Hunter to return to Bariavak with him?"

Madame looked at her, unblinking, long enough to make April want nothing more than she wanted to break the look. But she didn't. At last, Madame turned away. She sat on the bench at the foot of the bed, staring straight ahead.

April pulled the desk chair around to face the other woman, sat, and waited.

"I was in Bariavak at the time of the rebellion," Madame said, "not yet having come here to the embassy. My older brother was the closest aide to King Jozef. We had … grown up together.

"Laurentz was the head of the king's personal security. His wife had died, leaving him a young son, who spent time with a cousin's family while his father was on duty. When the fighting began, he received permission to bring his son inside the palace walls.

"He was everywhere in those hours, guiding the defense of the palace, leading the fighting. Everyone knew then and after that without Laurenz, there would have been a different outcome. He turned the tide. Only when he reported to the King that fact did he learn of the disappearance of Princess Josephine-Augusta. He immediately set out to try to find her."

Madame sat still and quiet for a moment. When she resumed, she needed to clear her throat.

"They must have come very close to those who took the princess, because they were killed. Laurentz and Anton Sabdoka, who was his second in command. My only child."

A gasp escaped April, but Madame's control and dignity did not allow for questions or sympathy. Madame would tell this as she had to.

"When the word was brought, my brother was with the king, as was the boy. The messenger blurted out the news. For a moment, the boy seemed not to understand, then he did. He cried out and he struck the king. His fists against King Jozef's legs over and over as he said, 'You killed him, you killed him.' And the king let him. Until the boy could strike no longer.

April wiped at tears on her cheeks but never took her eyes off the other woman.

"Amid all that was happening, with his own granddaughter missing and his daughter distraught, Jozef immediately ordered that Laurentz' son be cared for and brought up in the royal household." She shook her head. "There was such chaos. The boy ran away. No one knew where or even when. My brother had come to me … to tell me the news of my son. So he was not there to lead, either. Still, a search was made. For days they searched. But there were so few left, from those killed, those searching for the princess, those trying to have the country run again. Jozef was everywhere. Talking to everyone. Seen at all moments. Reassuring his people. Repairing damage to hopes as well as buildings. For all except Princess Sofia. She slipped away. Each day that her baby was gone a little farther."

She straightened her shoulders, which had sunk as if under the weight of grief.

"Rumors came, day after day, false rumors of his granddaughter. It tore at his soul. Then, one day, came word of a boy being sheltered by soldiers just beyond the border. Jozef—" April wondered if she knew she called him now by his first name alone. "—took only a few men with him. My brother among them. They found these soldiers and they found the boy.

"But one young soldier, with his arm around the shoulders of the boy who had become so skinny and ragged, said the boy was not going anywhere unless he wanted to. He said to this boy, 'What do you want?' Do you want to go with these people back to your country?' The boy said no. The boy said the man—and he pointed at our king— had killed his father, and he never wanted to see him or that place again."

April drew in a breath, feeling the king's pain. But also Hunter's. "He was a child," she whispered.

Madame might not have heard. "On the return from the border, before my brother and one other, His Highness wept. For the boy, for the boy's father, for his granddaughter, for his daughter, for all that had been lost. When they arrived at the palace, he put aside his tears forever. He put aside all that he had lost, and he put all that he was into our country. Still, he did not forget that boy. He lost track of him for a time after the young soldier's death. He roared such orders when that message reached him. Finally, he was told the boy had survived and was in a camp.

"I was given the task to get the boy to the United States. Twice I thought it was accomplished, then all crumbled to dust. But finally, he was brought to this country through a doctor. I came here to the embassy at that time as well, still with the task of securing the best that could be secured for the boy. An adoption was arranged with a good, kind couple. The boy refused to be adopted. A transfer to a better school also was arranged. He refused to leave."

A twist of her lips might have been a smile. "He was always a stubborn one. He did much on his own, making it difficult for any assistance more than small amounts to ease his path. The king ceased trying to provide that assistance once he began his career, but he continues to receive reports on the progress of the boy."

They sat in silence, April absorbing what she'd been told, hearing the words again in her mind. When she spoke, her question surprised her. "Why haven't you called Hunter by his name."

The older woman looked at her now. "Because that is not the name my niece gave the son she and her husband loved so much."

CHAPTER THIRTY-EIGHT

This time it was Derek who knocked on her door. "The king sent me, because we can't find—Oh, there you are, Madame. His Highness would like to see you both in his office."

At least to an observer the older woman had regained her usual rigid control. April wished she could say the same for herself, especially on the inside.

With all the emotions of that brief conversation, she found two thoughts repeating in her head. Hunter *did* have family. *Madame* was his great aunt.

Derek stepped ahead and opened the office door for them.

"April, come in," said the king. "I have introduced myself to your visitor, and await his introduction in return."

A man rose from one of the chairs by the fireplace.

"Michael? *Michael?* What are you doing here?"

He pulled her into a one-armed hug. "Checking things out."

The king, still seated, looked amused without actually smiling. "Would that mean you are *checking out* me?"

"Your Majesty, let me introduce myself. I am Senator Bradon's aide. Michael Dickinson."

April noticed—and saw that the king noticed—that Michael didn't answer the question.

"Do not be modest, young man. You are the senator's chief of staff. I had understood you were in Chicago for the holidays."

"I was. My family was. Except for April."

Her heart clenched and released.

"Perhaps," said King Jozef smoothly, "we have that in common, counting dear April as our family?"

"That seems highly unlikely."

"Not, however, impossible."

Michael's arm tightened around her shoulders. "A DNA test would resolve the question soon enough. However—"

"DNA," the king said, three fingers flicking away its significance.

"—nothing changes that she *is* part of our family."

"Yet she has passed the holiday with me."

"Yes, she has."

The two men exchanged a long look, then the king nodded.

April straightened out of Michael's hold. "Yes, *I* chose to spend Christmas with His Highness."

At her emphasis on the pronoun, both men turned toward her. The king smiled. Michael met her gaze, then gave a slow nod.

"I'd like to speak to you in private, April. Outside the grounds."

She understood the significance. "Really, Michael, that's not necessary. I'll be happy to talk to you. But I am here of my own volition. For heaven's sake, the State Department—"

"It was State's representative who informed us of your location."

"State's representative? What State representative? Informed you when?" She divided the questions between Michael and the king.

Michael's brows rose, and he looked to the king, who tried a half shrug.

"Sir—?" she insisted.

"I requested of Hunter further background on you."

"That's what he was doing while he was gone? But you knew—I told you I'm not your granddaughter. So why bother getting background on me? Oh. *Oh.* It was to make *Hunter* get the background."

"You told the king you're not his granddaughter?" Derek asked, stepping forward from near the door. "Then why is it popping up all over the Internet that you are?"

He held up his cell phone.

The house was white. Set back from a street with no sidewalks. In a wide lot, trees and bushes grew from beds that marked the side limits and buffered the front lawn from the street. The back yard seemed to stretch forever.

Hunter had no idea how he had come to be here.

He hadn't intended to come.

He'd picked up the paper, intending to crush it so hard that the memory of it would become dust. It was still warm from April's hold, and he'd found himself reading the words and numbers she had written. Reading them over and over. Until he knew them by heart.

Now he stood at the bottom of the steps that led to the porch that spread across the house. The door was red. There was an evergreen wreath on it with a big red plaid bow. April would like it.

He didn't belong here. He—

"Oh, there you are!" A woman stood at the partially opened door—he hadn't even noticed it opening. She was short, softly rounded, and there was gray threading through brown curls.

"Pierce! He's here." She called over her shoulder. She came down the stairs and took his hand. "My goodness, your hands are freezing. You should wear gloves."

She frowned when she said that, which is what made him realize she'd been smiling before that. Smiling at him.

And leading him up the steps.

A tall, angular man with thinning white hair held the door wide to let them both in.

"It's a pleasure to meet you, young man. I'm Pierce Ascot."

"Oh, Pierce, let him get his coat off first."

Her husband was hanging up Hunter's coat when a new voice came from the room beyond the small entryway where they stood.

"Good God, he's not a runt anymore! Remember me? Memphis."

And then his hand was being shaken by a burly man with a full beard and a bald head. He could just make out the shadows of the skinny twenty-year-old with a buzz cut.

"You were ... his friend."

"His best friend. And the last thing he said to me was *Take care of the runt.* Felt like sh—" He glanced toward the woman. "—crap about that ever since. After, we put you with the refugee group because we knew things were getting dicier and then we couldn't get back there for months. When we finally did, you'd been transferred somewhere else, and then the trail went cold. We hunted all the hell over for you. When Scotty's folks called and said they'd heard from you there was no way I was missing this. The last thing Scotty said, and I didn't…" The man blinked hard, pumped his hand even harder and said, "God, I'm glad to see you."

"Now, Norm, we're not going back over that. We're going to enjoy meeting Hunter." The woman smiled, then her eyes misted. "How wonderful that our boy called you Hunter Pierce."

"That's right," Memphis said. "We tried to get you to tell us your name, but none of us could tell what you were saying, and we started calling you one thing you said over and over, but then someone who spoke the language said we were calling you *Food.*"

They all watched him a little anxiously. He smiled, and they relaxed. "I don't remember that. Only being called Hunter Pierce."

"Pierce after me," said Scotty's father.

"And Hunter for my maiden name." His mother smiled widely, touching his hand again.

"Hey, let somebody else in, Memphis. We all feel like we know you from all the letters Scotty wrote home, and from what all the other guys in the unit told us."

A man with his father's height and his mother's smile edged around Memphis's girth, and for the first time since he'd been a starving seven-year-old who passed out at the feet of a group of American soldiers, Hunter Pierce thought he might faint.

"Let him sit down, let him sit down," ordered Pierce.

"Oh, you poor boy. Are you okay?" said his wife.

The man's smile went crooked. "I guess nobody told you I look like my older brother. I'm Doug."

Everything Hunter should have said. All the words that might have eased their pain. They all disappeared. He stood straight, and said what he had to say.

"I'm the reason Scotty died."

Rupert appeared at the open doorway before they could respond to Derek.

"I beg pardon, Your Majesty."

"Yes, Rupert?"

"I could not call. The phones are not working. There are people at the gate who wish to see Miss Gareaux."

"Excuse me, Your Majesty," Michael said. "I suspect they are some of my party. We could not all get on the same flights this morning."

The king nodded to Rupert.

"*All?*" April said. "You all cut your Christmas short?"

"Well, not all. Mr. and Mrs. M agreed to ride herd on the kids for a day or two until we were sure any confusion was sorted out the way you want it to be."

"Things are fine, Michael. Truly. His Highness knows I'm not his granddaughter. There's no confusion."

"Maybe not inside this room, but as this young man said——."

"Derek," she supplied. "Derek Kenton. State."

The men nodded at each other as Michael continued, "Reports that you are the long-lost granddaughter of King Jozef of Bariavak started showing up this morning on the Internet. Tris found it, showed it to Leslie and … here I am."

"But it's had no impact on us or—"

"Madame?" King Jozef said, looking past April.

She turned with the others to look at the older woman. "Reporters began calling some time ago. They would not stop. I unplugged the phones so Your Majesty would not be disturbed. The doctors said—"

"What did they ask?" the king asked.

"For comment on reports that April is Princess Josephine-Augusta."

"Reports? What reports?"

"From what's on the Internet it started with pictures and video from here yesterday," Michael said.

"The Receiving Hours," April said.

Michael nodded. "Someone compared photos of April and Princess Sofia. It exploded from there."

"But why—?"

April never finished her question. Rupert was there, followed by a woman and a man.

April went directly into Leslie Roberts' arms. Leslie folded her in a hug, then took her by the shoulders and held her at arm's length, studying her. Then Grady was hugging them both.

April half stumbled through the introductions to King Jozef and Madame—Derek and Rupert had disappeared—with Michael filling in the rest.

"Leslie would like to talk with April alone," Grady said immediately.

Madame swelled. April's gaze went from her to the king, who said mildly, "Of course. Perhaps the library, April?"

"The king seems like a remarkable man," Leslie said, following her into the library.

"He is." Then the carefulness of Leslie's words sank in. April spun around. "I'm not—There's nothing—It's not that kind of relationship."

"Wha—? Oh, no. April. You think that I think—? *King Jozef?* No."

"I know you think I have a thing for older men."

Leslie looked at her strangely for a long moment, then took both her hands and drew her to the couch. "Let's sit down a moment."

April sat, but she wasn't going to let this not be said. Not this time. "Leslie, I *know* you think I'm looking for a father figure."

"That's not precisely—"

"Probably see it as me trying to find a substitute because of my dad dying when I was six. Classic, right? Then Gerard and Reese. I can see how you'd think that, but I'm not. Really. That's not what these relationships have been. Well, with Gerard and King Jozef they haven't been relationships at all, not in that sense. And Reese was the furthest thing from a father figure there is."

April drew in breath to continue persuading her.

Leslie sucked the breath out of her with three words. "I believe you."

"You do?"

"Yes. So why do you think you've had these three important relationships with men so much older than you?"

"I don't know."

"I think you do."

April looked into the older woman's eyes. "I don't want to be Melly."

"Ah."

She heard the syllable as a released breath from Leslie, but it seemed far away. She hadn't known she was going to say those words. She hadn't known she thought them. And now more words were coming—

"I don't want to be Melly. Never growing up. Never being responsible. Never ... never *lasting*. Never *mattering*."

"You are not Melly. Oh, April, you have to know that. You are not, you have never been Melly. From the time we were children she couldn't slow long enough to see anything beyond the next adventure. You are not like that at all. You have always mattered. You have to know that."

"I feel so disloyal. You never say bad things about Melly."

"She's your Mama, honey. And there's no knowing whether she would have been better if Jeff hadn't died."

April looked at her directly. "But you don't really think so."

Leslie held her breath a second, then let it go, long and slow. "No, I don't. I thought they were heading for divorce. Jeff grew up when you were born. Melly didn't. Jeff would have put what was good for you ahead of anything else. Including Melly."

Fresh tears spurted. Leslie took her in her arms and rocked her. Then she chuckled.

"What?" April asked.

"Oh, honey, how you can think you're like Melly. She wouldn't have noticed any of these three men, much less have considered getting to know them." She held April away from her and looked into her eyes. "Or rescuing them."

"Rescuing? *Me* rescue somebody? *You're* always rescuing *me*."

"What?"

"I'm a mess and you and Grady swoop in and make everything better. Like when Gerard died—"

"You were mourning a dear friend. *And* sorting out his house and his mess of an estate."

"—and when Reese broke off the engagement—well, actually his mother did—"

"She *didn't*."

"She did. And when that happened my first thought was to run to you and Grady."

"That's what family's for. But you didn't run to us, did you?"

"And now you're here again, rescuing me. Just like when I was thirteen—"

"Thirteen—yes, a child who was already far too much of a grownup for her own good, taking care of herself and her mother."

"I was surly and sullen."

Leslie smiled slightly. "You were. As was your God-given right as a teenager. It was the one piece of your childhood you held on to, bless your heart. Grandma Beatrice, Grady, and I—"

"Took me in. Rescued me."

"Gave you a safe place to be while your years caught up with the adulthood you'd been pitched into, practically from the time you were a baby. And as soon as that happened, you set about taking care of everything around you. Gerard Littrell, Reese Warrington, Rufus and all the other dogs. Why you even tried to rescue Brussels sprouts and the Vegetable Consortium. And now King Jozef and Hunter Pierce."

"No. Not Hunter—" She stopped.

Leslie's gaze was knowing. She nodded slowly. "It might take some time for you to get used to the idea that you've been the rescuer, what with you thinking all this time that you were the rescued, but it's clear that what you feel for Hunter is different."

"What I feel for Hunter…" Tears slid down her cheeks, the only ending to her sentence.

Leslie put her arms around her. "Terrifying, isn't it? Terrifying and so very wonderful, when you can rescue each other."

CHAPTER THIRTY-NINE

As he pulled up to the back gates, Hunter saw a group start running toward them from the corner.

He drove in. Rupert stepped in behind the car, guarding the dwindling gap. The first of the running group arrived as the gates locked.

Hunter nodded to Rupert and sprinted for the back entrance.

"What's happened?" he demanded of Derek, who was rushing to meet him. "April? The king—?"

"They're fine," Derek said. "It's the media. All hell's breaking loose here. It's all over about April—."

"His Highness wishes to see you," Madame announced from the stairs, glaring at Hunter.

"Princess Found, they're calling her. It's all over the Internet."

"Where's April?"

"His Highness—"

"Where is April? *Now.*"

Apparently, the voices outside the library drew Leslie and April out.

Hunter took an automatic step toward April. "You're crying."

She smiled. "Not anymore." But then her eyes filled again.

Grady, who'd been studying Leslie's face, put a hand on Hunter's shoulder. Possibly comradely. Possibly meant to be restraining. He could have shaken it off. He didn't. "When you've been married as long as we have, you'll know that sometimes crying is a good thing."

Leslie gave him a special smile. "It is. Hello, Hunter."

He nodded curtly, but his eyes were on April. She gave him a small smile.

"Ah, bless your hearts." Leslie's words blended satisfaction, confirmation, and acceptance.

Now that he knew April was okay, they could get on with this. "We have a situation. Need to deal with it. Everybody in the office—"

"Not yet," April interrupted. "Not until I hear—Until we talk."

"April."

She looked back at him. "Hunter."

Grady put an arm around his wife's shoulders. "C'mon, sweetheart, let's let April win this round in privacy. We'll wait for you in the office."

April stepped back into the library.

"We can talk about this later," he tried again.

"What happened?"

He followed her into the room. "I told them. Told them I was the reason their son—their brother, their friend—died."

"Oh, Hunter."

He looked at her, frowning. "They said I wasn't. Memphis—he was one of the soldiers and he's stayed in touch with the family, lives nearby. He said I wasn't even there. I was back in camp. Could I have remembered all of it that wrong?"

"You were a child. You'd been through so much."

I'm the reason Scotty died.

His words had echoed in the silence that followed.

Then MaryLou Hunter stepped forward, said, "Oh, my poor boy," and wrapped her arms around him.

"Remembered all of it wrong?" April asked.

"They had a letter he'd written talking about me. A few letters. But this one ... He said King Jozef came after me. Wanted me to return with him. He said I'd blamed the king for my father's death. He said he felt sorry for the king, because he was torn up about it. He wrote to his parents about how did you explain to a kid that even a king wasn't always in charge of everything that happened around him."

She touched his arms, crossed in front of him. She slid her hand down between his arms and chest. He shifted slightly to make room for the touch.

"I did. I blamed King Jozef. For my father leaving me. For his getting killed. I know better now. I know things happen that even the best leader can't prevent. I know operations go wrong. I know…"

He looked at her then away. "But that was my head. That was what I know, what I learned. And that's not what's been in charge. Like you said, I had to look at the past as an adult. I blamed him as a kid and I never stopped blaming him because I never looked at what I was thinking—feeling."

She put her arms around his neck and kissed him. He held her tight.

Her mouth opened to him, and he took it with gratitude and pleasure. Sinking into her, into *them*…

He surfaced with a curse and a smile. "God, April. We can't."

She pecked him on the check. "We can. We *will*. Later."

Holding hands, they returned to the office.

April's calm took a hit when they entered the office to find it so crowded that she could only see the king's shoulder as he sat by the fireplace.

"Bette? Paul?"

The Monroes turned toward her. Bette hugged her, then Paul slung an arm around her. "How're you doing, kid. Sorry we missed the beginning of the fun, but we took a detour to pick up—"

At the same time April realized Susan was there now, and she was talking, too. April picked up the phrase, "…may I introduce—."

"—Grandma Beatrice," Paul said.

"—April's great-grandmother, Beatrice Craig," Susan said.

"What?" April jolted away from Paul. The crowd parted, and there was her great-grandmother, sitting in the chair next to the King of Bariavak. "Grandma Beatrice, what are you doing here? You don't travel."

"I no longer care for the hurly-burly of travel. That does not mean I am not capable of it when circumstances call for it."

It took several minutes to sort out the new arrivals, assure everyone that April was fine, and determine that Sharon had organized the media into a reception room with the promise of a news conference and the restraining presence of Bariavak's security detail.

"There were rumors before," Sharon said. "They quieted down with April and King Jozef less in the public eye since the White House party, but all it took were a few pictures to jump from rumor to major story. Slow news day."

Hunter gave Sharon a narrow-eyed look that he then turned on King Jozef.

"What's going to be said at this news conference? Because if you say you just discovered that April's not your granddaughter, the wolves will be after her in a heartbeat. She'll be accused of trying to scam you, and it won't matter how much anyone denies it."

"I shall not say I have just discovered it, because I have known it—" He met April's gaze, gave a suggestion of a bow of apology, and finished. "—from before I met her."

"You knew she wasn't your granddaughter before we brought her here that first day? Is that what you're saying? Then why on earth didn't you turn her away? Or refuse to see her in the first place?"

"Because," April said slowly, "I didn't come here alone."

"So? You were the one who was his possible granddaughter."

She placed a hand on his arm. "It was you. He knew you were involved. He knew you were in charge. He knew you would come to the meeting. He wanted to see you."

Hunter turned from her to the king. "Is that true?"

"Yes."

"Why?"

The silence stretched, the king staring thoughtfully toward the fireplace, Hunter staring at him unrelenting. The others still.

"Because he wants to make things right before he goes in for the surgery," April said. "He wanted to see you, to be sure you were okay. For himself and ... others."

There would be a time for Hunter to know of his connection to Madame, but this was not it. Not for either of them.

"You are a wise young woman, April," King Jozef said. At last he looked at Hunter. "I should have honored your father as he deserved by insisting on your return to Bariavak, by raising you in the royal household. I have regretted not doing so. Very much. Now ... now all I can do is to offer you your father's station in our country."

Hunter shook his head slowly. "Your country, sir. I didn't want that. I don't want it."

After a pause, Sharon Johnson said briskly, "It's a good thing, because I have plans for you at Diplomatic Security. But first what are we going to tell those hordes out there? I don't imagine you want to tell them your personal history, Pierce."

In another circumstance his look of horror might have been amusing.

"I'll talk to them," April said. "I'll tell them I'm not the princess, but that the king and I formed a friendship, and that's all there is to it."

"No." King Jozef stood. "After you have all safely departed, I shall take my place at the lectern that Sharon has prepared. I shall make an announcement that I have greatly enjoyed the company of a delightful young American whom I could only wish were my granddaughter. And I shall answer questions until they are bored with asking them."

"No, you will not," Beatrice declared.

Madame gasped. Beatrice cast a glance her way, then returned her attention to the king.

The King of Bariavak looked at her coolly. "Indeed?"

"Indeed," she confirmed. "My great-granddaughter is clearly very fond of you. The Craig family does not desert its friends, allies or—" She narrowed her eyes at him, as if in a dare. "—family when difficulties are encountered."

The two stared at each other, while it seemed everybody else in the room held their breath.

"Very well."

"Your Majesty." Madame's tone held a breadth of meanings, including a strong objection and a warning.

"My dear, do you not think you could call me Jozef in front of our friends?"

Madame flushed, while her eyes shone.

The King took her hand. She didn't pull away.

He led her toward the door, while the rest gathered behind him.

"Rupert, are they assembled?"

"Yes, Your Majesty."

King Jozef turned to Beatrice Craig. "I shall first announce the extension of an agreement with your government. On that matter, I shall answer all questions, if you do not object, dear lady."

"That's quite all right," she allowed graciously, her hand resting on Grady's arm.

The king's mouth twitched, but he maintained his countenance better than many of the others assembled.

At the door, Madame released his hand and stepped back. He looked at her. When she nodded, he looked around at the others, laid his hand briefly on April's shoulder, regarded Hunter for an extra moment, then faced the door once more.

"Very well. Let us proceed."

EPILOGUE

NEWS REPORT
Jan. 2

WASHINGTON—King Jozef of Bariavak had surgery that doctors termed "very successful" today for an undisclosed ailment. He is in satisfactory condition this evening. The king, who has ruled his tiny country for more than six decades, is 87.

While doctors would not comment on the cause for the king's surgery, they spoke at length about its success. "It could not have gone better," said Donald Effingham, the head of the surgical team.

King Jozef had been in the headlines this past week because of the unfolding of the story of a young woman who was first rumored to be his long-lost granddaughter after she attended a number of events with him in December. King Jozef said at a news conference that she was not his granddaughter and that he had never believed she was. He strongly denied all supposition that there had been any effort to mislead him, and the young woman, April Gareaux of Fairlington, Va., was at his side for the surgery.

The king's granddaughter was kidnapped and believed killed 30 years ago during a brief but bloody coup attempt by extremists in Bariavak....

Washington, D.C.

April was fifteen minutes late for her first day back at work.

"Well, if it isn't, Princess Brussels Sprouts!" Jason said, followed by his loud, braying laugh.

She looked him over coolly, and said nothing.

Zoe bustled up and enclosed her in a hug.

"Oh, April! Oh, baby! I'm so sorry. So close to being a princess and now—you didn't have to come back to work today. You could have taken a few days to get over—not that anyone gets over being so close to a crown and then having it fall apart."

April laughed as she disengaged from Zoe's hold, and gently placed the other woman in a chair. Still standing, she looked around at the faces in the other cubicles, all looking at her.

"I have something to say to all of you, and then we can forget about it."

Two phones rang unanswered, and Zoe didn't say a word.

"I had a wonderful month away. I had to come back to work today, because I need a couple days off next week to spend with a friend who is recovering from surgery."

Zoe's lips parted. April forestalled any words with a raised hand.

"I am not the least disappointed that I turned out not to be the princess. I have been enriched beyond measure—I have two dogs I love, a cherished friend, and the most wonderful and challenging man in the world who is going to become my husband later this year."

Zoe grabbed April's left hand, and gasped. "It's gorgeous."

"So's the man," April said with a smile.

Hunter had insisted on getting the man who owned the little jewelry store whose window display she'd enjoyed the week before Thanksgiving to open early. And then he'd insisted on spending entirely too much on a ring. She had put her foot down about the one that equaled a down payment on a house, but when it came to this one he was not to be budged.

Her smile deepened. It was going to be an interesting life.

"Oh, my God, it's the hunk from State, isn't it?" Without waiting for an answer, Zoe narrowed her eyes and propped her hands on her hips. "I knew adventure would suit you."

She laughed. "It has. But I'm ready to get back to work, and bring Brussels sprouts to the world. I have so many great recipe ideas to share. Did you know they are part of the Bariavakian royal family's traditional Christmas dinner?"

No one answered. They were all gaping at something behind her.

She spun around, already smiling.

Hunter didn't look at her, but said in his best official voice, "Ms. Holland, the Department of State would appreciate your employee's assistance for the rest of the day to deal with an emergency."

Zoe's mouth formed an "oh" for ten seconds before any words followed. "Sure. Absolutely."

He had her out the door before she could say, "Hunter, really? I know from your face it's not anything awful, but—"

"The emergency is I received a text saying we'd received a belated Christmas present from Maurice and Etienne of four nights in a certain suite in a hotel overlooking Lafayette Park."

She laughed. "Now that's my kind of emergency."

"There's also a stack of real estate listings so we can find someplace to live that will take two dogs. But first, there's a bed."

Ashton, Wisconsin

As befitted an impulse purchase, the magazine sat at the top of the grocery bag. The pages had flipped in the breeze from the car window that wouldn't close all the way, fluttering their temptation all the way home.

But Katie Davis put the chicken, ice cream, and spinach in the freezer before she let herself sit at the metal-legged kitchen table and look at the cover.

They'd been right.

All the people who'd told her all day that the woman on this week's cover of People magazine could be her sister.

She found the article and read it through quickly.

She felt oddly numb when she finished, yet her heart stuttered to a faster tempo the way her old car did sometimes when she shifted into fourth gear.

She studied the photographs accompanying the article. The young woman who looked so like her, smiling, between the strong-jawed man with his arm around her and the distinguished elderly man, who ruled a country but had lost a granddaughter.

The story was amazing. The magazine said the king had been struck by the resemblance of this young woman to his daughter at the same age. They had formed a bond and shared the holidays together. Now the king was going to walk the commoner down the aisle when she married.

A happy ending for all concerned, the article-writer had said, then added a final paragraph.

Or is it? King Jozef still searches for his lost granddaughter. And somewhere out there could be a young woman who doesn't know she has a grandfather and a kingdom.

Katie closed the magazine, resting her crossed hands on the sleek cover.

She had automatically placed her right hand on top, but now she reversed them, looking at the elongated little finger on her left hand. The family mark, her mother had called it.

Yet neither her mother nor father had had the trait. Skipped a generation, was the explanation.

There'd been other things her mother had never explained. At least not beyond cryptic utterances in her characteristic blend of her native language and English.

She'd always written them off as her mother's longing for drama in a life entirely devoid of it.

…Or maybe she hadn't completely written them off, she acknowledged an hour later as she moved yet another box in the attic looking for the battered old suitcase her father had spanked her so hard for daring to open that once.

Why she had thought of it now, and why she was digging through all this to find it, she couldn't say.

She swiped away cobwebs and pushed aside a box labeled "Baby

Cloths"—her mother never had gotten the difference between cloths and clothes. And there was the suitcase.

Without ceremony, she flipped open the latches. Then she realized a rope was tied around it to keep it closed. That took some more doing to loose, but she succeeded just before she thought she'd need to take the whole thing downstairs to cut it.

The top sprang up.

Thank you for reading April and Hunter's story!

My readers know that I never end my books with cliffhangers. Well, almost never. You meet Katie Davis at the end of *The Christmas Princess*, but you learn her full story in *The Surprise Princess*, Book 6 of The Wedding Series. King Jozef continues his search for his long-missing granddaughter, and Hunter is on the case again. This time the clues lead to Wisconsin, and the Ashton University athletics office. There, Katie works as an administrative assistant and Brad Spencer as a basketball coach. Both soon will be caught up in international intrigue and some royal matchmaking.

You are introduced to Brad and the Ashton campus in *Hoops*, the prequel to *The Surprise Princess*. Flash back a few years and Brad is a star on the basketball team, coached by C.J. Draper and tutored by Carolyn Trent. The latter two return in *The Surprise Princess* as mentors to Katie, and, okay, they might take part in a little matchmaking themselves.

The Surprise Princess
Hoops (prequel to The Surprise Princess)

April, Hunter, Jozef, Madame and friends ask if you'll help spread the word about them and The Wedding Series. You have the power to do that in two quick ways:

Recommend the book and the series to your friends and/or the whole wide world on social media. Shouting from rooftops is particularly appreciated.

Review the book. Take a few minutes to write an honest review and it can make a huge difference. As you likely know, it's the single best way for your fellow readers to find books they'll enjoy, too.

To me—as an author and a reader—the goal is always to find a good author-reader match. By sharing your reading experience through recommendations and reviews, you become a vital matchmaker. ☺

For news about upcoming books, as well as other titles and news, join Patricia McLinn's Readers List and receive her twice-monthly free newsletter.
www.patriciamclinn.com/readers-list

And for you Wedding Series readers, I have a special incentive. If you join my readers list at www.patriciamclinn.com/lp-su-tsk, you'll receive an exclusive offer to download a free short story. ***The Soldier's Kiss,*** a prequel to ***The Forgotten Prince,*** introduces Harmon Reed, the heroine of ***The Forgotten Prince,*** and shares how her father, Lt. Col. Brooks Reed, discovers his true love, artist Ann-Elise Jerakenko … with help from a cat.

The Wedding Series

Prelude to a Wedding

She's all work and no play. He's an expert at fun. Their romance could be the biggest game of all.

Wedding Party

As one couple ties the knot, the best man hopes to find love with the bridesmaid.

Grady's Wedding

Marriage can be catching. Will the last bachelor take the leap?

The Runaway Bride

Escaping a bridal disaster in Illinois, her life takes a wild, wild turn in the West.

Hoops (prequel to The Surprise Princess)

Can the coach and the professor play on the same team?

The Surprise Princess

She's an ordinary young woman living an ordinary life in small-town Wisconsin … isn't she?

Not a Family Man (prequel to The Forgotten Prince)

City girl Jenny, the ranch's attractive new owner, spells trouble for foreman Tucker.

The Forgotten Prince

Karl and Harmon have a history, but a royal matchmaker helps them rewrite it.

Praise for The Wedding Series

"A wonderful series that will make you laugh and cry. Each page is filled with love that will eventually come to the people who so need it. A must read!"—*5-star review*

"McLinn is an expert at revealing the layers enveloping her characters. With each reveal, sometimes exquisitely subtle, we are pulled in deeper to be active participants in the emotionally charged, yet heart-melting romance."—*USA Today*

"Love this series … so many twists and turns that take you all over the world!"—*5-star review*

"Fun and serious all at the same time. Love how the friends intertwine and add new along the way. It was refreshing to read the different stories and having them all come together. Really enjoyed this series!"—*5-star review*

"Perfect. The characters were multi-dimensional and played off each other in warm, thoughtful, loving ways. Each couple faced a different situation and overcame their obstacles together and with the insightful comments of their friends. … Heart-warming."—*5-star review*

"Full of warmth, understanding of human nature, and great characters. They are connected, following the lives of college friends, and by the time you are finished, you feel as if you are a part of their extended circle. A dash of sex here, but not to the point that it overshadows the well thought out storylines. Definitely a feel good experience."—*5-star review*

Also by Patricia McLinn

Marry Me Series

Wedding of the Century

The Unexpected Wedding Guest

A Most Unlikely Wedding

Baby Blues and Wedding Bells

Seasons in a Small Town series

What Are Friends For? (Spring)

The Right Brother (Summer)

Falling for Her (Autumn)

Warm Front (Winter)

Wyoming Wildflowers Series

A Place Called Home Series

Bardville, Wyoming Series

Explore a complete list of all Patricia's books

patriciamclinn.com/patricias-books

Or get a printable booklist

patriciamclinn.com/patricias-books/printable-booklist

Patricia's eBookstore (buy digital books online directly from Patricia)

patriciamclinn.com/patricias-books/ebookstore

About the Author

USA Today bestselling author Patricia McLinn spent more than 20 years as an editor at The Washington Post after stints as a sports writer (Rockford, Ill.) and assistant sports editor (Charlotte, N.C.). She received BA and MSJ degrees from Northwestern University.

McLinn is the author of more than 50 published novels, which are cited by readers and reviewers for wit and vivid characterization. Her books include mysteries, romantic suspense, contemporary romance, historical romance and women's fiction. They have topped bestseller lists and won numerous awards.

She has spoken about writing from Melbourne, Australia, to Washington, D.C., including being a guest speaker at the Smithsonian Institution.

Now living in northern Kentucky, McLinn loves to hear from readers through her website, Facebook and Twitter.

Visit with Patricia:

Website: patriciamclinn.com

Facebook: facebook.com/PatriciaMcLinn

Twitter: @PatriciaMcLinn

Pinterest: pinterest.com/patriciamclinn

Instagram: instagram.com/patriciamclinnauthor